Rave Reviews for the Lumby Novels

"For lovers of Americana—a series featuring the old-fashioned country town of Lumby populated by relentlessly quirky residents who remind us just how crazy normal life usually is."

— Forbes

"There's a quality to the writing that lends an unrushed, meandering feel to the narrative as evildoers are dispatched and equilibrium is restored. Fraser's story is pleasantly easy reading and as smalltown cozy as they come. There are plenty of light chuckles to be found."

—Publishers Weekly

"At a time when we seem to be taking ourselves all too seriously, Gail Fraser pulls a rabbit out of the hat that charms while it helps us relax. *Lumby* strikes just the right balance of playfulness, satire and drama. A thoroughly enjoyable read!"

—Brother Christopher, Abbot, New Skete Monastery

"You will be amazed by the great imagination of the author... The reader is in for a treat. This book is a delight to read and one that you will thoroughly enjoy."

—Bestsellersworld.com

"In the tradition of Jan Karon's Mitford series, this engaging inside look at small-town life will draw a bevy of fans to its old-fashioned story combining a bit of romance, a bit of mystery and a multitude of quirky and endearing characters."

—*Booklist*

"Lumby goes straight to the heart. The simplicity, humor and downright friendliness of the book make reading it a pleasured. Readers will close this book with a sigh of contentment and a desire to visit Lumby again. The author has faithfully carved out a slice of small-town living and topped it off with a large helping of humor. This reviewer can't wait for her next visit to Lumby!"

—Christian Book Previews

"This was by far one of the most delightful books I have read in a long time. A very well-written light fiction filled with great moments of reflection... a great way to spend a relaxing, lazy summer afternoon swinging in a hammock. While simply composed, the writing flows like a dream, including witty and fast-paced dialog, resulting in a carefully woven tale that brings to life small town life and quirkiness."

—Seattle Pi

"Readers who have traveled to Mitford with Jan Karon will find the trip to Lumby at least as pleasant and marked with a lot more laughter. If the world of cozy fiction has a capital, it's Lumby. Gail Fraser tells wonderful stories that have kindness at their core—and are a gentle reminder of the goodness in people's hearts. Lumby will astound readers with its sense of humor, quirky charm, its aura of magic and possibilities and happy (if unexpected) endings."

—Cozy Library

"If Gail Fraser's little town of Lumby could escape the confines of her imagination and be put on the proverbial map, I'd move there in a moment. Until then, I'll have to be content with my vicarious visitations. What an agreeable world she's created!"

—Philip Gulley, Author of the Harmony series

"A visit to the charming, whimsical town of Lumby is a refreshing change from our fast paced lives. Challenged to host a hot air balloon festival, its residents rise to the occasion: lives change, love blossoms, a wild and irrepressible young man matures. A delightful read."

—Joan Medlicott, author of The Ladies of Covington Series

"Gail Fraser deftly carries the reader through a rich venue of interwoven storylines and memorable characters set against the backdrop of small town life while deftly leading the reader towards the core message of tolerance, forgiveness and redemption. Grab a hot cup of cocoa, snuggle under a favorite quilt and enjoy!"

—Katherine Valentine, author

"Full of good fun, drama and characters so richly drawn that you'll swear you know them, or wish you did. Wrapped in its compelling pages are real emotions and page-turning situations that keep the reader involved in the pure joy and quirky lives of Lumby's residents."

—Saratogian

"Drop in on the sweetest small town since Mayberry, where the worst people are still nicer than the best people you know, and life's problems are solved by a backhoe, an industrial sewing machine or monks wearing light-up tennis shoes. Your own troubles will melt away."

—Bob Tarte, author

"You'll find yourself and a sizable portion of your own whacky relatives attending this hysterical family reunion filled with food, fun, and familiar truths. Every which way you turn, you'll find a Lumby laugh and a sideways quirky glance at you and yours."

—Charlene Ann Baumbich, author

"Gail Fraser's Mitford-esque settings and engaging characters will charm readers of all ages. Pack this thoroughly enjoyable novel in your beach bag this summer—you won't want to miss this amusing adventure!"

—Christian Book Previews

Books by Gail Fraser

The Lumby Lines

ა

GAIL FRASER

Lazygoose
Publishing

Lazygoose Publishing
Published by Lazygoose Publishing, a division of Lazygoose USA, Inc.,
305 Cottrell Road, Greenwich, New York, 12834, USA

Copyright © Gail Fraser, 2005, 2017
www.lumbybooks.com
Illustrations copyright © Art Poulin, 2005
www.artpoulin.com

Library of Congress Cataloging-in-Publication Data:
Fraser, Gail
The lumby lines / Gail Fraser.
ISBN: 978-0-9986301-1-3
Printed in the United States of America

In memory of Nick.
Dedicated to Jodi, Brother John
and my husband, Art.
Thank you.

ॐ

ACKNOWLEDGMENTS

My deepest gratitude to Art for his genuine encouragement, support and kindness in our daily lives. And thanks to Pam Purcell who, without knowledge or intent, stirred the air that began an amazing butterfly effect which led me to Lumby. And, as always, a world of indebtedness to Brothers Christopher and John for sharing so many thoughts and details about monastic living.

I would also like to acknowledge and thank my past agent(s), editor(s), and Penguin NAL for their respective contributions in stewarding my first five Lumby novels through their early editions. And steadfast appreciation goes to John Paine for being both an outstanding editor and an insightful adviser. Finally, many thanks to Ron Toelke and Barbara Kempler-Toelke for their contributions and layout support of this edition during our transition to Lazygoose Publishing.

The
Lumby Lines

ONE
Goatish

One could describe Lumby as one would describe, with unreserved fondness, one's own small town in our vast and diverse country: quaint, with enough quirk to make it interesting. It is a town that holds strong to the belief that the oldest apple tree in the country is firmly rooted on the corner of Cherry Street and Farm to Market Road, and a town that reacted adversely when one of its more entrepreneurial youths put the tree up for auction on the Internet a few years back.

It is also where, one winter, the Chatham Press distributed its annual calendars, which inadvertently showed the preceding year's holiday dates, so although the twenty-fifth of December remained sacred, most other significant religious and historical celebrations were off by as many as six days. The residents of Lumby, though, decided that it might be interesting to be out of sync with the rest of the country for just one year, so for the next twelve months, followed the written word to the letter.

And finally, Lumby is a town in which the greatest pastime is reading the Sheriff's Report in the local paper.

The Lumby Lines

Sheriff's Complaints

SHERIFF SIMON DIXON   **MARCH 23**

9:42a.m. Woman from Hunts Mill Road reported a bat hanging on her screen door.

10:55a.m. Lumby resident requested that her grass be measured by front walk.

1:13p.m. John Morris reported two dogs trying to down a steer. He shot at them, chasing them off.

1:15p.m. Reverend Olson reported three bullets going through stained glass windows at Holy Episcopal.

3:39p.m. A Lumby caller reported that two draft horses had wandered into his pasture.

4:17p.m. Caller reported that aluminum ladder stolen yesterday had been returned bent.

6:43p.m. JoEllen McKee, 44, was arrested for disorderly conduct at Jimmy D's. Bond: $115.

10:01p.m. EMS responded to a report of a man having a diabetic reaction and in a semi-conscious state.

10:22p.m. Received report of a burning bush on fairgrounds property. LFD dispatched.

11:22p.m. Pickup vs deer. Pickup wins.

11:58p.m. Moose damages car State Road 541.

Sheriff Dixon is as steadfast and dependable as the paper in which his name appeared that day. For more than a dozen years he has been the patient guardian of the residents and activities in and around Lumby. A brick of a man, with a tall, solid body and square shoulders, he demonstrates as much kindness toward the innocent children as he does firmness toward those who jeopardize the tranquility of the town.

In his younger and, as he readily admits, more foolish years, his only focus was his career advancement during the years he spent in the Seattle police department. He ultimately became the youngest lieutenant in the department, spending most waking hours at the downtown station. When not in uniform, he dedicated his few non-working hours to either police study or physical improvement. He was, overall, a very disciplined and focused man.

Until he met Anna, who came into his life one summer when she was in the fish market, smelling salmon. Within weeks they were good friends, and they became inseparable by the end of the summer. In late August, Anna returned to her hometown ten hours away to continue teaching, leaving Simon alone and, for the first time in his life, unmotivated.

During the following year, when Simon visited Anna in her small town, he came to embrace Lumby's pace and "unique way of life," as Anna called it. That second summer Simon asked Anna to marry him, and they began to plan their future together. Job prospects looked limited after Simon's first conversation with Sheriff Dumont, who explained that the "Lumby police department" was, in fact, one person who worked part-time until just two years prior.

However, Simon was quickly able to get a position in Wheatley, a small city south of Lumby, and bided his time until Dumont retired. During those first three years he and Anna bought a small home off Loggers Road and had a son and then, eighteen months later, a daughter, who has the same dirty reddish-brown hair and dark brown eyes as her mother.

Within a year of little Sarah's birth, Dumont announced his retirement, and Simon accepted the town council's offer to become Lumby's second sheriff in its unblemished history. And so Simon came to learn patience from two new forces in his life that he held dear: his children and the quirkiness of the residents of the small town of Lumby.

"And how are you this morning?" Simon asked, walking into the station shortly after seven a.m. that early spring day.

"Fine, Sheriff," Dale answered, as he does every morning. Dale Friedman was hired four years prior, doubling the town's police resources from one to two.

"Anything to report?"

"Rob Steadman called a few minutes ago. Seems there are two goats locked in the bank vault that are enjoying a breakfast of ten- and twenty-dollar bills. Can't get them out until the vault timer allows entry at nine."

Simon smiled, shaking his head as he occasionally does when he hears about some of the town's stranger mishaps. Patience and humor.

"Anything else?"

"Principal Harris called earlier to report that the nine-foot cata-pult built by Mrs. Escher's tenth-grade class had been moved from the back parking lot to the football field."

"Who would want a catapult?"

"Probably the same kids who took six chickens from Bill Henry."

"Let me guess: catapulting chickens over goalposts?"

"Seems so. Bill Henry said that all his chickens have been returned, mostly defeathered and shook up, but alive."

"Next."

"One other. Cindy Watford called to complain about the electri-cians from Rocky Mount. Seems after they did some work in her house yesterday, each time she turns on the kitchen light, the door-bell rings."

"Poor woman," Simon responded. "That must be driving her

nuts. Would you call Chris and have him go over and fix it?"

"Already done," Dale said.

"Great. If that's it, I'll be across the street if you need me."

Directly across from the police department is the Chatham Bank, best known, or perhaps only recognized, for being the smallest bank in the state, with reserves of slightly over twelve million dollars. Simon loved this time of morning, when the school buses were beginning their routes and town merchants swept the sidewalks on the main street. Within a month, the store owners would plant spring flowers in the raised beds that line the road, and the town would be vibrant with colorful blooms and waving banners hung from awnings.

Simon was proud of the town and its residents. Although Lumby lacks the economic benefits of some of its neighboring towns, the little community has steadily grown while keeping the same values as had been instilled by the town's ancestors a hundred years before.

Simon was equally proud of the role he had in Lumby. He had done a good job. During the twelve years that Simon had protected Lumby, only once did his integrity fall short. Had the monastery fire never happened, had "private" conversations that told him to back off never taken place, he would have a spotless record. Even though that was a year ago, he was still haunted by the events of that week, especially this time of year, when the winter was releasing its cold grip.

"The *Post* called to ask for a comment about your goat situation," Simon teased as he approached Rob Steadman, shaking his hand. Rob, the president of Chatham Bank, was a man who could make coffee nervous, but he was also one of Simon's closest friends.

"Damn things are eating my money!" Rob said, looking at the security monitor on his desk.

"So, that's a 'no comment,' I assume?" Simon joked. "Should I even ask how they got in there?"

"We're using them this morning for an advertising campaign,

but Mcnear had to drop them off last night. When Dora was locking up, she thought they would be safe in the vault for the night."

"No doubt," Simon said.

"And those conniving goats. One actually jumped on the back of the other to reach the lower shelf where there were two money bags that were prepared to be taken out this morning. See, you can see one of them there," Rob said, pointing out a canvas bag on the bottom shelf behind the goat's back legs.

"Where's the other?"

"Eaten," Rob paused, still watching the monitor. "The bottom is under the goat's hoof. They must not like premium leather," Rob said sarcastically.

Right then the goat on the shelf relieved itself, splashing everything within a six-foot proximity, including the money bag.

"Wonderful," Rob grunted, sitting down.

Simon became transfixed watching the smaller goat chew a ten-dollar bill.

"I think those are the same goats that ravaged the bookstore last year, and they still look hungry," Simon commented.

"They shouldn't be," Rob said. "They've been eating for hours. Must have swallowed thousands of dollars between the two of them."

"Why not call Dr. Campbell and see if she can anesthetize the goats through the air ducts so they sleep for the next few hours?" Simon suggested.

"Best idea I've heard all morning."

The goat picked up a twenty-dollar bill and began chewing in leisure. "Really nothing else I can do. I'll check in later," the sheriff said, waving his hand as he left the bank.

Simon walked out to see Allen Miller sitting on the bottom stone step of the bank.

Allen turned when he heard the door open. "Mr. Dale said you were here," he said.

"And what can I do for you, Mr. Miller?" Simon asked, sitting down next to him.

"Can you talk to Billy?"

"Sure, about what?"

"He put a pea in my ear last night."

"Is the pea still in there?"

Young Allen shook his head. "Mom took it out after dinner, and she gave me an extra scoop of strawberry ice cream."

"Well, that sounds like a fair deal," Simon said, leaning into the six-year-old's body. "Where's your mom now?"

"She went next door."

"Well, let's go find her," Simon said, taking the small hand of one of his favorite young residents and walking him over to Dickenson's food store. Allen's father had died the prior fall from a car crash at Priest Pass, and Simon had made a concerted effort to befriend Allen, and his older brother, Billy, who was beginning to test his boundaries and independence, not to mention his mother's good nature.

After returning Allen to safe hands, and visiting with Linda for a few minutes, Simon walked back to the police station.

"So, are the goats under control?" Dale inquired.

"Not quite," Simon answered.

"How much money is gone?" Dale asked, just as Scott Stevens walked in the door.

"Money—stolen in Lumby?" Scott asked excitedly. Scott Stevens is the lead reporter, of the two reporters in town, for the local paper, and is always looking for a story. The young man should be, no doubt, let loose in New York City, as the slow, sometimes humdrum life of Lumby doesn't offer the excitement and chaos that Scott believes his type of reporting needs. Born and raised in Rocky Mount, he never had the opportunity to venture far from home, and took the job at the paper only because of his father's friendship with William Beezer, the owner.

But he sends out resumes every now and again to various papers, all in large cities, just waiting for a job offer to be made. He has been waiting for more than six years now. It has been rumored

that he was offered a few jobs along the way, but no one has directly asked him why he is still here in Lumby.

The townspeople can sense his degree of restlessness through
his writing, which serves as a barometer for his level of frustration to be reporting on small town events. Scott has been known
to exaggerate the facts, or, on at least three occasions, totally fab-
ricate a front-page story to "liven up the place a little." However,
Mr. Beezer finally pulled his fiction-written-as-fact plug when he
ran a three-column exposé entitled "Mafia Connections Implant
Cocaine in Local Cows."

"Hellooo?" Scott said, after getting no response from Simon or
Dale.

"No money was stolen," Simon calmly explained.

"So, what money is gone?"

Simon didn't especially like Scott, but always admired his tenac-
ity, although misguided at times: very ferret-like. "I need to return
some calls, Scott. Why don't you come back in a few hours?" Simon
asked politely.

"I saw you walking out of the bank, that's why I came over."

At times, Simon thought, there are disadvantages of having the
police station, the Chatham Press and the bank at the same intersection in town. This was one of those times.

"No comment," Simon said.

"Fair enough. I'll be at the bank if you want to be quoted," Scott
offered as he walked out the door.

Hearing Scott's voice, Dennis Beezer looked up as he was just
stepping into his car, which was parked in front of the police station.

"You're out chasing news awfully early this morning," Dennis
said.

Scott sauntered over. "Same old, same old," he said with a shrug.
"Lumby's just not a hotbed of illicit activity these days. How are
things down at the *Sentinel*?" Scott liked Dennis, who was many
years his senior and, being the editor of the largest newspaper in

Wheatley, could someday be in the position to hire him—a fact that Scott always appreciated.

"Same old," Dennis concurred.

"I assume you're not in town to see your father?" Scott asked, never hesitant to turn over any rock to find any worms he could write about.

Dennis laughed. "Your assumption is correct," he said, shaking his head. Although his father, William Beezer, owned the Chatham Press and *The Lumby Lines*, he had not talked to his father for decades—more than Dennis cared to remember. As they were in the same profession, social and professional etiquette would occasionally require a handshake or a polite, albeit strained greeting, but no other words were shared between them.

When Dennis and Gabrielle, his wife, and their young son, Brian, came to Lumby eighteen years ago after living in Central America for a short time, Dennis extended an offer to introduce his father to his daughter-in-law and grandson, but William said nothing, and when Dennis paused during that brief one-way conversation, his father quietly hung up the phone. A year afterward, Gabrielle sent William an invitation to the grand opening of her restaurant, The Green Chile, but it went unanswered. So, no, he thought, he wasn't in town to see his father.

"Well," Dennis said, getting into his car, "I need to head off. Have a good day."

"Hey, would you give me a call if something opens up at your paper?" Scott asked.

Dennis was always amazed by Scott's unabashed brazenness. "I may forget, Scott. So best you call the paper every month or so, and if you hear of a position that interests you, you can call me to discuss it."

"Will do," Scott said as Dennis started his car.

Then, as he did every weekday morning, Dennis turned left onto Farm to Market Road, which connects Lumby to Wheatley, thirty minutes to the south. The drive is one of the most beautiful in the country. After leaving Lumby and its small farms on the outskirts of town, the expanse broadens to a large range of gently rolling hills that gradually drops down to Woodrow Lake. To the west, some distance away, the rolling terrain gives way to the extraordinary Rocky Mountains.

Only occasionally on his drives would Dennis take note of Montis Abbey, an old stone monastery five miles south of Lumby, which had been vacant for at least a year. He would see the blackened, scarred remains of the flames that consumed much of the building. He then would think about the fire and wonder how his son, Brian, grew up to be a teenager who totally lacked good judgment and moral fiber.

TWO

Coved

The Montis Abbey compound was originally built as a monastery in 1893, one of the older in our country, and it sheltered an order of as many as twenty-eight monks at its most active peak in the last century. At that time Farm to Market Road was a narrow dirt lane for horse-drawn carts that came to a small village north of Woodrow Lake (close to what is now the town of Lumby) for fishing and trade. While making their dusty way along the road, travelers would stop by the abbey for food and lodging, knowing that the monks were a hospitable, albeit quiet, lot.

The primary grounds of the abbey consisted of ten well-maintained acres on which seven buildings stood, one being across the road. An additional twenty-four acres comprised twelve acres of agricultural fields, four acres set aside for livestock and horses, and the remaining as dense woods that surrounded the complex and were used daily for hunting. Among a complex of assorted buildings and outhouses, the largest was the chapel and community house, which fronted Farm to Market Road. A short distance away stood the monks' sleeping quarters and private annex. The other large building was the dining room and grand kitchen, with "grand" referring to the size of the room rather than any comforts or conveniences it had. Remaining were two smaller buildings: a guest lodge and library.

The monastery was stark at best. The monks worked hard, ate hearty meals and, above all, prayed in song and prayed in silence. Their prayers continued through many of our country's most trying times until 1986, when the abbey was finally dissolved by its four remaining brothers.

Montis Abbey was then sold by the Church for a song, and for the next decade was used, on and off, as a private girls school for the few wealthy families of Wheatley. The school, though, met its demise shortly after two of its young, unworldly charges became pregnant by two boys from Lumby.

Over the next few years, the buildings gradually became lost in the overgrown landscape, but remained a target of stones that were thrown at those few windows that were still intact after the fire. It was understandable, then, that anyone driving Farm to Market would give the monastery no notice.

Mark and Pam Walker were no different. For the past four years they had driven to Lumby each Sunday for lunch during their four-week vacation in Wheatley. They would often stop, as they did on that specific morning, and park their car at the bridge over Fork River, halfway up Woodrow Lake, and walk down to Gunther Cove. From where they were standing, they could have seen the main house at Montis Abbey had they just looked.

But they were looking downward, carefully watching their footing as they made their way over large boulders and loose rock and traversed a steep embankment that brought them down to the cove's bend. The cove was one of the many treasures Mark and Pam had found during their first time exploring Woodrow Lake—a small stretch of white sand no more than a few hundred feet long and thirty feet wide. As it was nearly impossible to access by land, and well hidden from view by water, the cove was seldom visited.

Mark and Pam had kept a travel magazine article about historic inns across America, and every now and again they would bring it out to plan a vacation that never was taken. Then, four years ago, their professional and personal lives had become so rocky that they knew they needed more time for each other. In particular, Pam agreed to set aside her work, as best she could.

Beginning that year, and each year thereafter, the Walkers came to Wheatley for their spring break, staying at the Cedar Grove Inn, a polished pale yellow and white mansion on the outskirts of Wheatley. Each Sunday they returned to Gunther Cove.

The hike to the cove was strenuous, but Pam was tall and lean and maneuvered over the boulders with ease. Mark would occasionally look up and see his wife several yards ahead, her ash blond hair catching the wind blowing off the lake. He always thought she was an incredibly attractive woman, and he felt that age was bringing out her finer qualities. As he told her many times, she was as captivating as the day they married.

Reaching the last of the boulders, Pam stepped down onto the smooth sand, marked only by the imprints of the animals that had been there the night before. They walked along the water's edge until they came to a level area where Pam spread out the blanket that Mark had been carrying. Mark, in turn, poured coffee from the thermos and they sat down to enjoy another quiet morning, listening to the geese on the lake.

The first year they had come to Wheatley, they sat in that exact location on that same blanket and had one of the most heart-wrenching conversations either could remember. During those early morning hours, words were spoken in fear and in anger, in desire and regret, but what ultimately mattered was that Mark and Pam still loved each other and neither wanted to get a divorce. On that morning, both agreed to try to recapture what had been lost during their fifteen years together.

Their marriage had become a disconnected shamble. After so long, momentum had done what it always does: it had carried them forward to a point in time when they no longer recognized where they had gone.

Pam never fully evaluated the toll that her work was taking on their relationship. She felt that it was a marriage to which she had committed heart and soul a long time ago. She had learned along the way that marriages are as different as the people who enter into them, and she knew hers was bound both by Mark's love, patience and empathy and her strength and motivation. That morning, four years ago, was the beginning of a better phase in their lives.

The following year, in that same location, they had decided not to proceed with their application for adoption. For nearly eight years Mark and Pam had sought the finest medical treatments that would allow them to begin a family, but, as they came to accept, there were problems even the most advanced technologies or procedures couldn't correct. Even though Mark had long relished the thought of having several small children underfoot, he ultimately abandoned the notion much more easily than did Pam.

∽∾∽

"I think it's a matter of balance," she said logically, continuing a conversation that they had started that morning in bed, a conversation that actually began several years prior at Mark's insistence. She gazed up at the mountains that were reflected on the still water of Woodrow Lake. The peaks were still snow-covered, but the air was becoming warmer as each day passed.

Mark moved closer to Pam and put his arm around her shoulder.

"That, and timing," she added.

"But don't we make our own timing?" Mark asked rhetorically.

And therein was the greatest difference between them: Pam was methodically going through life's journey to reach a final "resting point" when there would be no worries and they could afford to follow their hearts. Mark, though, simply appreciated each day, changing direction on a whim, because in his mind it wasn't the final destination that ultimately mattered. Mark knew they had reached a point some time ago when they could do something totally different, but he couldn't break Pam free of the compelling force that had made her so successful in business. Only on vacations, when she was removed from that momentum, did she feel a twinge of uncertainty for laying her path so carefully and, at times, inflexibly.

"Perhaps when we go home, we can . . ." Her sentence trailed off, not wanting to make any promises she couldn't keep, not wanting to disappoint her husband yet again. She looked up at Mark. His brown eyes were tired, she thought. He still had that same rugged handsomeness that first attracted her, but now his thick dark brown hair was speckled with gray, as was his well-kept mustache, which he allowed to grow in during their vacation.

"As we didn't last year?" he asked gently. Everything seemed so simple to him: they were both forty-four, healthy, and had more money than they could ever have hoped for. Resting point.

"Are you happy?" Mark asked after they had been sitting in silence for quite some time.

"Yeah, I love it here," Pam answered easily.

"No, I mean, are you happy with your life?"

Pam was initially taken aback by the question, perhaps by the tenor in which it was asked, but then thought carefully. "I feel it's right," she finally answered.

He pushed harder. "But are you happy?"

Pam was staring at the sand she was fingering next to the blanket. "It's not that simple," she answered.

"I don't see any complexity in the question."

"There are so many layers that most of the time I can't even separate where one ends and another begins."

Mark had heard this same argument many times before. "All right, let's simplify: do you enjoy your work?" Mark prepared himself for another noncommittal answer, but Pam surprised him.

"No longer," she said softly. "It's changed so much these last few years." She paused. "I sort of resent who I need to be and what I need to sacrifice just to play par. But—"

"There isn't a 'but,'" Mark interrupted.

"There is. The 'but' is that it affords us a life we like to live. The 'but' is the security it guarantees."

"At what cost, though?"

"I'm willing to see it through for another five years, regardless how much I dislike it."

"Pam, I don't want you to be miserable just because you've convinced yourself we need more *things*. We have what's important: each other."

Pam felt trapped by decisions of her own making, and Mark so wanted to help his wife find her way out of the maze that they had jointly built.

"Look," Mark continued, "your happiness is much more important than anything your job might offer in the next few years."

Pam gazed at the sand running through her fingers, and then turned to Mark. His eyes were so gentle, she thought.

"Are you happy?" she cautiously asked him.

"When we're together, yes. But those times are few and far between."

"And do you still love your business?"

"Being a landscape architect is what I know, and I enjoy it a great deal, but I could easily try something different. I'm willing to forgo what I've built up in Virginia."

"I wish I could say that as easily."

"But if you're unhappy, why is it difficult to let go?"

"It's what I'm good at. . . . . It's who I've been for longer than I want to remember." Pam shrugged heavily and then leaned her body into his. "It's defined me, and I wouldn't know where else to turn," she added.

"You can turn to me."

∞

Well before noon, they packed up their belongings and continued hiking around the cove, stopping every few minutes to appreciate their surroundings, the soaring evergreens, the smell of moss. They finally reemerged on Farm to Market an hour later. As they drove toward Lumby, they were just passing Montis Abbey when they saw Hank.

Hank the flamingo came by way of Johnnie D (Jimmy D's youngest son), who one day received a large box from Amazon. Having
ordered a few books the week before, he was surprised as any in the
post office to get a box that was at least four and a half feet long and
two feet wide and equally high. Opening it, he found a tall, lanky
plastic pink flamingo with long legs and a black beak, which had
gotten lost and wrongly stamped in Amazon's shipping department.

Being the restless and imaginative boy that he was, Johnnie decided to keep the flamingo, and after careful consideration named him
Hank, after a hound puppy he had lost several years back. Over the
course of that early spring, Hank, an otherwise well-behaved flamingo, found himself the victim of numerous pranks: being named as an
altar boy in the Presbyterian Church Sunday bulletin, applying for a
shift manager position at Lumby's Sporting Goods and, worst of all,
being accused of making sexual advances on a stone goose statue
owned by Mrs. Bowman on Grant Avenue.

Hank continued to be seen about town every now and again: at
the voting booths being as politically involved as a plastic bird can,
taking the eleventh-grade final English exam, on the picket line in
front of the lumber mill demanding better health insurance, and in
a canoe paddling solo on Woodrow Lake. After a month of wild and
carefree adventures, he finally landed on the front lawn of Montis
Abbey, nesting in the overgrown foliage. Had one thought that pink
flamingos were indigenous to the area, he would have been a candidate for the cover of *National Geographic*.

Over the weeks Hank became the honorary caretaker of Montis. Undiscussed with Johnnie D, someone began dressing Hank
in appropriate, and occasionally inappropriate, attire, and soon
several of Lumby's finest sewers got involved to give Hank a well-
turned-out wardrobe.

ʝʘʑ

On that fateful morning when the Walkers took notice, Hank was
basking in a pair of bright red shorts, a Hard Rock Café T-shirt tai-
lored to his unique physique, a sun visor, sunglasses, and a towel

loosely draped over his wings. They were so amazed at what they saw that they hit the soft shoulder going a little too fast.

When the car finally careened to a stop, they instantly broke into laughter.

"What was *that?*" Pam asked.

"A pink flamingo."

"In Lumby?"

"Only in Lumby," Mark said, still laughing.

At that moment, someone tapped on Mark's window, which startled both of them, which got Pam laughing even harder—she now had uncontrollable giggles. "You folks all right?" a man asked loudly, still pecking at the window with his index finger. "I was driving right behind you when I saw you run off the road."

Mark lowered his window, fighting back laughter, hitting Pam's leg to quiet her down. "We're fine, thanks," he said.

"Looks like you'll need a tow," the man said, leaning forward to look at the car's front end.

Mark got out to assess the damage; the tire was flat and the wheel looked very bent.

"Can you recommend someone we can call?"

"Oh, no phones up here," the man said, not used to cell phone technology. "I'll give John a call when I get home. If he didn't go to church with Lilly, he should be here in about thirty minutes."

"Thanks very much," Mark said, shaking his hand, giving an evil eye to Pam, who was still in the car laughing.

While waiting for John & Son to drive the short distance down from Lumby and bring them a new tire, Mark and Pam Walker passed the time by strolling around the Montis property and peering in the dingy and frequently broken windows. The grounds were so overgrown, it was difficult walking through many of the fields, but they could still make out the abandoned orchard, the collapsing raised beds where the monks once tended to their summer vegetables, and the rose garden planted by some of the schoolgirls while boarding there.

The condition of the buildings appeared to range from "still standing" to "not still standing." In back of the main building where the fire had been, two-by-fours were nailed together to support a massive tarp thrown over the charred roof opening. Over time the tarp had given way to bad weather, resulting in serious water damage to the inside. The outbuildings, though, were untouched by the fire, and had kept their condition as well as could be expected.

As the Walkers made their way around the compound, an idea that had lain dormant for years awoke and danced in the air like static electricity. Their first, hesitant words must have been so softly spoken no one would have been able to hear; the words were more of a heavy exhale with sound than anything.

"We've talked about it for a long time, you know," Mark said, "talked about doing something different."

"Yeah, but this is just too much. And we don't even know if it's for sale.

"But this is what we said we wanted in our phase two, and now's a good time for both of us to make the move."

Pam wasn't so sure. "It would take everything we have to just rebuild it, let alone turn it into a profitable business."

"But we *could* do it."

"Do you want to leave the East Coast? That's where all our friends are."

"But this place is incredible," Mark said.

"And we don't even know if there's enough tourism to support an inn."

"Then we don't rely on tourists. We can get some local businesses to rent out space for meetings."

Pam didn't respond.

"And we can bring back the orchard . . . start making some cobbler." Pam, who still wouldn't respond, just stared at her husband in partial disbelief.

"And, during the summer, we can have a farmers market."

ာတ

When they finally worked their way around to the front of Montis Abbey, Pam stood transfixed as she looked at the old chapel. A shiver went down her back. She stared at the massive stones that had been stacked a hundred years ago to form the walls and support the roof of gray slates, now worn and cracked from time and weather. She carefully walked up onto the front porch and ran her fingers over the handblown glass of the windowpane, feeling the ripples and small air bubbles caught in time when the glass was liquid, and noticed the window's gentle tint of color that softened the view within.

What awed Pam the most, though, was the front door: a massive piece of redwood five feet wide and eight feet tall, carved with tremendous skill and precision. Scrolled columns were engraved into both sides of the door with an intricate pattern of spirals encircling a large cross that was centered between them. Above that, the word "MONTIS" was cut deep into the wood in detailed calligraphy. The hinges were of forged iron, each one of such size and weight that Pam thought they must have been hammered several centuries earlier and somehow made their way to this monastery, this door.

She turned to ask Mark a question, but saw that he had crossed the road and was making his way through what they presumed was once a vibrant and well-cultivated orchard. She watched as he stumbled over fallen limbs that were hidden under a carpet of wild vines and knee-high weeds. Mark was a fit, athletic man, but he had clearly met his match with this orchard, and Pam heard him laugh, swear, and then laugh again as he tried to make his way to the top of the hill.

Standing on the porch watching her husband, Pam allowed her heart to take hold and sweep away all logic, leaving her defenseless against the exhilaration of pure excitement. Here she could live a life that would bring her joy, a life shared with the husband she loved. She finally saw what Mark had envisioned, and she knew, in that one moment, that this was the compelling reason she needed to finally break away from her golden handcuffs.

ʕʘʗ

THREE

Lumby

The Lumby Lines

What's News Around Town

BY SCOTT STEVENS   **MARCH 30**

A busy week in our sleepy town of Lumby.

Last Thursday, two goats hired by the Chatham
Bank enjoyed an expensive breakfast on the town.
Eating their way through $1,012 while held captive
in the bank vault for twelve hours, the goats were
finally released at 8:48 a.m., no worse for wear.
Mcnear, the goats' owner, made no comment when
asked if he would reimburse the bank for its losses.
However, Rob Steadman, the bank's president,
has assured all account holders that their funds
are secure, and that the bank's insurance company
would cover any losses, eaten or otherwise.

There have been an abnormally high number of complaints from local residents that an unknown assailant has been applying hot-red nail polish to their horses' hoofs. Dr. Campbell has confirmed that nail polish presents no immediate danger to the equines, adding that it's probably best for the owners to allow the polish to wear off instead of attempting to remove it.

Chris Donnelly has launched the Lumby Time Capsule project, and requests that anyone with something to add to our town's time capsule should bring it by his house on River Bank Road. The capsule, which will actually be a donated coffin from the Wheatley Funeral Home, will be filled and ceremoniously buried in the northeast corner of the Lumby Fairgrounds next Saturday evening. The burial will be immediately followed by the semi-annual tractor pull. Jimmy D's will provide the refreshments at both events.

That same week Scott Stevens also submitted to his editor an exposé on Jeremiah Abrams, whose daily buggy rides into Lumby were causing the town merchants increased concern. Jeremiah's mare, Isabella, was becoming quite blind, as was Jeremiah, and was unable to differentiate road from sidewalk, tree from awning, and trough from bicycle stand. Further, the mare had been inadvertently given goat grain in her bucket (as Jeremiah could no longer read the small labels on the feed bags), and the change in diet left a long and odorous trail from Hunts Mill Road to the Wayside Inn, which Jeremiah certainly could not see, and probably could not smell given the sinus problems he has had since being a young boy himself. To Scott's dismay, the article was never published.

ഗ

One of the few factors separating Lumby from most other villages that dot the landscape is its apparent anonymity, being hidden away in a less-traveled part of the Northwest. Lumby is also extraordinarily beautiful, reminiscent of the landscape canvases painted by young college artists when told to envision paradise on earth. The sounds and smells are just as enticing, reminding one of childhood walks through fields of lavender and honeysuckle with the low hum of pollinating bees and dragonflies all about.

In a visually broader sweep, Lumby is both a town and the valley in which it rests. The influences of the town and the valley on each other are so strong that one archaeologist, passing through years ago, called it an "eco co-dependency," which most folks who attended his Lions Club presentation that evening didn't understand at all.

Woodrow Lake, although not officially within Lumby's town borders, is sometimes represented on area maps as being part of the township, and is usually shown to be within Chatham County, which is flagrantly incorrect.

The fact that a third-generation Lumby resident owned the Chatham Press, which the U.S. government subcontracted to print local street, municipal, geographic and topographic maps, had direct bearing on how some town and county lines were drawn. It never occurred to anyone involved in these misrepresentations that the U.S. government might someday audit the work. That was good fortune for owner William Beezer, as it had never occurred to the government either.

"Do you think he knows?" Carrie asked Scott, surveying the revised county map that she had just pulled from the press, with the ink still wet.

"Of course Beezer knows," Scott answered. "He approved the final galleys."

"But the county line has been extended at least six miles to the west."

"It's all uninhabited state forest. No one will know."

"But it's nearly doubled the size of our town!"

Carrie Kerry, the other reporter for *The Lumby Lines*, continued to gaze at the map, very concerned. Had the paper and the printing press not been owned by the same man, she would have a great story to write.

"Well, I think this is worse than the brochure," Carrie said, referring to the new Lumby town brochure that had been printed the prior month, using on its front flap a spectacular photograph of downtown Banff, Alberta, and the surrounding Canadian Rocky mountains. To her amazement, no one had registered a complaint; all of the residents appeared to like the slight enhancements that the Banff photo offered. If one glanced at the brochure, just seeing a blur of mountains and a small town, the mistake might have been innocently overlooked. Admittedly, the Canadian flag above one of the stores was barely discernible through the evergreens. But it was hard to imagine how anyone could overlook the fact that a twelve-mile lake was missing from the photograph, a lake just south of Lumby that might or might not be within the town's limits.

Woodrow Lake, regardless of its true geographic orientation, is a tranquil, very long but irregularly shaped reservoir that offers some of the finest fishing in the entire area. It is occasionally remembered that the U.S. Army Corp of Engineers significantly modified the lake, eighty years prior, by cutting coves and inlets to facilitate better runoff when the valley had a spring deluge. But most residents prefer to think that Mother Nature was the only architect of this beautiful and efficient body of water.

Here, too, occurred the infrequent tragedies that beset the town, such as the young, freckle-faced child learning to swim but slipping deftly out of her father's embrace, or the high school Merit scholar who desperately tried to save his retriever that had wandered too far from shore onto the thinning March ice. Each time the victim had been driven back to Lumby to a mourning community.

The only road that passes Woodrow Lake is Farm to Market Road,

which runs, quite loosely, north and south. Heading south, a thir-
ty-minute drive from Lumby, is the small city of Wheatley, named
by the Indians for the natural grasses that were abundant in the
area. Heading north from Woodrow Lake, Farm to Market follows
Goose Creek, passing Montis Abbey by mile marker 5, and then to
the south end of Lumby, where the creek veers northwest and the
road continues straight into this quaint-quirky town of 4,200.

�ç૦ૢ

Having just driven up from Wheatley, Dennis Beezer pulled up
and stopped directly behind Isabella, Jeremiah's mare, who was
eating some flowers in the raised bed outside Wools Clothing Store.
Giving it not a second thought, he reversed his car, leaving a safe
distance between the mare's hindquarters and the clean hood of
his vehicle.

As he stepped out, Dennis heard his wife, Gabrielle, chatting idly
with Jeremiah, who was sitting on a stool he had placed in front of
his mare while she ate.

"More than fifteen years ago," Dennis heard her say to Jeremiah
as she swept the sidewalk in front of her restaurant, "when we first
came to Lumby, it was difficult. We had very few friends and Dennis spent much of his time in Wheatley. But one day Joshua—well,
Brother Joshua at that time—suggested we go to the county fair.
And so we packed up young Brian, as well as two Mexican dishes I
had made for the town's potluck dinner, and ventured into Lumby."

She continued with her story. On that same evening, she and
Dennis met Charlotte Ross after Charlotte had tasted what she
called the most extraordinary enchiladas and quesadillas she ever
had. As they came to learn, Charlotte loved three things: great Mexican food, a strong margarita, and a new proposition that sparked
her keen instinct for business success. Sitting in the back of an old
pickup truck parked by the picnic tables that night, Charlotte Ross
and Gabrielle Carillo Beezer, two women of vastly different ages
and even more dissimilar backgrounds, launched the concept for
The Green Chile, a Mexican eatery.

Dennis smiled at hearing the story again. After that initial margarita whenever Gabrielle used the expression "tough old bird," he was never quite sure if she was referring to a four-day-old chicken or her new business partner.

"Hi, honey," he said, walking up and kissing his wife. "Good morning, Jeremiah," he added, putting his hand on the old man's shoulder.

"Is that you, Dennis?" Jeremiah looked around, although he saw only blurred patches of light and dark.

"Yes, it is. And how are you doing?"

"Very well. Just resting a bit before heading home."

"Do you need anything? Perhaps another carrot for Isabella?" Gabrielle asked as she and Dennis headed toward the door of the restaurant.

"You're too sweet. Thank you anyway."

Once inside, they sat at a front table. "What are you doing here? Is everything all right?" Gabrielle asked Dennis, concerned.

"I'm not sure. Simon Dixon called me at the office and asked if we could meet him here at eleven." He looked at his watch. "In a few minutes."

Gabrielle was watching Jeremiah get into his buggy when she saw Simon and Joshua walk out of the police station with their son Brian, following behind, his hands pushed deep in his pockets and his head hanging low.

"Oh, no," she said.

"What is it?" Dennis asked as he turned and looked in the direction of Gabrielle's stare. He got up and opened the door, shaking hands with Simon and Joshua and leading them to a back table.

"Thanks for driving up, Dennis. I thought it would be better if we talk here—it's more discreet than the station. We don't need Scott Stevens turning this into a front-page article."

"Turning what into a front-page article?" Dennis asked.

Simon turned to Brian. "Would you like to explain to your father?"

Brian shook his head and sloughed down farther into the chair.

"Brian and one of his cohorts, Terry McGuire, drove to Rocky Mount and put several gallons of food dye into one of the smaller water sheds at Ross Orchards last night. It wasn't noticed until dawn this morning after the sprinklers had been running for a few hours. In the north corner of the orchard, all of the trees are bright blue and will be for some time. The Rosses are unsure of the damage to the crop, but they believe this year's fruit will be lost."

Brian chuckled under his breath.

"Are you sure it was them?" Dennis asked.

"Show him," Simon firmly told Brian.

Brian shrugged his shoulders and pulled his hands from his pockets, raising them in the air. Both hands were dark blue.

"Damn it, Brian," Dennis said in exasperation.

Joshua leaned forward. "The Rosses asked if I would talk with you about this since they know we have a longstanding friendship."

"Which is understandably being tested to the fullest," Dennis said in embarrassment.

Joshua went on, "I've worked for them a long time, Dennis. They're fair people, but I must admit, they're incredibly angry right now. I don't know if they'll formally press charges, but perhaps Brian could recommend some kind of repayment to encourage them not to."

"Such as?" Gabrielle asked.

Simon answered. "I believe Terry McGuire is going to offer working in their orchards as free labor each Saturday and Sunday for the next two months."

"What a chump," Brian said under his breath.

Dennis stared at his eldest son in disbelief. "Joshua, please tell the Rosses that Brian will work twenty hours each weekend for the rest of the summer—for the next four months," he said angrily.

Brian bolted upright. "But, Dad—" he whined.

"Not a single word," Dennis snapped back at him.

Simon stood up from the table. "Joshua, would you let me know if the owners want to legally carry this forward?"

"I'll be talking with them tomorrow and then will call you."

Dennis walked Simon to the door. "Thanks for handling this so quietly."

"Not a problem," Simon said.

Dennis continued to hold the door open. "Brian, go home. We'll talk about this tonight."

After Brian left, Gabrielle said quietly to Joshua, "I don't know how to apologize. Perhaps we can go and talk to Chris and Lilly tomorrow."

"That might help."

"Should I call Charlotte?" she asked.

"No, I don't think so. She's no longer involved in the orchard's operations, and it would just upset her."

"I just don't know what to do with him," Dennis confessed.

"For what it's worth, I did some crazy things in my youth as well. Far worse than tinting some trees," Joshua said with a chuckle.

Dennis leaned back and tried to calm himself. "Well, my father never gave me the opportunity. Maybe it was outright fear that kept me out of trouble."

"I hear William Beezer still keeps an iron fist over those around him," Joshua said wryly.

"Well, please don't go to Brian's defense with your employer. I don't want you to jeopardize your position there."

"Let's see what happens."

Changing the subject, Joshua said lightheartedly, "I believe you owe me some money, Dennis."

"For what?" Dennis asked, confused.

"My garage is finished," Joshua said, raising his arms in triumph.

Dennis started laughing, and Gabrielle shook her head. "Why two grown men would make a bet on who drywalls their garage first is beyond me. You guys really need to stop doing this."

"Fine," Joshua said. "But only after he pays me."

"How much this time? Five dollars? Ten?" Gabrielle asked.

Dennis wrapped his arm around his wife's neck. "You make it sound like I lose every time."

"Well, you do, don't you?" she teased him. She got her purse, knowing that Dennis seldom carried any cash. "By the way, I heard rumors in town that an East Coast couple is looking to buy your old residence."

Joshua looked perplexed. "The rental property in Wheatley?"

"No. Montis Abbey."

"Really?"

"It sounds like they plan to turn the old monastery into an inn."

"Wow, that's amazing." Joshua paused, thinking about the abbey. "I thought the property couldn't be sold. Wasn't there some confusion over its reinstatement into the National Historic Landmarks Association?"

"Possibly, but they're certainly asking a lot of questions around here."

"Oh," Dennis said in a low voice. "I bet that won't sit well with some of our more illustrious town residents."

Gabrielle knew exactly who he meant. "No, not well at all."

FOUR

Montis

Their investigation into Montis Abbey led Mark and Pam during the following week to courthouses in Wheatley, Lumby, and the county seat, plus the archives at the local papers. In this way they began to draw a true picture of the property's past and current ownership. When they first met with adjacent landowners, word began to spread, so by the time Mark and Pam walked into the real estate office, their intentions were well known.

A few significant issues rose from their investigation, any one of which should have been a deal breaker, but the possibility of converting Montis Abbey into a historic inn was now so close at hand the Walkers were as hooked as a trout on a dry fly.

ᔕᗝᔕ

"I still don't fully understand," Mark said during dinner in Wheatley that week.

"There seems to be an issue about the property's historical landmark status," Pam answered, doing her best to repeat what the attorney had explained to her earlier that day.

"But the abbey is a hundred years old. Is that not enough?"

"Yes, but the fire damaged the property to such an extent that

Montis Abbey was removed from the landmark registry last year."

"So, worst case is that our inn won't be on the registry," Mark responded. "It would be nice if it were, but if not, that's all right. I don't think it would substantially change the amount of business we would get."

"Unfortunately, it's more chancy than that."

"How so?"

"The attorney examined the property deed and ordinance going back to 1894, and he believes that the abbey is currently protected under a grandfather clause with the National Park Service. If the property were to permanently lose its historic landmark status, the land and buildings would revert back into the Bureau of Land Management ownership."

"Well, if it doesn't have historic status now, why hasn't that already happened?"

"The current owners requested, and received, a five-year waiver, buying time to either be reinstated into the registry or sell to someone who could."

"So we could actually buy the abbey, restore it, and then lose it?" Mark asked with serious concern in his voice.

Pam tried to give a reassuring smile. "It's possible, but in my opinion, not probable. Assuming we are diligent in restoring Montis to its original condition, there should be no reason why the abbey would not be reinstated." Mark relaxed slightly, easing back in his chair. "But that type of true restoration is tremendously expensive," Pam continued. "And unfortunately, from what I researched this afternoon, there are no federal grants or loans to assist us."

"Do you think we could financially handle it ourselves?"

"I'm not sure, but I think so," Pam said. "Certainly it would burn through a lot of our savings. Once the inn opened, we would need to have full occupancy of all twelve rooms in the summer to carry our operating costs."

"And the winter?" Mark asked further.

"I only estimated a ten percent occupancy rate, which I think is very conservative given the numbers I saw at the chamber of commerce."

Mark didn't answer but returned to his meal, pondering the risk they would be taking.

"But if this is it, the 'it' that we've been waiting for—" he said, almost arguing with himself.

"Then it may be worth the gamble," Pam finished his sentence. "So, how was your meeting with the building inspector?"

"Perhaps we should wait until after dinner to discuss that," he chuckled. But seeing the worried look on Pam's face, he added, "Really, no better or worse than what we thought. I have his report in our room, and you can read it tonight. Very thorough, and in places, almost encouraging."

꒰ꕤ꒱

At two o'clock in the morning Pam gently woke Mark.

"Who will cook?"

"What?" Mark asked through a sleepy haze.

"Who will prepare the meals?"

"I will," he said, rolling over and taking his wife in his arms. "Now go back to sleep."

"Honey, I think I'm the only person on earth who can appreciate your jalapeno and sardine omelet surprise."

Mark yawned. "Okay, then you will," he mumbled. "You make wonderful Tuscan pork."

"And so begins and ends my culinary expertise."

"And great rum cake," he added.

"Mark, seriously."

"So, we'll need to find a chef. But not in the middle of the night."

Pam had been awake for several hours, and she continued to wrestle with the problem. "We need to offer a wonderful breakfast to our guests."

"French toast stuffed with liver and mango," he said slowly.

Pam cringed like she was being forced to eat frogs from the

blender. "Yet another one of your originals that we won't want to put on the menu. But if we hire a chef, why not open a charming country restaurant that offers spectacular dinners? The kitchen is large enough, and the dining room could seat well over thirty people. It may be a way to increase our revenue during the slow months. Perhaps we can even print a cookbook of the inn's recipes." Pam waited for a response. "So, what do you think?"

Not much. Mark had fallen back to sleep.

It took Pam another few hours to think through other alternatives.

"Honey? Are you awake?" she nudged him.

It was 4:15.

"No," he groaned, placing a pillow over his head.

"I think we could offer all-inclusive vacation packages to the inn: a honeymoon weekend or a midweek getaway."

"That sounds fine," Mark said from under the pillow.

Two hours later, Pam leaned over and kissed her husband. She had already been to the bakery and bought several croissants hot from the oven, walked back to Cedar Grove Inn, and made fresh coffee in their room. Had the kiss not awakened Mark, the fragrances would have.

"A bit excited, are we?" Mark teased Pam after looking at the clock.

"Well, I've been thinking about a wine cellar, and how that may be one way to advertise: international cuisine with a broad international wine list."

"Great idea. Can we go back to sleep for a while longer?" Mark pleaded.

"There's too much to do. I think we need to see the realtor this morning and finalize the deal."

"We do?" That was encouragement enough for Mark to jump out of bed and enjoy coffee and croissants with his wife. After breakfast, Pam and Mark went back to bed and made love, and it was as it used to be when they first met.

So, over the course of the next few weeks, consuming their remaining vacation time, the Walkers negotiated the purchase of Montis Abbey. It entailed endless discussion, leaving them sleep-deprived and nervously exhilarated. Never had Pam even entertained the idea of making such a radical move so impulsively. But Mark was right, as he normally was about matters of the heart: this kind of opportunity might only come once. Carpe diem.

Once their decision was made, she led their efforts in acquiring Montis Abbey. She approached the task as relentlessly as she did any project, with steely precision and analytical thinking that always assured Mark that their best interests were protected.

As word of the deal spread through Lumby, one early morning someone dressed Hank in a banker's pinstripe suit and tied a briefcase to his wing—he looked quite debonair.

The Lumby Lines

Old Montis to Open New Doors as Inn

BY CARRIE KERRY   **APRIL 19**

The Montis Abbey at mm 5 on Farm to Market Road has been sold to a Mark and Pamela Walker of Falls Church, Virginia, for an undisclosed amount. The closing was conducted at Russell's office yesterday morning.

The property consists of 34 acres split on both sides of the road, and has seven buildings. The largest of those buildings suffered extensive damage from last year's fire.

In an interview conducted yesterday by this reporter, the Walkers said that they will start restoration immediately, and hope to open the Montis Inn by March of next year.

Their plans are to have sixteen bedrooms, most with private baths, and two restaurants. Mark Walker also added that he will be personally overseeing the recultivation of the abbey's extensive orchard.

It's said that the Montis Abbey has the best views of Woodrow Lake in the state.

ನಿಂ

FIVE

Antlers

In addition to Woodrow Lake, Mill Valley, called that for the hundred-year-old bright red water mill rising from the banks of Goose
Creek, spread before Montis Abbey as a gentle offering: twelve
square miles of rolling pastures, agricultural fields, farms and
grasslands. Surrounding the valley on the west side are protective hills of evergreens and hardwoods, occasionally scarred by
clear-cutting for lumber. Beyond those hills are low mountains
that, very distant on the evening horizon, grow and ultimately become the Rockies.

Lumby rests at the north end of Mill Valley where Farm to Market
Road forms a junction with State Road 541. Main Street, shown on
some maps as Lumby Road and referred to by the residents simply
as "Old 41," is a tree-lined road that was one of the last in the state to
be paved. Small storefronts and restaurants, with colorful awnings
that flap in the summer breeze and warm stoves that burn within during long winter months, line sidewalks of raised flower beds,
scattered fruit trees and brightly painted wooden benches.

This, the main downtown intersection, is the only intersection
busy enough to warrant a blinking stoplight. One could easily argue

that the light was not then, nor ever, required, but the townspeople voted overwhelmingly at last year's annual town meeting to have it installed. For many, it was a social and economic forecaster—a blinking indicator that the town was going places: yes, no, yes, no. But this light that controlled the epicenter of activity for sleepy Lumby hadn't worked for several months, and there were no immediate plans to look into the problem. Regardless, the Chatham Press saw the streetlight as another opportunity to print and sell "The New and Revised Lumby Town Map."

Outside S&T's Soda Shoppe on one of the brightly painted benches, Mackenzie McGuire and Joshua sat and quietly talked.

"I really appreciate your involvement during the orchard incident. I don't think the Rosses would have been as lenient had you not stood up for my son."

"I think you're giving me far more credit than what's due. But I thought Terry showed good character when he met with the owners—even if his hands were still tinged," Joshua kindly acknowledged.

"Instead of the scarlet letter, he showed his crime with blue fingers." Mackenzie shook her head. "He certainly resents having to spend his weekends at Ross Orchards. How is he doing?"

"Well. He has a good attitude and learns quickly," Joshua said encouragingly.

She looked down at her hands. "You know, he's really not a bad kid. But when he gets together with Brian Beezer, he just stops thinking. They're not good together—they egg each other on."

Joshua laughed thinking of the harmless rivalry he'd had with Brian's father for well over a decade. "Boys will be boys," he offered as solace.

"Well, he'll have very little time to get into trouble now," she said with satisfaction. "He'll be working for me full-time this summer. I have a few jobs, so we don't have to be working side by side, which he considers a crime."

"Give him time—he'll grow up. I hear he's becoming a fine carpenter."

"Like his father," she paused, "in far too many ways."

"So are you going to bid on the Montis job?"

Mackenzie turned and looked at Joshua in surprise. "I didn't know they had speced out a job. Are they asking for proposals?"

"I don't know. It's just an assumption on my part. They have a tremendous amount of framing to be done because of the fire last year."

"That would be a huge contract," she said, already thinking about what the project would entail. "I haven't been in Montis for years. How are the other buildings?"

"Poorly weathered, I think, but it's been years for me as well."

Scott Stevens, who had been standing behind the bench, interjected, "Talking about Montis?"

"More about the weather, actually," Mackenzie tried to redirect him.

"I heard several townsfolk are up in arms that it was sold to an East Coast couple." Scott flipped the pages in his notepad and pulled out a pencil, preparing to write. "Brother Joshua, your opinion would be greatly valued since you are one of the few who lived there."

"I'm no longer a brother."

"But you must think something of what is happening to Montis Abbey. Rumor has it that the new owners are going to open it as a cheap hotel, very brothel-like."

Knowing Scott's perseverance, Joshua carefully selected his words. "I think any person who is willing to commit the time and money to restore Montis should be given the benefit of the doubt." He then stood up. "Excuse me, I need to run some errands. Good seeing you again, Mac."

Joshua looked apologetically at Mackenzie before leaving her alone with Scott, and then escaped down Main Street and quietly entered the police station, where he saw Simon lost in paperwork at the front desk.

"Shouldn't you be out arresting goats or something?" Joshua laughed.

"And such unruly citizens they are!" he responded in kind.

"I just wanted to tell you that the Rosses agreed to have Terry and Brian work in the orchards during the next few months as reparation for their prank."

"So, no charges?"

"No."

The phone rang, and Joshua heard Dale Friedman's muted voice coming from one of the back offices of the station.

"It's for you, Simon," he called out.

"I'll talk with you later," Joshua said, hearing another call ring on the second line.

Simon answered the phone. "Lumby Police Department."

"Simon?" a faint, aged voice said.

"Yes, this is Simon. How can I help you?" he responded.

"This is Martha Ellers."

"Morning, Martha," Simon said. "Is there something wrong?"

"There's a moose in our backyard, and he's eating up Gordy's new azaleas."

"Is your husband there now?"

"No. He and Will Barr had to go into Rocky Mount for some supplies, he said."

"And no one is outside near the moose?"

"I'm in the kitchen."

"Good. Let's see if we can get him to move on. Why don't you open the window and bang two pans together?" he gently instructed her.

"Okay. I need to put the phone down. The cord won't reach that far."

"That's fine. I'll hold on."

Simon heard the rustling of pots and pans, and then silence.

"I can't open the window. It's stuck."

"Try another one. Any one that faces your backyard is fine."

"I'll be right back."

Within a few seconds, Simon heard two weak "clanks" of the pans hitting each other, followed a few seconds later by an equally weak "Oh my."

"Martha?" Simon said loudly into the phone.

"Yes, I'm here," she said, picking up the receiver.

"What happened?"

"When the moose turned, he kicked little Emma's tricycle," she said. "Oh, wait. . . . He just poked it with his antlers. . . . It just fell over."

"The tricycle?"

"Yes," she said tentatively. "Oh, my word. . . . He's poking it again, but really hard." More silence. "Now he's flipping it over. . . . And he's poking it again. . . . Oh, look! The antler broke the spokes and went right through the wheel. . . . It's stuck! He's shaking his head, but it won't come off!"

"The tricycle?"

"He's shaking his head really hard, but the tricycle's stuck on his antler," she explained. "Oh, and there he goes. He's walking through our garden. He just crossed over into Cindy Watford's yard."

"Are you all right?" Simon asked, knowing her frail health.

"Yes, but he took my granddaughter's little bike. Can you get it back?"

"I'll call the county wildlife extension to report the incident. Just to confirm, when the moose left, the tricycle was still hanging from his antler?"

"Yes, a pink one with yellow and red streamers on the handle-bars."

"That's fine. When is Gordon due back?"

"Before noon, he said."

"Well, I'll call you later today if we hear anything," Simon said.

"Thank you so m—" Martha responded, hanging up the phone before finishing her sentence.

SIX

Brooke

For 48 years, the local paper, *The Lumby Lines*, had always held steadfast to its motto: "It's worth the paper it's written on," but occasionally locals heard the founder, Mr. William Beezer, refer to it as "useless as wet toilet paper." But many things in Mr. Beezer's life had become twisted or lost in translation.

The best remembered was when the paper was first published, Vol. 1, No. 1, as *The Lumby Record*. Getting feedback from his staff and friends that the name sounded more like a police blotter sheet than a newspaper, he instructed his printer to change the paper's banner to read *The Lumby Times*. However, over the sound of the running presses, that wasn't quite what was heard. And so, the following week, Vol. 1, No. 2, of *The Lumby Lines* was printed. Everyone initially laughed, but somehow, in the time Mr. Beezer spent trying to think up yet a third name, it settled on the people of Lumby, and they all but insisted it not be changed. It was, after all, unique.

Dale Friedman was reading *The Lumby Lines* when Simon walked into the police department at seven a.m. "And how are you this morning?" Simon asked.

"Fine, Sheriff," Dale answered, as he does each morning.

"Anything to report?"

"No. It's been disturbingly quiet," Dale said, looking at his log. "But Charlotte Ross is waiting for you in your office."

"Do you know what she wants?"

"No idea," Dale responded. "But it's always interesting, isn't it?"

Simon walked down the hall and into his cramped but comfortably organized office, where he saw Charlotte, a small woman, sitting quietly in the chair in front of his desk, her hands crossed on top of a sunhat that was lying on her lap. She was wearing a simple flower-printed dress with stockings rolled just below her knees. Her shoes looked very worn, and her long hair was tied loosely in a bun with gardening twine.

"Good morning, Miss Ross," Simon said loudly, walking over to her and taking her hands in his, noticing the dirt under her nails.

"Good morning, Mr. Dixon. I'm sorry for intruding so early."

"That's never a problem," Simon assured her. "What can I do for you?" He crossed the room and stood behind his desk.

"I have a personal favor to ask, if it's not too much of an imposition."

"I'm sure it won't be. What is it?"

"I would like you to witness the signing of my prenuptial agreement."

Simon sank slowly into his chair, trying to process that one sentence, but there were too many disconnects.

"Charlotte, I didn't know you were getting married again." He paused, groping for the right words to say. "Ah, congratulations! And who is the lucky man?"

"What?" Charlotte asked, cupping her ear.

"And who is the lucky man?" Simon repeated, a little louder.

"Zak Taylor, over on Hunts Mill Road."

Simon tried to control his surprise. "Well, Zak's a good man," he finally said. "Good for you, Charlotte," he almost yelled, in a tone as if she had just won a swim meet. "And I would be honored to be your witness, but wouldn't Russell be a better choice?"

"Lawyers are just a bunch of crooks. They don't even trust other lawyers." Charlotte always spoke her mind. "And in a dream last week, Zeb, rest his soul, told me to come to see you." She paused and then asked, "Do you think it's unusual that all of my husbands' names begin with a Z?"

Simon smiled warmly. "Not at all," he answered. "Regarding Russell, he's a good friend of yours, you know, and I'm sure he will look out for your best interests. Did he draw up the agreement for you?"

"Yes, of course, but I want you to sign it, Simon. Everyone trusts you."

"Well, thank you, Charlotte," he paused. "When would you like me to do this?"

"Russell asked me to come to his office Thursday afternoon at two o'clock. Can you join us then?"

"That would be fine," Simon said, getting up from his chair.

He helped Charlotte up and walked her to the front door, chatting casually. But then at the door she reached into her purse.

"I nearly forgot," she said. "Would you be sure that Linda Miller is given this anonymously? I heard that she has had such a difficult time trying to raise her sons alone since her husband died." She handed Simon a cashier's check.

"May I?" he asked.

"Certainly," she nodded.

He opened the folded check and saw that it was made out to Linda for five thousand dollars, with no reference to its benefactor.

"This is very generous of you, Charlotte. I spend quite a lot of time with her sons, and I can assure you that this will be very helpful."

"Shhh," she said, putting her thin index finger to her lips. "Not a word that it came from me."

"Promise," Simon guaranteed her.

She turned and he watched the small woman shuffle down the sidewalk. Quite an amazing person, Simon thought. At ninety-something years old, her mind was frequently as clear as those thirty years her junior, and she certainly had her wits about her regarding this marriage.

If one was to see Charlotte on the street, shuffling to S&T's for her morning coffee, one might mistake her for being destitute, for being a burden to the small town of Lumby. She always dressed modestly, no longer drove, but when she had, always drove a twenty-year-old Volvo, and frequently had dirt on both her hands and knees.

Those who knew Charlotte, though, knew that in addition to being an avid gardener, she was the town's wealthiest, and most generous, resident, who had amassed a small fortune that began on a shoestring budget with the two-acre orchard her first husband, Zeb, planted when they were both eighteen.

Since then the orchard, which was put into her name when Zeb died of a heart attack at the young age of forty-one, had grown into an eighty-million-dollar business, with Charlotte buying more land, starting new businesses and selling unsuccessful subsidiaries. The core company now consisted of twenty independently run orchards in three states and two vineyards in Washington, which had a combined land ownership of close to four thousand acres. Her company also owned the second largest gourmet fruit and fine wine catalogue business in the country.

No one would have guessed during those first days after Zeb's death that Charlotte would have a great business mind, perfect timing, and her share of good luck. And now she was getting married for the fourth time—for companionship, possibly for love, but definitely not for money.

As Charlotte shuffled down Main Street in the direction of Zak's home, she stopped at S&T's for a light lunch: a bowl of soup, a cup of milk and the local paper since she had not already read it in the library. And on that day, Charlotte made a special note of the article about Montis Abbey being sold.

∞

In addition to raising Charlotte's curiosity, that news clip in *The Lumby Lines* appeared to have two effects: first, it enticed several of the more curious townspeople to pay a friendly visit to the new owners. Those who ventured down Farm to Market within the first few days were disappointed to find no one around and no activity in sight. Second, it prompted Hank to change his attire—he was now wearing carpenter's overalls, which just barely covered his knotty knees, no shirt, and a nice orange hardhat. A hammer hung from his beak with duct tape.

After the closing, Pam returned home to Virginia for a month while Mark stayed in Wheatley, coordinating contractors and subcontractors, and trying to set up a construction schedule that worked within their resources of both time and money. He soon missed his wife's innate skill with project management.

"I don't understand how two bids for the exact same framing job can be twelve thousand dollars apart," Mark said to Pam during one of their twice-daily calls to each other. He was becoming frustrated in the detailed planning, and impatient to have the work begin.

"Which one did you feel you could work with?" Pam asked.

"I like Mac McGuire a lot," Mark answered.

"Which was his bid?"

"Actually, it's a *her,* Mackenzie McGuire, and her bid was the lower of the two."

"A female framer?"

"Yeah, with flaming red hair and a back as strong as any man's. She has outstanding references and a good crew. She just finished a job for Gabrielle Beezer expanding The Green Chile. I went over and saw her work before they drywalled and it looked really good."

"Why do you think her bid was so much lower?"

"I don't know. It's a small business, and she and her crew are local. But she agreed to a penalty if she ran over. In return, we agree to structure the draws and final payment to provide for a bonus if she comes in under budget or earlier than committed. Plus, she and her crew can start immediately."

"That's great. I like the idea of our framer being a woman—very open-minded. I wish I was there to see them begin," she said glumly.

Sensing her sadness, Mark asked, "So, what are you doing this evening?"

"I'm in our bedroom, beginning to pack the books and pictures." She was holding their wedding photograph, about to wrap it carefully in packing material. "We've come a long way, haven't we?" she asked, looking down at the picture.

Pam was remembering the day when they first met, on a bitterly cold afternoon in January with six inches of new snow blanketing Boston. To temporarily escape the drudgery of her graduate work, she had walked to the university bookstore, which was open but totally empty. While looking down at a book she was going to purchase and walking toward the register, she inadvertently stepped on and into the only other customer in the entire store—a man who would have enjoyed his cup of coffee had the impact not jarred it from his hand and sent it tumbling onto the discount book table. Regrettably, the cup was full, so no less than a dozen books were victims of their first encounter.

"Yeah, we have come a long way. But think about what awaits us." He paused. "Are you okay?"

She didn't respond right away. "I'm just packing up some of our personal items and became a little melancholy, I suppose." He waited for her to continue, and at last she did. "I've been trying to call Brooke—left her two messages, but I haven't heard from her. And I finally called Mom to tell her."

"How did she take the news?"

"Happy for us, but tremendously sad that we're moving away," she replied. "Moving away from *her,* as she put it. She thinks that she'll never see us again."

Pam's relationship with her mother, Kay, had changed dramatically from a distant bond to a strong friendship after her father passed away ten years before. During Pam's youth, she had seldom spent time with either of her parents, who were both focused on their very demanding careers. After school, she was frequently alone in a large, empty Connecticut estate, obediently completing her homework while awaiting her parents' return, which often did not occur until days later, as their successes required them to travel throughout the world. Although they would occasionally bring Pam in tow during the summer months, she was usually left behind with a dependable guardian. Given Pam's upbringing, it wasn't surprising that she had become such a self-starter, very much like her mother.

Kay's strong sense of independence and single-minded determination to carry on allowed her to maintain a happy and purposeful life after becoming a widow. Those qualities, which Pam always admired, and Kay's excellent health had served her well in her senior years. It was in Kay's older years when Pam became determined to hold tight to the bonds between them, a tie between an only daughter and her mother.

By comparison, Mark's childhood was mostly spent in a tiny country kitchen filled with the endless laughter of relatives and friends and wonderful aromas from poor-man's stew. Four generations of his family lived under one small roof, and although food was frequently scarce, love and music were abundant. It was, no doubt, their opposite upbringings that had formed their opposite definitions for the term "living richly."

Mark could hear the guilt and uncertainty in Pam's voice. "Tell Kay that she'll be with us at the inn for a month or two each year over the holidays. And she would so enjoy coming out in the summer."

After a long silence, Pam finally said, "I think we may be making a mistake." The words poured out in a rush, only to be followed by another silence. "Did you hear me?" she asked cautiously. "Mark?"

"I did hear you." He had prepared for those exact words, and thought it best to just let Pam talk it out.

"I think we maybe getting in over our heads," she said. "Neither of us has ever done this kind of restoration, and I'm sure it will deplete every dollar we have." She marshaled up her other doubts

before continuing. "And we don't know anything about running
an inn. Even if we did, I don't think people can just pick up and
change like that. Also," she hesitated, "we've never worked together, and those times we've done projects around the house, it always
ends in a fight." She sighed, fighting back the tears. "I don't want
this to be the end of us."

"I promise you it won't be."

"How can you be so certain?"

"Because we've stayed together in far worse circumstances," he
assured her.

"Unhappily, at times," she added.

"But what if it's beyond our wildest dreams and it offers a quality of life we both want? And what if we grow *into* Montis Inn and
have fun learning along the way?" Pam didn't respond. "Honey, you
need to come back to Lumby. Once you're here and we're together,
everything will be all right. You'll see."

"Damn it, Mark, you keep on saying, 'You'll see,' but what happens if you're wrong? This is turning into a financial wreck that just
may be our last."

After ending the call with Mark, Pam again dialed Brooke's home
phone, but only got her answering machine. "Hey, it's me. I really need to talk with you as soon as possible, so when you get in,
please call. Hope all is well."

ಌ

During the next few days, Pam continued the tedious process of
packing up and closing down. Knowing what was awaiting her in
Lumby quickly turned familiar comforts into unwanted burdens.
Falls Church, Virginia, where they lived, now appeared overly con-
gested with people in ultra-high gear.

Pam's separation from the Baltimore consulting firm where
she was a partner ultimately required more time than she had
planned. As Pam specialized in new product and market development for start-up companies, those clients who were days or weeks
away from launch insisted that she remain engaged through the

whirlwind and fanfare of their initial marketing campaigns. Mark assured her that her time in Virginia simply bought him more time to convert one of the smallest buildings, the guest lodge, into a temporary home for them to live in while the main building was restored.

"Will it have a roof when I arrive?" Pam asked Mark one night.

"Why? Do you object to looking up at stars from your bed?"

"I hope you're not teasing."

"Get out the telescope," he said jocularly.

"Mark, this is serious," Pam said, getting more agitated. "Please stop joking about everything. You keep sending me copies of the estimates being given. Do you have any idea how much this is adding up to?"

"Don't worry. We'll just sell more apples."

"Mark, stop it!" she snapped. "We're jeopardizing our life savings and you don't seem at all concerned."

"Honey, that's not true," he said more soberly. "I am concerned, but I'm doing the best I can. We knew that there were going to be a lot of unexpected expenses."

"Which are now more than double our budget."

"Which are necessary for us to restore Montis."

"Well, maybe the idea of restoring Montis was a bad one from the beginning," Pam said coldly.

Mark was getting frustrated. "You know that's not true."

"No, I don't know. I'm not sure anymore."

"We need to see this through, Pam. We have no other option."

"Even if it means putting everything we have at risk?" she asked.

"It won't come to that."

"But if it does?" Pam pressed.

"It won't."

∞

As the weeks passed, the home in which they had lived for nine years was transformed into a house that strangers would venture through and inspect for possible purchase. Pam's spirits were lifted by reading *The Lumby Lines*, which Mark faxed to her on a regular basis.

After spending two of her planned four weeks in Virginia, Pam was still knee-deep in boxes and paper, but finally saw an end as she began to pack up the kitchen. When the phone rang, she had to push boxes aside to get to the receiver.

"Hello?" she said, still fumbling.

"Honey, it's me." Mark sounded hurried and agitated.

The Lumby Lines

Politics: It's a Dog Eat Dog World

BY SCOTT STEVENS   **APRIL 21**

With town elections still several weeks away, the political race is becoming more interesting as the candidate list grows.

As is well known from the numerous flyers and signs about town, Jimmy Daniels is making a bid to fill the shoes of our recently departed and deceased mayor, the honorable David Miller. It was assumed that this was going to be a one-man race.

However, yesterday afternoon two additional candidates registered at the courthouse and were officially added to the ballot.

Toby, a four-year-old, well-behaved golden retriever owned by Sally Mae, has declared his nomination as an independent. Toby received some notoriety two years ago after appearing in a local television ad for The Feed Store.

At campaign headquarters, Sally Mae's garage, posters are being spray-painted with the slogan "A Vote for Toby is a Vote for Old Yeller."

A protest filed by Jimmy Daniels yesterday
afternoon was quickly overturned after confirming
that there is no law on the books to prevent a canine
from running for, or taking, office.

A third candidate, Hannah Jones, 15, of Pine
Street in Lumby, also declared her nomination, and
is running on the Republican ticket, she thinks.

"What's wrong?"

"The county just notified me that we will have to get separate
occupancy permits for each of the buildings."

"So, we won't be able to live in the lodge while we restore the inn?"

"Not until it's inspected and approved."

"What does that entail?"

"Bringing some things up to code. The work that the school did
was shoddy at best, so we will need to . . . hold on."

After a long pause, Pam asked, "Mark, are you still there?"

"Yeah, I'm here," he said, but Pam heard a man talking to him.

"Mark?"

"Yes?"

"So, does that mean more money or a delay?"

"Both, I'm afraid."

"God, Mark, this is becoming a nightmare," Pam said, but she
didn't think he heard because at the same time he was yelling,
"Watch the cable!"

"I've got to go," he said in a rush, and hung up on her.

Almost shaking in frustration, Pam threw the phone into one of
the open boxes.

"Hey, girlfriend," she heard a familiar voice say.

Pam saw her closest friend, Brooke Shelling, standing in the doorway. Several years older than Pam, Brooke was also several inches
shorter. She had long, dark brunette hair that covered her shoulders.

Her most distinguishing feature, though, were her light brown eyes, or more specifically, her expressive eyebrows whose movements reflected her emotions as clearly as a still pond on a cloudy day.

"Brooke, oh my God! I've been trying to call you for days! It's so good to see you." Pam pushed her way through the boxes and gave her dear friend a hug.

"I just flew in this morning and picked up your messages. I tried your cell phone."

"Mark has it in Lumby. In fact, Mark has almost everything that's good in Lumby," Pam said in a tone of mild resentment.

"I know. I just talked with him, and he told me your big news. That's just amazing."

They were still standing by the kitchen door. "Come in, come in," Pam said, pulling her friend through the clutter. She was unsure if she was about to laugh or cry. Experiencing so many emotions on top of being so physically tired made her confused about everything. "Let's have some coffee, and I'll tell you all about it."

Over the next hour, Pam told the whole story about Lumby, the orchard and the fire, the dream she and Mark now shared to restore Montis Abbey and open it as a historic landmark country inn, and how costs had begun to tumble out of control. Pam vacillated between excitement and fright. Also, she desperately needed Brooke's help, but was unsure how to ask.

"So, what do you think?" Pam asked, looking for reassurance.

Brooke started walking around the room, her eyes filling with tears, trying to process everything she had heard. "I think I'm going to miss you," she said.

"Are we crazy?"

"Absolutely not. You guys have talked about this for the longest time, and you have such a good business mind. I'm sure if you think the numbers can work, it will happen. I just didn't think it would be all the way across the country."

Pam's insecurities surfaced again and she dropped her shoulders heavily. "Neither did we."

"So when does the construction begin?"

"Mark has hired a few contractors to start on the outer build-ings. But . . ." Pam paused.

"But what?" Brooke prompted her to continue.

Pam's strong veneer cracked slightly. Without Brooke's knowl-edge, many of their financial assumptions rested on her friend's shoulders. "We can't begin on the main house."

"Why not?"

In almost a whisper Pam said, "Because we need you."

"For what?" Brooke asked. Before Pam began to recite the words she and Mark had scripted and she had practiced on the flight home, Brooke gave her a shrewd look and said, "Ah . . . I see. I get it. You need me to watch over the house until it's sold."

"No," Pam corrected her right away. "We need you to come to Lumby." She paused before continuing. "We need you to resurrect Montis Abbey."

It took Brooke a few breaths to understand what Pam was asking of her, and she halted in the middle of the room with her mouth agape.

∞

Brooke Shelling and Pam had known each other for the last ten years. When Mark and Pam moved into the area, they purchased a beautiful five-acre lot on a quiet dead-end street and went look-ing for an architect. After meeting with some of the larger firms from McLean to Washington, they were still left searching for some-one with whom they felt comfortable, someone who would listen to them and not build just another large showplace. While antique shopping in Leesburg one winter afternoon, running from store to store to avoid the chill, they inadvertently rushed into an office that they thought was yet another mom-and-pop shop. Brooke was lying on the floor, an eggroll in one hand and Chen's Chinese food cartons scattered about, intensely studying some blueprints.

So began a long and loyal friendship. Over the following months Brooke and the Walkers worked to design a gracious and livable home, which was completed by the following fall. Although Brooke lived farther out in the country, the three met for dinner at least weekly, and sometimes more frequently if their schedules allowed.

ΩΩ

So, there Brooke stood, in the middle of the library that she had designed and helped build, looking down at Pam, who never wanted to test their friendship as she felt she was doing now. Brooke wanted to ease her friend's mind, to say that friendship was for the asking and anything she could give them was there for the taking.

"So, when do we leave?" Brooke asked simply, and both broke into spontaneous laughter.

"In nine days. Does that work for you?"

Brooke squinted for a moment, trying to visualize the calendar in her office. "I think I can manage. I can only stay for a couple of weeks, but that will give me enough time to get everything I need to come back and finish the plans in Leesburg. Do you have any original documents that can give me a start?"

"Mark and I found lots of photos of the abbey taken thirty or forty years ago. All outside shots, so we know how the back looked before the fire. We also found some rough blueprints that were submitted to the county when the school wanted to make some alterations, which were ultimately turned down."

Brooke began scrutinizing the papers that Pam passed to her. "Well then, while you're packing, let me wrap up some business and start doing some research and see if I can get a jump on your project."

"Brooke." Pam walked over to her friend. "I can't tell you how much this means to both of us."

ဢၢ

SEVEN

Speeding

After talking with his wife most mornings, Mark drove up to the
inn and either walked the fields if the weather was nice or, if it was
raining, sat on the front porch conversing with Hank, who usually
kept his opinions to himself, as some long-necked birds do. Mark
walked carefully on some of the floorboards. An engineer had cau-
tioned, during three separate meetings at the property prior to
closing, of the structural problems due to the fire and long-term
neglect. They needed to hire a carpenter who would immediately
set massive beams and posts to better support the remaining joists
and roof rafters.

Mark loved being in the midst of all the action—he felt direction and purpose. Because his family had not had much money, a
traditional college education had not been available to him. That
wasn't where he wanted his path to lead, anyway. Instead, he spent
his young adult years building expertise in a trade of his choice:
landscaping. In those initial years, it was hard, laborious work, but
the solid background it offered allowed Mark to transition from a
young unskilled laborer to the highly desired landscape architect
that he later became. During those early transition years Mark met

Pam, and his life was forever changed. After they moved to Virginia, he started his own business and momentum carried it forward. But now at Montis, walking through the tall grasses from one building to another, he knew in his core being that this was where he was meant to be, doing exactly what he was meant to do.

"You're not meant to do that," Mac McGuire yelled at Mark after he picked up a bucket of nails and headed for the roof.

"What do you mean, 'I'm not *meant* to do that'?" he protested, belligerently taking a step up the ladder.

"Don't do that," she warned.

"Says who?"

Mackenzie tilted her head and gave him a cold stare.

"Alex?" Mark yelled up to one of the men on the roof. "You need me up there, don't you?"

Alex turned, caught by surprise, and let go of a shingle he held under his knee. The shingle slid down the roof and missed hitting Mark's head by a few inches.

"Please get down from there, and leave my men out of it," Mac said firmly.

"Well, perhaps we can talk about it further," Mark said in a friendly, lighthearted tone.

"No, we can't, Mr. Walker."

"For the umpteenth time, you can call me Mark."

"Mr. Walker, we're here to do a good job for you. About the only thing that will interfere with that plan is . . ." she paused for emphasis, "you. I don't mean to be rude, but I don't have time to watch over someone who knows nothing about construction."

"I'm a fast learner."

"But I'm not a teacher," Mac replied quickly.

"You just wait. I'm sure I'll come in handy one of these days."

"Perhaps when we're done and long gone," she said politely.

Mark laughed because he knew she was right, and he knew there was no way for him to win this specific argument. He liked Mackenzie a lot. Her mass of bright red hair could be spotted a half mile away, so she was always easy to find on site. She was very good at her craft and was, from what Mark could see, fair and honest with her workers.

However, he wished she was not so reserved whenever she was around him. On the rare occasions when their discussion strayed from work, Mackenzie quickly backed away, sharing hardly any information about herself. The little Mark knew about her he learned from her workers: she was a single mother whose husband had wandered off to greener pastures years before, leaving her to raise an unruly young boy named Terry who had become a tempestuous teenager. Mark heard other mutterings as well, something about a fire, but he assumed they were referring to how much harder their framing job was because of the fire damage.

The following week flew by for Mark. He hired an electrician from Lumby, a skilled worker who came with good referrals but was down on his luck after being struck by lightning, of all things, the summer before. He and a few helpers, working closely with Mac's crew, began wiring repairs on the old guest lodge. The building was in better condition than the others, probably due to being closed up for so many years, but still needed upgraded circuitry, repairs to the roof and the replacement of some of the beams and supports in the crawl space. Additional labor was brought in to strip and reseal the hardwood floors, as well as to repair and repaint the plaster walls. Work on the lodge proceeded as quickly as Mark had expected; it was a small, five-room rambler with manageable problems. He was happy to report to Pam that it would be ready by the time she and Brooke arrived. He deliberately omitted from the discussion some of the events surrounding the lodge's return to livability. But, on the positive side, Mark had ample opportunity during this time to get to know some of Lumby's finest Emergency Medical Services and Fire Department volunteers.

Pam reported that Crest Van Lines was scheduled to pack up and load everything at the beginning of the following week,

The Lumby Lines

Sheriff's Complaints

SHERIFF SIMON DIXON **MAY 15**

5:19a.m. Ford vs deer mm8 Old 41.

6:14a.m. Cindy Watford on Cherry St. reported that someone had messed with the wiring in her car. She said that anytime the car is running, the horn blows.

2:33p.m. EMS responded to call at Montis Abbey, where someone had fallen through the roof and couldn't get up. Caller said he was stuck in floor.

3:18p.m. LFD put out fire in one of the fountains at Lumby Fairgrounds.

5:11p.m. Brian Beezer and Terry McGuire, both 18, arrested for shooting trout in Goose Creek. Bond set at $85.

10:48p.m. Sophia Meyers, age 76, but address unlisted, was arrested for no insurance and driving 82 mph in 45 mph zone on Loggers Rd. No bond listed.

11:03p.m. Car vs. deer City Service Rd.

MAY 16

8:04a.m. Lumby resident reported that his mail box had been repainted and his Sunday newspaper was missing.

10:12a.m. Complaint reported against Donna Fowler for backing up over ten-foot cross in front parking lot at First Presbyterian.

1:14p.m. A caller reported that someone had stolen his daughter's lawn mower and left an older one as a replacement.

1:36p.m. Deer damages Datsun on 4th St.

9:09p.m. Wheatley resident reported finding a moose calf on Farm to Market Road at mm 2 with small-caliber bullet wound in butt. Mother was nowhere to be found. Dr. Campbell responded and has the calf under good care at her vet clinic.

MAY 17

8:14a.m. Montis Abbey reported two goats in their apple orchard, and wanted to return them to their rightful owner.

and then she and Brooke would be driving out together. Pam's remaining evenings were spent saying goodbye to friends over home-cooked meals. As she was making these final visits, she thought about the many times her various employers had moved her in the last eighteen years. She believed it was far easier to leave than be left.

When the final Wednesday morning came, Pam walked through the now empty and silent house one last time, turned off the lights, and locked the door behind her. The Jeep was loaded to the roof with just enough space for Brooke, whom she picked up twenty minutes later.

"So, do you think you could stuff anything else in here?" Brooke asked, looking cautiously at the Jeep, which had various objects sticking out of various windows, including the sunroof. She kicked the front tire in teasing protest.

"If I tied you to the roof, possibly," Pam laughed.

When Brooke opened the passenger door, a large bag of chocolate-covered doughnuts rolled out and hit the pavement.

"Great, a culinary delight for lunch," Brooke said, picking up the doughnuts and crawling in the car, shoving her articles into the already crammed backseat.

"Are you ready?" Pam asked.

"More importantly, are you?" her friend responded.

The last week had been such a whirlwind that Pam had neglected to step back for even a moment and appreciate the magnitude of the change that was upon them. With Brooke's one question, all came into clear view: this was it.

She tightened her fingers around the steering wheel and checked the rearview mirror, which reflected Route 7 leading down to Falls Church, to the life she had comfortably grown into.

"More than ready," Pam said with a huge smile. "Let's go."

Driving out of Leesburg, leaving everything behind, the two friends set off on their way to Lumby. Unfortunately, the same could not be said for Crest Van Lines, whose driver was headed to Southern California, having received a dispatch to the wrong destination address.

Pam was so excited that she had difficulty staying within the speed limits, and unfortunately she was pulled over in four consecutive states. Brooke complained that it was becoming monotonously repetitive. She eluded all tickets, though, with her charm and genuineness, and a ten-minute soliloquy about the monastery, Woodrow Lake, Mark, and of course Lumby. One amazingly patient officer stood in the pouring rain to hear Pam's description of Hank, while another looked through Pam's small photo album, interested in what kind of fishing the lake had to offer.

When the trip was done, one could draw a fairly straight line from Falls Church to Lumby and pinpoint those police stations in which the story of Montis would be retold time and again.

The same held true for the hotels that Pam and Brooke visited en route, with specific fondness for the desk clerk at the Starlight Motel, which was in the middle of nowhere somewhere in Illinois. Unlike the officers, though, he was far more interested in Brooke. He went so far as to ask her to dinner when his shift ended at one in the morning.

"He's cute—should we ask him in for a drink?" Pam teased as they settled into their room.

"Very funny."

"Maybe there's enough water under the bridge. Maybe it's time to start dating again," Pam suggested with more of an undertone.

"And it starts here? At the Starlight Motel with Erskine from the front desk?" Brooke laughed. "God, has my life become that pathetic? What a sad state of affairs."

"Affairs . . . that's exactly what I'm talking about."

"With a married man?" Brooke was shocked that Pam would suggest that.

"No, of course not. But how long has it been since Taylor left?"

"Not long enough to forget the pain," Brooke said. She slumped down on the edge of the bed. "You know, I've thought about it a lot. I understand why he left. In fact, I was the one who most encouraged him to take the job. But the six years we were together were great. . . . I don't think I could have ever turned my back on it and just walked away like he did."

"I know how happy you were," Pam said. She started to unpack her small suitcase.

"And I suppose that's why it's hard leaving Leesburg, even this morning. We formed that business together. In fact, I still think he was the better architect. He certainly was the better half of us."

Pam gave Brooke a sharp, disapproving stare. "I don't think that at all."

"But don't you sometimes think that about Mark?"

"That he's the better half?" Pam sat down beside her, thinking about the question, understanding what Brooke was asking. "Well, I certainly feel I married upward. He's a kind and forgiving person, and has more empathy in one day than I do in a year, but I wouldn't say either of us are the better or worse half."

"Are you at all concerned about how this move, how Montis, will change your relationship?"

"It couldn't be any worse than never being together like it has been the last few years." Pam paused. "You know, looking back on it now, I have no idea how our priorities—okay, my priorities—got so twisted."

"Natural momentum. It's hard to break a pattern."

"Exactly my point to you. Sometimes we need to force ourselves to crack the mold."

"Erskine?" Brooke asked with an expression of dread on her face.

"Not specifically," Pam reassured her. "But in concept, yes."

∞

The next two days on the road would have been uneventful had it not been for the cow incident in South Dakota, or those two unexplained hours spent at the Lazy J bar. It was almost noon when Pam and Brooke finally drove through Wheatley, deciding not to stop but to continue directly up to the abbey. Passing over the Fork River bridge on the east side of Woodrow Lake, one could see the old abbey a distance away, perched on a rolling hill.

"This is breathtaking," Brooke said. She had heard Pam's numerous descriptions of the scenery, the lake, the old buildings, and she had, over the last week, studied photographs of the property, but the raw perfection had to be seen firsthand.

They slowly pulled up to the abbey, and Pam parked the car.

"This is just unbelievable," Brooke said, stepping out. If she'd had any doubts about Montis Abbey, she now knew why they had jumped at the opportunity.

As promised, Mark had finished the guest house, now called Taproot Lodge, identified by a wonderfully hand-carved sign on the front door. He had converted the lodge's main room into a spacious but warm kitchen with a wood-burning stove and a large oak table that would be used more for laying out plans than eating meals during those first few weeks. Mark was adding the finishing touches, which included installing a working toilet, the morning his wife returned.

When Mark ran out of the lodge, smiling from ear to ear, he was drenched from head to foot with the toilet seat ring hanging from his neck, bleeding from one hand, and waving a plumbing wrench as if it was a victory flag from the other.

"My God, what happened?" Pam blurted out. So much for a romantic reunion.

"Just a little water issue I had to fix in the lodge," he said triumphantly.

"All by yourself?" Pam asked with concern. Mark hoped the concern was for him and not the plumbing fixture that he had just conquered.

Mark took his wife in his arms and held her tightly, which got Pam as wet and as bloody as he was. He then removed the toilet seat from around his neck and placed it on the roof of the car.

"I'm so glad you're back," he said, kissing Pam again.

"Me too," she said, and she wouldn't let go of him.

"Brooke," Mark called out, still in his wife's tight grasp, "welcome!"

Brooke, who had been standing quite transfixed looking at the old chapel, walked over and received a huge embrace from Mark, who had always been like a brother to her—far closer, in fact, than her own brother.

"We're so glad you came," Mark said.

"Well, I love what you did to the place," Brooke teased him.

"Yep. It has a touch of that burned-out fixer-upper something, don't you think?" he said proudly. "Pretty cool, huh?"

"That's an understatement," Brooke said, walking toward the main house to inspect the scarred remains of the fire.

"Are you all right?" Mark asked, turning back to Pam.

"Yes, why so?"

"You look like you're about to cry."

Then the tears started, quickly and easily. "It was such a hard month. I've missed you. And I'm sorry." she said softly.

"Sorry for what?"

"For doubting what we have here . . . and for getting angry at you because of it." She paused, wiping her eyes. "I felt so far away from you in Virginia, but now that I'm here and see everything that you've accomplished, I know that all my . . ." She searched for a word.

"Angst?" he jokingly offered.

"More like panic—it was all for nothing." She breathed out loudly, as if exhaling all of her past uncertainties.

He didn't say anything but just smiled and held her tightly.

∽∾∽

While the women unpacked the car, Mark showered and, in doing so, proved to those doubters that his handiwork had not, in fact, irreparably harmed the plumbing system at Montis.

When they convened on the front porch, Mark brought out a bottle of white wine and some sandwiches he had purchased in Wheatley that morning. Before beginning the full inspection of the property, they ate lunch on a makeshift picnic table, waving to passersby and talking about the future.

"So, how's life been treating you, Brooke?" Mark asked.

"Blessing me sometimes, kicking me in the pants the others," she answered with a laugh.

"And how's everything in Leesburg?" which Mark always pronounced with an extended *ee*, as if it was spelled Leeeesburg.

"Great, but it's growing too quickly. We now have two Starbucks and a Cold Stone Creamery."

Mark waved a hand at the scenery all around them. "Hope you got your fill before you left. I doubt you could find either within a hundred miles of here."

"There's something to be said for that, isn't there?"

"Tomorrow morning we'll make you a great latte with milk I bought at Mcnear's Farm this morning. You'll never taste anything as fresh."

"And the coffee beans?" Brooke inquired.

"Brazilian, by way of the Lumby Coffee Hut," he laughed.

After lunch, wine glass still in hand, Brooke went to the car to rummage through her papers for the handwritten plat map faxed to her the prior week. It was time for her to explore on her own, and give her good friends an opportunity to be alone.

As she walked through the debris of the main building, she could easily see where the chapel was, and where the monks had added a community room in back. Occasionally she would look out a broken window and see Mark and Pam sitting close to each other, holding hands, talking quietly. This is a very good place, she thought with a smile.

"I've missed you," Mark said. "Hank has missed you. He almost said as much the other day."

Pam laughed. "You look like you haven't had a good meal in a while," she said, putting her hand on his thinner face.

"That's probably true. But we've been so busy that when I finally get back to Wheatley, it's late and I just collapse into bed."

"I suppose I didn't think how hard this last month has been on you."

"It was physically hard, but each day was always such an emotional high," Mark assured her. "You'll see what I mean tomorrow evening. You'll know the progress they made during the day. It may be almost negligible, or it may appear to be a quantum step forward. Either way, it's a great feeling." He eyed her drawn face. "I have a sense you may need a great feeling like that right about now."

"Probably. But you've done an amazing job in such a short time," she said. "The lodge looks great."

"I think it's a precursor for what's to come. I couldn't get over the number of questions the workers asked, or worse, the amaz-

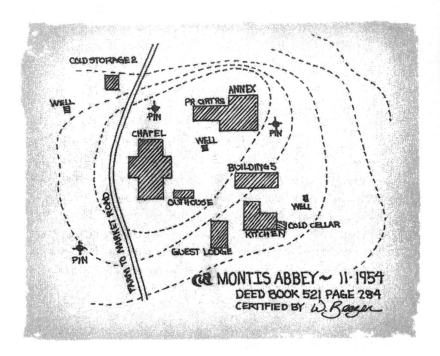

ing assumptions they made without even talking with me. I was either on the floor laughing or walking into the woods to scream in total frustration," he said. "I never told you about some of the less than shining moments of the refurbishing of the lodge."

"Oh, really?"

"Let's just say that I now know Sheriff Dixon and the county inspector better than the best man at our wedding. Both are really nice guys, by the way. But I'm pretty sure that the Wheatley paint store won't be at all interested in working with us on the main house. We had a yellow bathroom issue, so best we stay away from them for a while. Oh, and we'll need to find a new stonemason, but everyone said Lincoln was close to a breakdown before he started working here." He shrugged. "And, I think we both need a few more glasses of wine before we look at some of the bills."

Pam winced. "Are they that bad?"

"About double what we budgeted for the lodge." He didn't know a gentler way of breaking the news.

Pam sat up, becoming almost rigid. She was about to lash out in frustration and concern before she caught herself. She took a few deep breaths and tried to put everything into proper perspective. Within a few seconds her body relaxed and she patted Mark's knee. "It will be fine," Pam reassured him.

"God, I'm so glad you're here," he said, pulling her close.

"Me too."

∞

The fire damage was as extensive as the photographs showed. Clearly the back center portion of the building was lost, and there didn't seem to be a clean break between salvageable and unsalvageable. Brooke estimated that approximately a quarter of the total square footage would need to be designed and completely rebuilt, with another quarter needing to be gutted to the frame, rewired, heating and air added, plus drywalled. Finally, the remaining walls needed to be washed down and repainted.

After spending an hour walking through charred framing rubble in the main building, she went to the old sleeping quarters: a T-shaped building eighty feet long with an attached room of 600 square feet at the top of the T. Walking down the main hall, with bedroom cells of identical size on each side, Brooke was struck by the almost painful austerity of the architecture and trim work. She imagined this to be the monks' sleeping chambers, two dozen men quietly retiring to God each night, falling to sleep on hard horsehair mattresses after final prayers. The air was still stale, although Mark had opened the windows weeks ago.

The hallway emptied into one large room, the monks' annex, where they probably socialized after dinner. Aside from some hard corners, the room had tremendous potential. The eastern wall was lined with large original windows, still intact, that would allow the morning light to flood in. Unlike the austerity of the sleeping quarters, this annex had beautiful stained hardwood wainscoting and crown molding. Perhaps this was added when the school assumed ownership.

Brooke then walked down an overgrown path to the building directly behind the chapel-community house, which was obviously used as the library when it was a school, but of unknown use during the monks' tenure. Very close on the south side was another building that had served as the kitchen, dining room, root and ice cellars. Prior to electricity, the monks had cut large one- to two-hundred-pound blocks of ice from the lake and brought them up to the compound on a horse-drawn wagon. These kept the ice cellar, which was twenty feet deep, cold for weeks during the late fall and early spring. During the winter only a few blocks would be brought up at the beginning of each month.

The dining room and kitchen, which made up the L-shaped building, were in very good condition, having been fully renovated and updated by the school. Although functional, Brooke was unsure of the original design of the building. She sensed that although the monks cooked and ate here, sections of the rooms had been significantly altered. Again, she wished she had more to go on.

Leaving the remaining two buildings for later exploration, Brooke headed back to the main house and walked one more time through the burned ruins. Her clothes and hands were black from soot by the time she rejoined her friends on the porch.

"You guys have a gorgeous place here," she said, sitting down at the corner of the picnic table. "I'm almost stunned by its peacefulness."

"We think so, too," Mark said. "What do you think about the damage? Can you draw up some blueprints for us to get a permit within the next few weeks?"

"Designing a retrofit section of the building isn't the problem; I could do that in a few days. But I'm concerned that it wouldn't be historically correct." She poured herself some more wine. "But, yeah, I think we can have something rolling by the time I leave."

With that, they toasted their friendship, the inn, and the good fortune of being there that spring afternoon.

While Mark and Pam continued to talk, Brooke picked up the copy of *The Lumby Lines* that was lying on the picnic table, read for about thirty seconds, and started laughing uncontrollably.

The Lumby Lines

When Pigs Fly

BY SCOTT STEVENS   **MAY 21**

To the bewilderment of many in town yesterday, a haltered pig, tethered to nine helium balloons, floated along Main Street, staying approximately fifteen feet off the ground. When caught by a gust of wind, the squealing pig rose another twenty feet and flew over Jimmy D's, who was serving Sunday brunch with eggs and bacon (perhaps one of the flying pig's siblings) at the time.

Crossing over Mineral Street, several of the ropes became caught up in the tree branches, which punctured two of the balloons, dropping the pig halfway down to earth in a matter of seconds. At which time, the other ropes became entangled in larger branches, and seized the pig in midair.

Lumby Fire Department used ladders to rescue the pig after Dr. Campbell was brought in to sedate the frantic animal.

Animal rights activists are on the warpath to find and hold accountable those people involved. Additionally, Mr. Knowles, who was given a ticket for rear-ending a parked car during the episode, is also looking for those responsible.

The drugged swine, branded #5371, was returned to Mcnear's Farm without further incident. Lumby Police have launched an investigation. Anyone having information regarding the pig's flight of fancy should contact Sheriff Simon Dixon at police headquarters or his home.

EIGHT

Settling

"Mommy, we're out of goldfish food. Can I give them some guacamole?" young Timmy called out to his mother, who was sitting at a front table in the restaurant.

She laughed at her six-year-old son and rolled her eyes at her husband, who was sitting across from her, his back to the restaurant windows. "The fish told you they want that?"

"Yep. Through their bubbles. They said 'gua-ca-mol-e.' I heard 'em with my own ears."

"And do they know that their water would turn green and slimy if you fed them avocado?"

"But they don't want avocado, they just want gua-ca-mol-e," he corrected her.

"Sorry, sweetheart, but they really wouldn't like that," Gabrielle said. "After lunch we'll all walk down the street and you can pick out new fish flakes."

"Okay," Timmy said happily, and went off on another important mission: encouraging the cat to try a stuffed red-hot pepper.

"I wish Brian was that agreeable . . ." Gabrielle said quietly, putting her head down. On this Saturday late morning, The Green

Chile was empty of customers, and Gabrielle and Dennis were enjoying a few minutes alone.

Dennis regarded his wife fondly. He was as in love with her as the first day they met when Gabrielle was a graduate student who was completing her master's degree in languages as Dennis was entering his senior year at Stanford. Since he was one of the few men who didn't try to Americanize her name (she deeply resented being renamed Gabby, or worse, Gabs, which she believed obliterated both her heritage and her culture), and who intently listened to what she said without his eyes straying to her long legs, she took an immediate liking to him.

She was eight years his senior, and he was intrigued by her depth of wisdom and international experiences. He was constantly amazed by her ability to easily converse in four languages, and to move between them as effortlessly as she moved between his sheets. Well into the nights Gabrielle would tell Dennis about her home in El Puerto de Veracruz, about the banana plantations with the humidity so high that all one can do is run naked through the fields.

In one word, Dennis would describe Gabrielle as "passionate." It was a passion he couldn't live without. So on a balmy Thursday afternoon in March of their final year at college, Gabrielle and Dennis married in a civil ceremony a few miles from campus.

That news, and the fact that Dennis was not returning to Lumby to work at *The Lumby Lines*, came to his father by way of a hastily written letter from his son a few days after graduation. For the first time in William's life, his son was out of his control, so not knowing what else to do, he resentfully corrected the spelling and punctuation of the letter and sent it back to him, with no further comment. Dennis never received his father's response, or lack thereof. He and his wife were already settling into their first, modest home in Boca Del Rio, a quiet town south of Veracruz.

During the four years that followed, Gabrielle worked as a translator, always having more job offers than she could accommodate, while Dennis worked as an independent reporter for several U.S. newspapers. Their lives were full and happy, and when Gabrielle unexpectedly became pregnant, they embraced the news as they did everything else: with ease, flexibility and humor. That temperament changed, though, one afternoon in February 1975, when Gabrielle was helplessly involved in a political coup that overflowed into the headquarters offices where she worked. Although she escaped, two of her colleagues were killed, and her faith in her country was shattered.

Within the week, with young Brian in tow and an offer in hand from the *Wheatley Sentinel,* Dennis and Gabrielle returned to the only other place either had called home: Lumby.

". . . but Brian was never agreeable, even as a young child," Gabrielle continued. She took his hand and stroked the back of it idly. "I don't know what I did wrong. He's so angry and so controlling."

"He's like his grandfather," Dennis said with some resentment.

"But he's eighteen, not eighty."

Just then Mackenzie McGuire opened the door and leaned in. "Too early for lunch, Gabrielle?"

"No, not at all. Come sit down and join us. We're commiserating about Brian's latest antics."

"Wherever Brian is, you can be sure my Terry is right there, egging him on," Mac said, taking a chair next to Dennis.

"You two worry too much. They'll grow out of it."

"I'm worried Brian won't," Gabrielle said, with Mackenzie nodding in agreement. "He's walking a fine line right now."

"They both are," Mac chimed in.

"And I think Simon is reaching his tolerance level for bringing them into the police station."

"They're all minor pranks." Dennis tried to sound reassuring, but even he had some doubts.

Mac looked at him with a somber expression. "The fire wasn't minor."

He sat forward in his chair awkwardly. "That was an accident."

Neither of the mothers responded.

The tension was relieved when Joshua walked in. "Tomorrow, six a.m. in front of the library," he said, pointing a finger at Dennis.

"Tomorrow," Dennis nodded, giving Joshua a dark look, and he was gone as quickly as he arrived.

"Oh, God, what was that about?" Gabrielle asked in dismay.

"Nothing important."

"I somehow doubt that." She frowned at her husband. "What inane bet do you two have going on now?"

"Don't look at me like that. It was his idea." He quickly realized how much he had just sounded like his son, and laughed. "It really is nothing. Joshua made the wild claim that he could get to Wheatley using back roads in less time than it would take me to drive it on Farm to Market."

"So you two are racing at dawn tomorrow?" Gabrielle asked in disbelief.

"Well, not exactly racing," he corrected her.

She looked at Mackenzie. "And we wonder where Brian gets his tendencies?"

Mackenzie's cell phone rang.

"Yes? . . . Yes. . . . Is anyone hurt? . . . In a few minutes." After hanging up, she turned to Gabrielle. "I need to go. Terry just swung the backhoe through our front window."

Gabrielle gasped. "Is he all right?"

"Yeah. He was actually going to surprise me by planting an oak tree he bought from the nursery."

"At least his heart was in the right place," Dennis said.

"Too bad the same couldn't be said for the backhoe bucket."

∞

After assessing the damage at home, Mac drove down to Montis Inn. Although it was the weekend, Mark had asked her to come by to meet his wife and discuss some work that Pam wanted done in the building behind the main chapel.

"I'm so glad we finally meet. Thank you for doing such an amazing job," Pam said, shaking Mac's hand. Turning so Mark couldn't hear, Pam asked under her breath, "How much extra do I owe you for keeping my husband unharmed through all of this?"

Mac chuckled, liking Pam's humor. She obviously knew her husband all too well. "More than you could possibly know."

"We'll settle up later," Pam said with a quick wink.

◌

During the next few days, as Pam, Mark and Brooke settled into Taproot Lodge, they separately began their respective missions. Brooke's fervor for the project was, in no other word, relentless, combing every corner of Lumby, Wheatley, the county seat and the Internet for any information she could find on the abbey.

In the Wheatley library she located entries for two journals, both single copies handwritten in the early twentieth century, that would have discussed Montis Abbey in great detail. However, both volumes were missing with the last recorded library usage to be around 1958 on each. Another reference document, catalogued by the State Department and compiled by the U.S. Army Corps of Engineers, made numerous references to the monastic compound, located so close to the lake on which they were working, but the information was cursory at best.

Assuming little more information would be found, Brooke began outlining the house on her laptop CAD system that she had brought with her from Virginia. Mark had converted one of the spare bedrooms in the lodge into a makeshift office, complete with a table made up of spare plywood resting, unsecured, on sawhorses. Knowing that Brooke fancied reading *The Lumby Lines*, Mark also nailed up old newspaper racks: two-inch dowel bars over which to hang newspaper. She had never worked in such rough surroundings, but nothing had ever felt more comfortable or more satisfying in her life.

While Brooke continued at a steadfast pace, Pam was working directly with Mac's carpenters and other tradesmen on refurbishing the old kitchen and dining room. Both rooms were in good working order, so minimal repairs were needed. Most of the work on that building was focused on reframing and conditioning the cold cellar that was attached to the kitchen. Within a week Pam was already turning her attention and labor to the next building: the old library.

Mark was where he wanted to be since originally surveying the property more than a month before: he was inspecting the trees in the orchard. It covered the better part of six acres, with another half acre set aside for saplings. The mature trees, untended for years, showed enough signs of distress and disease that even a newcomer like Mark recognized that all was not fine in that corner of heaven.

With the weather just beginning to warm the deeper soil and awaken the plants to the coming summer, the trees were now showing their full bloom. The best that Mark could do was to identify the type of tree, and they had, in his rough estimation, at least a thousand apple trees, five hundred peaches, and half that again of pears and nectarines. Still, as he confessed that night over dinner, there were approximately a hundred trees of unknown origin in a separate field—the Darwin Discovery, as he called it.

"Do you think it's possible that the monks cultivated a new line of fruit tree, never before seen or tasted?" Mark asked, simply because he had drunk too many glasses of wine.

"About as probable as them growing marijuana up in high pastures," Pam retorted.

"Boy, wouldn't that make a story for *The Lumby Lines*. I can just imagine the headline: 'Pope Knew about Dope.' Mr. Beezer would go nuts," Brooke said.

"Who's Mr. Beezer?" Pam asked, raising her brow.

"A very odd, angry old man I met today, must have been about eighty. He stared at me like he knew me . . . almost like he had seen a ghost or something," she said, trying to shake off the weirdness of the encounter.

"Strange name . . . Beezer," Mark said, extending the *ee* in the name, making it sound almost sinister.

"Yeah, I've only heard that name once before," Brooke said.

"How did you meet him?" Pam asked.

"I went to Lumby to look at some of the earlier issues of the local paper, and it turns out William Beezer owns not just the local paper, but also the printing press, the bookstore and the bookbinding company."

"Why do you say he's angry?" Mark asked.

"Well, when I introduced myself and told him I was working with you guys on the restoration of the abbey, he said that the place should have burned down to the ground last year."

"God, that's a little disconcerting," Pam said.

"You would have thought it was more than that if you had heard the tone in his voice. It was a little creepy."

"Did you talk to him for long?" Pam asked, now more engaged in the discussion than Mark, who was beginning to look at the blueprints Brooke had generated before dinner and laid out on the kitchen table.

"No, less than a few minutes. Smart man, though, and he definitely knows his business. But he has a real attitude toward this place."

"Well, that's not good that the owner of *The Lumby Lines* has it out for our inn," Pam said.

"We'll send him an apple peach pie and be done with it," Mark joked. Turning to the prints, he pointed to the back of the main building. "Brooke, why did you bring out the wall so far? I thought the photos only showed a ten-foot bump-out."

Brooke walked over to the dining table and leaned over Mark's shoulder. "I agree with you about the photos, but I dug around some yesterday. Finally I had Mackenzie use the backhoe, and we found stones that I think were the original old foundation walls from a hundred years ago. That would place the wall about six feet farther out than what we see in the photos."

"Do you think the front entrance bump-out is original?"

"I'm not sure, but I think so. If I'm correct about the back wall, that would make the building a perfect cross, which makes sense."

ध्छ

The following morning, while Pam and Brooke were having coffee, Mark walked in with the local paper he had just retrieved from
the mailbox.

"Did one of you goof with the mailbox last night?" he asked.

"What are you talking about?" Pam asked.

"Well, seems we had a hit-and-run van Gogh in the neighbor-
hood last night. Our mailbox has been repainted—fine job, but
lime green isn't my favorite color. You guys really need to go look.
It probably can be seen for miles. And," Mark continued, "seems
Brooke made quite the impression in town yesterday," laying down
The Lumby Lines on the table.

Their jaws dropped to the ground in disbelief. Brooke grabbed
the paper, her hands trembling slightly as she reread it.

"'Confidential information regarding the future business
intent,'" she quoted out loud. "Is he serious? I jokingly said that if
construction costs run over, we might have to sell peach pies and
apple cider by the roadside." She looked up at Pam. "Can they really issue a stop-work order?"

The Lumby Lines

Letter from the Editor:
A Town's Choice

BY WILLIAM BEEZER   **MAY 24**

There are times, such as these, when one cannot
stand idly by and witness a wrongdoing to the
community.

I had the occasion yesterday to meet the architect
hired to restore Montis Abbey, which the new

owners, Mark and Pamela Walker, have renamed
the Montis Inn (as we first reported in the April 19
issue of this publication). A Miss Brooke Shelling of
Virginia mentioned that construction was well under
way to restore the outer buildings and that blueprints
for the chapel and community house were close to
being submitted to the county for a building permit.
She also disclosed some confidential information
regarding the future business intent for the property,
which may have significant impact on our town.

As it was impossible, during our brief
discussion, to determine what information she
was withholding, our town should insist that all
work stop immediately so that the town council
has the opportunity to review and approve not just
the blueprints, but also the business intent and
plans. Simply because the Walkers have obtained
a business license does not mean their plans are a
good thing for Lumby.

"I don't think so," Pam said, totally annoyed, "but if they do, we can always take them to court."

Calm and gentle-mannered Mark suddenly stood up and started to forcefully pace the room. The mention of court, of having to put their dream in the hands of the legal system, scared him.

He had once relied upon the courts to right a well-planned wrong, and painfully learned that the outcome of any trial depends upon the competence, or incompetence, of the lawyer rather than the truth. His one legal misadventure had taken place many years prior, when he sued his brother-in-law, who had stolen several hundred thousand dollars from Mark's company, leaving the firm in such financial ruin that it had to declare bankruptcy. After five days of lies told by his brother-in-law, five days of stupid and inexcusable errors made by his attorney, the judge ruled in favor of the defendant. Not only did that ruling crumble Mark's belief in the legal system, but it also damaged his relationship with most members of his family, who were as deceived as the judge. Only a few strong enough to face some unpleasant family truths supported Mark, while the others turned away, or worse, pretended nothing ever happened. In the end, he felt he lost all but one of his sisters because a quarter of a million dollars had been stolen from him.

"No, we can work this out another way. We're not going to put everything at risk in front of a local judge because one man has a vendetta against Montis Inn," Mark said firmly.

"I have an idea," Brooke said, still holding *The Lines*. "I think we can use his own paper to sway some public opinion in our favor. Since I accidentally initiated all of this, if you guys don't mind, I'd like to take the next step."

"Sure, as long as it doesn't involve the Lumby jail for any of us," Pam agreed.

"You know, I was planning on going home this weekend, but things are under control in Leesburg, so if you don't mind, perhaps I can stay on a little longer? Then we can finish the prints here, and I can answer any questions the county inspector may have."

"You can stay forever if you want," Pam assured her friend.

NINE

Robes

Having completed his business at the Lumby Police Department, William Beezer walked out abruptly, leaving Simon Dixon and Dale Friedman standing by the front desk with their mouths agape.

"Was he serious?" was the first thing Dale could bring himself to ask.

Simon, still looking at the door, was dumbfounded. "I actually think he was."

"But how could he possibly think that we would issue an injunction against Montis Inn?"

"I don't know. Sometimes a person sees his control as a little broader than what it really is."

"So, are you going to?"

"No, not right now, at least. But he's serious about his demand and, knowing William, I'm sure he won't let it be swept under the rug." Simon put on his jacket. "I'm going to stop by and see Russell Harris for a few minutes."

"Ah, good idea. Get some legal advice," Dale said supportively.

"I just want to make sure we're standing on solid ground."

The phone rang, and Dale answered, "Lumby Police Department."

Simon listened to the first few seconds of Dale's conversation to ensure there wasn't an emergency that would require his immediate attention.

"Hello, Martha," Dale said, and then covered the phone and mouthed "Martha Ellers." "No, Martha, we haven't found the moose that stole your granddaughter's tricycle yet."

Simon waved to Dale and left.

ﾟﾟﾟ

As it happened, Scott Stevens overheard William Beezer from the jail cell where Scott was interviewing a town resident who had been arrested for riding his horse drunk to Jimmy D's bar the night before. As William was the owner of *The Lumby Lines* and Scott's immediate boss, Scott thought hard about how he could play that particular card. So he headed to S&T's for lunch in his regular booth, where he had drafted many exposés. This one, though, would actually be sent to the *New York Times*, or, at worst, the *Wheatley Sentinel*.

"BLT with fries today?" the waitress asked Scott.

"That would be fine. Thanks, May."

As Scott took out his pad and began jotting down the "facts," he eavesdropped on a discussion taking place at the back tables between several town residents.

"I think it's just good business. Good for us and good for the town," Cantor, a local contractor, said.

"I agree," Mackenzie McGuire chimed in. "The folks who own the abbey have a lot of work to be done, and they pay their bills on time. That's all I care about."

The owner of Brad's Hardware stood up. "Look, guys, I can benefit from their business more than most of you," he said firmly. "But I don't want Montis owned by a bunch of East Coast yuppies who know nothing about us. They obviously don't want to be a part of the community—we never see them in town."

"I think they're really busy," Mac said, not defending them but just making a simple observation.

"I've seen the man several times out in the orchard," Charlotte Ross said in a crackling voice. "He doesn't seem to mind getting his hands dirty."

"All the same, Charlotte, I agree with Brad," Jimmy D said politely. "It would have been better if someone from the area bought the monastery."

"How so?" Charlotte asked.

"Less risk," Jimmy D answered. "People who live here know our values—they know when they have to put the town and the residents ahead of themselves."

"They wouldn't be absorbed with only making money for themselves," Brad added.

Scott was so engrossed in the argument that he almost missed Dennis Beezer walking right past him.

"Oh, hold on, Dennis," Scott said, grabbing his arm. "You have a second?"

"One," Dennis said dryly. "What's up?"

"I just saw your father at the police station."

"Oh, was he finally arrested?" Dennis asked with a chuckle.

"No, he was kicking up a storm about Montis Inn. Claims the new owners don't have the necessary permits to be doing the renovation."

That made Dennis stop and think. "I doubt that very much," he finally said.

"Doubt he was kicking up a storm?"

"Oh, no. He can create storms. What I meant is that I doubt the owners haven't followed county building regulations. I hear they're both pretty smart and honest folks."

"Well, one of William's many claims is that the monastery is within town borders and they never submitted a business plan to the Lumby Town Council. Says he'll sue anyone involved if work's not stopped immediately."

Dennis shook his head. "Don't quote me, but I'm quite certain that my father would sue just about anyone under any conditions simply to make a point."

ʃↃↄ

Mark, still angry about the trial years ago and irate with a Mr. William Beezer whom he had never met, decided to spend the rest of the morning in the orchard. He crossed the road with a plan for attacking the wild vines that were strangling his wonderful trees. That would be a good release of his frustrations. Gazing down at the wonderful expanse of Woodrow Lake, where some fishing boats trolled the waters, he took several deep breaths and felt better.

The orchard consumed most of the acreage on the other side of Farm to Market Road, and was only slightly higher in elevation than the inn, so one could see the fields clearly from almost any point on the property. After pulling out several vines, Mark continued to walk up the rows, and in the process wandered into a much smaller back field, adjacent to but set higher than the other, where the Darwin trees were planted. He had only taken a cursory look earlier, but now he wanted to walk all the rows and begin to cut back the tall weeds and wild growth. If time allowed, he also would begin cutting off dead wood and unbridled vines there.

When he reached the farthest corner of that smaller orchard, he noticed a narrow path leading through some trees into another clearing. Walking through, he came into a small quarter-acre field with a dozen or more white boxes scattered about. Each box, on stilts, was about two feet in height, width and depth. Curious, he unlatched and opened the lid of the nearest box. In that moment he realized what a mistake that had been.

The low buzz emanating from the box became almost deafening. "Oh, my God," he blurted as he dropped the lid and began running for his life. He tore through the trees, not knowing if he was being followed by a swarm of bees. As he reached the orchard clearing, he turned to look over his shoulder—and ran into what looked, in that split second before crashing, like a black tree trunk.

The trunk gave slightly, but not enough to prevent Mark from toppling backward to the ground. Slightly dazed, he saw a hand reach out from the tree trunk. Mark looked up and realized that the hand was extended by a man in a long black robe.

"I'm sorry. Are you all right?" asked the tree that had turned into a man.

"I don't know," Mark said, stunned and a little disoriented. "Are they coming?"

"Are who coming?"

"The bees."

"Oh, no, they won't hurt you," he said with assurance. "They're honeybees."

Mark accepted the extended hand and pulled himself up, brushing dirt off his jeans. As he stood, he was struck by the height of the man assisting him, maybe six feet four inches. Mark, slightly over six feet himself, still felt very short. Perhaps it wasn't the man's actual height, but more the illusion of height due to the hooded black robe he wore.

"Hi. I'm Matthew," the man said, shaking Mark's hand.

"God," Mark said.

"No, not God, just Matthew," the monk replied with a smile.

"I thought you were Mr. Beezer." Mark forced out the words, not meaning to be impolite, but just devoid of social graces for the moment.

Matthew let out a hearty laugh. "Well," he said, "given that Mr. Beezer is at least twenty years older and a foot shorter, I won't consider that a compliment."

"Oh, I'm so sorry," Mark said in embarrassment. "It's just that . . ." but he decided not to try to explain. He recovered enough to finally say, extending a fresh handshake, "Hi, I'm Mark Walker. Are you all right? I hit you pretty hard."

"I'm fine, thank you. And you?"

"Unsteady, but not stung," Mark said, patting himself all over to make sure. "And I'm guessing you know something about those bees?"

"Yes, I was one of the brothers who lived here, and beekeeping was my monastic chore, although it was more a labor of love. They are quite harmless when undisturbed."

Mark stared at him in disbelief. Over the last month he had heard many stories about the abbey and the religious brothers, and now here was one standing before him. He had never met a monk, and paused, unsure of the protocol.

Matthew sensed his confusion. "Are you sure you're all right? I didn't mean to startle you, but as we pulled up in the car, I saw you walking through the orchard and assumed you were the new owner. So I thought I'd follow you up here," Matthew explained.

"Yeah, really, I'm fine. It's just been a rough morning. I can't quite get over you being here. Come on," he said, finally coming to his senses. "Let's go down to the house so you can meet my wife. We have so many questions to ask you." They headed back down through the main orchard.

Matthew was carefully looking at the fields he used to tend, and remarked, "It's been many years. The trees are in need of pruning."

Mark was unsure if Matthew meant it had been many years since he had been there or since the trees were pruned. Probably both.

"I thought that I would lose the entire season's crop if I pruned them now," Mark answered.

"You probably would, and yet forgoing one season in the life of an orchard isn't giving up so very much. Perhaps you might tend to the wild vines and weeds now, and prune in the late fall," he said with due consideration. "If you have no objections," he continued, "I'd enjoy joining you." Again, Mark was unsure if he meant joining him that day or in the fall for pruning. "The aspens in the lower mountains turn brilliant yellow in October, and the air chills with the warning of winter's approach." He continued to survey his former fields of toil. "I do miss it," Brother Matthew said in reflection.

Mark continued on, only to realize that Matthew had stopped. He turned to find the monk many yards behind him, standing deep in thought. As he came closer, he judged Matthew to be in his sixties, with lines on his face drawn by a good balance of contemplation and laughter. His eyes, behind the bifocals that he wore, were clear and dark gray, similar in color to his thick hair and the closely trimmed beard that covered his square jaw. There was little else to see that was not covered by the robe, tied at his waist with a black belt.

"I came to Montis when I was nineteen years old," Matthew reminisced. "I still remember how difficult it was to leave my family in Denver, to leave my brothers and sisters who were still young and impatiently waiting for their own lives to begin. But that first night at Montis," he continued, looking down the hill at the abbey, "that first night when I was alone in my room praying, I knew that I had followed the right path, and that I had finally arrived home."

Matthew then searched the sky intently, and Mark wondered if he was praying.

"Looks like rain this afternoon," Matthew said, and began to walk down the hill.

As they approached Farm to Market Road, another man, much younger than Matthew but also in a black robe, emerged from a car parked on the shoulder and casually walked up to meet them.

"Hi, I'm Brother Michael," he said, smiling, extending his hand to Mark.

"Michael, this is Mark Walker," Matthew said.

"Oh, wonderful," Michael said sincerely, still shaking his hand. "By the way, nice mailbox," he kidded Mark as they crossed the road. Mark immediately pleaded innocent, and told his story of mailbox woe.

"And very nice pink flamingo. It certainly gives the abbey a serene touch," Brother Matthew added. Mark half expected Hank to defend himself, but when the bird stayed silent, Mark just shook his head and said, "Thanks."

Both Pam and Brooke turned when they heard the lodge door open. In walked Mark, smiling ear to ear, which was quite the change from when he had left earlier that morning. Immediately behind him followed Brothers Matthew and Michael. Pam, standing by the sink, nearly dropped the pot of coffee in her surprise. Brooke, who was sitting at the kitchen table leaning over some papers, her knees bent under her, sat back with an expression of cautious amazement.

"The monks of Montis Abbey, I presume?" Pam asked, recovering. Walking over to Brother Matthew, she shook his hand and gave a warm smile.

"Brothers, this is my wife, Pam, and our close friend and architect, Brooke Shelling." Mark paused. "And this is Brother Matthew and Brother Michael."

As it was noon, Pam asked if the brothers could stay for lunch, which they accepted with appreciation.

The monks laughed as Mark and Pam retold some of the taller tales they had heard about the brothers' adventures, tales that had been passed down over the years, getting more bent from the truth with time. The stories had become so outrageous, given the conservative and contemplative nature of the monks, that it would not have surprised Brother Matthew if one such tale had him walking on water, on Woodrow Lake, no doubt.

"I guarantee that we would have been excommunicated," Brother Michael laughed. "We really kept very much to ourselves, going into town for food and supplies once a week, and then sharing Sunday service with the community. It's surprising so many funny stories could have been concocted over the years about such a quiet and, truthfully, boring group of men."

"I think people are just curious, maybe a little fascinated, with your simplicity and separation from life," Brooke responded, quite fascinated herself.

Matthew leaned forward. "But then again, Brooke, we feel we are the ones very close to life, while others are separated from its true meaning and value."

"Touché," Brooke said.

While they finished coffee and dessert, the brothers addressed a seemingly endless string of questions asked by Mark and Pam. Answering why they had returned to Montis, Matthew explained that that morning they had heard about the article in *The Lumby Lines*.

"We actually haven't read William Beezer's article, but we received several calls this morning about it, which prompted us to drive over, hoping to find you here," Matthew explained. "I fear you may have become the unwitting targets of the older man's anger, and we thought we would offer any assistance we could."

"Pray hard," Mark quipped with a grim smile.

"Do you have a copy of this morning's paper?" Matthew asked.

Pam took it off the counter and gave it to Matthew, who read the editorial.

"Oh, William," he said softly. After finishing, Matthew laid the paper down on the table, shaking his head but still smiling slightly.

"We must have missed the humor in his article," Mark said, perplexed by Brother Matthew's reaction.

Pam sensed Mark's anger was coming dangerously close to the surface, and Mark did not manage his anger well.

"He wants to—" Pam began to explain the obvious.

"He can't," Matthew gently asserted before Pam finished.

They all stared at him.

"He can't what?" Mark asked.

"He can't do what he has threatened and what you are worried about. And I'm sure he is fully aware of that fact," Matthew said.

"I don't understand," Pam said.

"Montis is not in Lumby," Matthew said simply.

"But the map clearly shows the town line circumventing the Montis property," Brooke corrected Brother Matthew.

"And that would be a map printed by whom?" Matthew inquired.

"The Chatham Press," Brooke answered.

"Which is owned by whom?" Matthew continued.

"William Beezer," Brooke said, nodding her head as she made the connection.

"Not only is Montis not within the town boundaries of Lumby, but further, it doesn't even have a county jurisdiction, because the land was owned by, and may someday, a hundred years from now, be returned to, the National Park Service."

"So—" Mark began.

"So, William is bluffing," Brother Michael inserted in his direct style.

Mark sat still for a moment, taking in what this meant, and then leaned back in the chair and let out a sigh so deep and so long that everyone felt the anguish leave his body. The shock was still too fresh to be laughed about, but Mark was able to close his eyes and smile.

"Do you know him well?" Brooke asked.

"No, not very well, but he and his family had a long relationship with the monastery," Matthew answered.

At that point the conversation abruptly turned. Michael asked Pam and Mark how they came to purchase Montis Abbey, and Mark recited the tale of Hank and the momentum that took over their lives immediately afterward.

"Is converting a monastery something you always wanted to do?" Michael asked.

Pam and Mark laughed. "It was never a consideration," Pam said.

"But we had been, for a few years, looking for a different lifestyle that would allow us to share more time together than apart," Mark added.

"If the truth be known," Pam teasingly corrected her husband, "Mark was looking for that from the day we first met."

"And when was that?" Michael asked.

"Almost twenty years ago," Mark answered. "Pam was finishing graduate school in Boston, and I was working for a small landscaping firm north of the city, and we literally walked into each other in the university bookstore."

"One of the few things we have in common: a love for books.

Other than that, we simply complement each other by our strong differences," Pam said, leaning over and patting Mark's hand, resting on the arm of the chair.

"New England is a wonderful area," Michael said. "I was brought up in Nashua, New Hampshire."

"Not far from Boston," Mark commented, to which Michael nodded.

"How did you find your way out here?" Brooke asked.

"I initially heard about Montis from the priest at our town's parish, who was good friends with the monastery's abbot. And it was all downhill from there," Michael joked. "But, seriously, it was a great order. Many very dedicated, good men built and sustained this compound for so long, I still find it amazing."

Both brothers then began speaking at great length about different aspects of Montis. They discussed in detail the history of the compound, the buildings, even the footer Brooke had found. Brother Michael, more of a historian than Brother Matthew, had been responsible for much of the compound maintenance, and went so far as to make notations and minor corrections on the blueprints lying on the kitchen table.

As Michael was explaining the final improvements made to the compound shortly before leaving, Pam asked why they ultimately sold the monastery.

"After Brother Joshua left in 1986, the remaining four of us could no longer maintain the abbey, and we ultimately decided to move and join a monastic community an hour away."

"Saint Cross?" Pam asked.

"Yes." Brother Matthew looked down solemnly. "It has been a good home for us, even though it may not last forever." He gave a helpless shrug. "But then, what does last forever?"

ॐ

T E N

Scribing

The five spent the next several hours walking through the compound, discussing the buildings' histories and the lives of the
men who lived in them. Brooke took copious notes as the monks
recalled in detail the construction, repairs and renovations made
during the years.

When they finally came to the library, Matthew paused before
he entered. The simple building consisted of only one room with
large windows in all four walls. Brooke was intrigued by its form,
and Pam was more than curious about its purpose.

"This was our scribing room," Matthew answered, walking
through the door.

"I don't understand," Pam said.

"Well, most monastic communities have a source of revenue.
Some make food products, such as breads, cheesecakes, choco-
lates and jams. Others make clothes, candles, greeting cards. The
list is almost endless. In fact, one wonderful monastery in upstate
New York breeds dogs. Our primary vocation was calligraphy,"
Matthew explained, "and this was our writing room."

"Did only a few brothers scribe?" Pam asked.

"All of the brothers were very skilled calligraphers, some perhaps more gifted than others, but we all wrote," Matthew explained, looking around the room that had changed so much from the candlelit chamber he remembered from so long ago.

"Within a community such as ours," Matthew continued, "one does what one needs to do for the good of the cloister. Brother Michael, for example, was always very mechanical, very good with construction, so that was—and still is at Saint Cross Abbey—his primary responsibility, although he also wrote several days a week and assumed other chores when one of the brothers fell ill or was on retreat."

"A perfect commune," Brooke commented.

"Far from perfect, but a way of life that allows each community member to contribute to the benefit of the whole," Matthew responded.

"And if someone disagrees about their contribution, being unequal or wrongly directed?" Brooke asked.

"In many orders it becomes a common concern, to be resolved within the community with the help of all of the members. We are all there for one purpose, which both precedes and supersedes all other needs. So we seldom face the situation you described," Matthew explained.

Michael nodded his head in agreement. "In some ways it's an ideal life, but at times it's trying. Occasionally, I personally feel like it's a crapshoot. But those hard times strengthen both our spirit and our community, and we hopefully come through it for the better," he added.

"Well, not all of us." The voice came from behind them, from the vicinity of the front door. "And my fingers still ache from the scribing."

Everyone turned to see a man enter into the room. He was not tall but had a strong, self-confident casualness in his stride. Perhaps it was his thick, sandy-auburn hair that made Brooke take notice, or his intense dark blue eyes, or even his open, relaxed smile. For whatever reason, she watched intently as Michael gave the stranger an embrace. Then the man walked over to Matthew and said with an even broader smile, "You look well, my old friend."

"Oh, how good it is to see you again, Joshua," Matthew said, laying a hand on the younger man's shoulder. "It has been too many years."

"It has," he said, nodding in agreement.

"Let me introduce you," Matthew offered.

On that same morning Joshua Turner, who, many years before, was known as Brother Joshua, had read the article regarding Montis Abbey and drove over from Rocky Mount to also offer whatever help he could.

∞

After introductions were made, Mark, Pam and Brooke went back to the lodge to give the monks an opportunity to reacquaint in private. An hour passed before Michael stuck his head in the lodge door and asked if they wanted to join the brothers for a walk around the property. All three jumped at the opportunity. They hurried to join Matthew and Joshua, who had already crossed Farm to Market Road and begun to walk up into the orchard.

While they walked slowly, the monks continued to talk about the history of Montis Abbey, stopping to examine different limbs, or a small outcropping of wild berries. They explained that at one time, fifty or sixty years ago, the abbey produced some of the finest jams, syrups and honeys sold in the Northwest, but many of those projects had ended as the number of brothers decreased.

Brother Matthew took Mark aside several times to show him the different types of apple trees that they had planted: the well-known Macintosh, Cortland and Gala, but also the lesser-known Elstor, Criterion, Shamrock and Jonagold. The orchard also contained a variety of cherries: Bing, Lambert, Lapin and Rainier, with ten trees of the very sour Pie cherries. Mark was unsure if that was the actual name or just the purpose of the cherry, and his head swam with names he feared he'd forget by nightfall.

"And what are those trees with the beautiful white flowers?" Mark asked, pointing to his Darwin Discovery.

"Oh, those are Japanese-American hybrid plum trees. I think we have Alderman, American and Toka. For better fruit production, the plum trees need to be cross-pollinated with other plum trees of a different variety," Matthew explained.

"Ah, the bee thing," Mark said.

"There's always a connection between different points of nature," Matthew answered, nodding his head. "Let's go over to see them."

As Mark and Brother Matthew separated from the others to examine the plum trees, Brooke and Joshua continued walking through the rows of apple trees, well behind Pam and Michael, who were deep in conversation about New England, specifically Maine clam chowder.

"Has it been a while since you've been here?" Brooke asked, noticing how Joshua was savoring the walk through the orchard.

"It has been," Joshua confirmed. "It must be well over ten years now. I drive by every so often, but have never stopped, even when the abbey was abandoned."

"Bad memories?" Brooke asked.

He looked back toward the monastery and smiled. "No, just the opposite, actually. Montis Abbey was a wonderful experience."

"But you left anyway?"

"That's a long story," Joshua sighed, not at all minding her questions.

"We're on a long walk," she responded, looking up at him with a sly smile.

"Ah, a curious mind," Joshua said. "That's a good thing." He paused for a moment, trying to decide where to begin. "When I was in my early twenties, growing up about thirty miles away from Wheatley, three related events occurred within a few weeks of each other: the army had changed my brother's status from missing-in-action to killed-in-action, my mother passed away after being ill for many years, and my father withdrew from life, preferring to grieve his losses rather than embrace what he still had." Joshua had his head cast down, absently kicking at the larger stones in his stride's path.

"Perhaps that was the best he could do at the time," Brooke said, trying to console him, but feeling tremendously inept.

"I'm sure it was, and I never carried a grudge," Joshua agreed. "But I had lost both my wind and my rudder, and for six months I lived . . ." he paused, thinking of the right word, "recklessly. One night in the middle of January, after having far too many drinks, I decided to take a swim in Woodrow Lake. I can vaguely remember walking out on the ice, stark naked under a full moon, and slowly sinking into the frigid water that enveloped me. And when I woke, I was lying on a cot covered in warm blankets, and the only thing I could see was the small fire burning in the fireplace."

"The brothers rescued you?"

"No, not right then. Some friends who had followed me pulled me out of the lake and brought me, by that time unconscious, to the monastery, where the brothers were awakened at an ungodly hour to tend to an ungodly young man." He paused, looking up to see where they were headed. "I intended to stay for only a few weeks, but that turned into months."

"And months into years," Brooke concluded.

"I owed them my life, and I felt I owed God reparation."

"Reparation for what?"

"For allowing my brother to go to war. For allowing my mother to die," Joshua said.

Without thinking, Brooke reached over and touched his arm. "But that wasn't in your control."

"I know that now, but it took me a dozen years to understand. And when I finally did, and when I made peace with God and accord with my father, I felt it was time to leave Montis, to begin the next part of my life. The brothers supported me and wished me well."

Brooke didn't know what to say, and Joshua wondered if he had said too much. They continued walking among the apple trees in silence.

ͼͽ

Mark, Pam and Brooke paid close attention as Matthew and Joshua talked about beekeeping, or apiculture, as they referred to it. When a bee approached them, they would very gently wave a hand and make a comment as if talking to a friend: "Go back and make honey" or "I'm not sweet like the flowers."

The brothers spoke of colony types, flight patterns, drone production, wax grafting, apiary management, and even free-flight mating. Pam and Mark, to be polite, resisted making comment, but Brooke, never missing an opportunity, made several jokes that had them all laughing aloud, Joshua especially.

Ending the first of many apiary discussions that would eventually continue through the summer and into fall, they walked to the far end of the field, where four hives appeared to be unusually close together, banked directly in front of a thick forest.

Matthew led the way between the center two hives and into some dense trees. Only when they followed him did they discern an old, poorly maintained path. It led in a few hundred yards to another field about the same size.

"Oh, my God!" Brooke exclaimed as she looked around.

Matthew turned to Mark and joked, "See? I get that a lot."

"We can explain," Joshua said, almost stumbling over his words. "It's not what it appears." He paused, and then sheepishly continued. "Well, actually it is what it appears to be."

"It's marijuana!" Brooke burst out. "Now, this takes the cake."

Then Matthew said calmly, "A long time ago, one of our oldest members, Brother Jacob, was diagnosed with cancer. As the disease began to ravage his body, the pain became unbearable. We were a poor monastery with no medical insurance, so we couldn't afford many of the drugs that were available to reduce the pain."

"So we took care of our own," Brother Michael added.

"And the crop just kept growing, perhaps a sign from God that we were doing the right thing," said Joshua with a smile.

"I'm sure it was," Pam said with a chuckle.

"I'd like to show you one more thing," Matthew said.

ॐ

Returning to the abbey, he led the group behind the annex and well into the woods. They were now on the opposite corner of the property from the field of illegal crops. As with much of the surrounding woods, any path had long since been lost to young trees and wild thorn vines that engulfed the formerly open space. After a few minutes, Matthew slowed his walk, and they came upon a small opening, overgrown with tall grasses through which they walked.

It was a cemetery. More specifically, it was Montis Abbey cemetery, which had received its deceased monks and close community members for the last hundred years. In all, there were eighteen small headstones, some so old that the granite had worn flat, making it impossible to read the words that time had worn away.

Brother Michael carefully began pulling tall weeds from a headstone that simply read "Brother Jacob." Brother Joshua, with Brooke following behind, went to another site, kneeled and began weeding around that headstone. As the weeds were cleared away, they revealed a gravestone whose granite was still polished and carving still clear. Her breath stopped when she read the engraving.

BROTHER BENJAMIN BEEZER

1917–1962

ELEVEN

Editorial

Hearing Brooke's hard intake of breath, as if someone had knocked into her, the others turned and saw the gravestone. Sensing their surprise, Brother Matthew said, "This is both the end and the beginning of one of the stories I feel I should tell you. Let's go back to the lodge," he suggested, and led the way, slowly and silently, back to the compound.

Upon entering the lodge, Brother Matthew was offered the easy chair in the corner, around which the others arranged their seats.

"The Beezer brothers," he began, "like everyone else born around 1915, entered the world in a time of tremendous contradictions. On the tragic end, as many as thirty thousand youngsters were paralyzed by polio in the prior two years, and shortly thereafter, twenty-one million people died in a worldwide influenza epidemic."

He paused, his gaze sweeping all of them. "However, even with these adversities, the human spirit was able to prevail. Stravinsky completed *The Rite of Spring*, Einstein wrote his Theory of Relativity. James Joyce and T. S. Eliot kept us in amazement with their writings. It was a time of darkness with occasional sparks of brilliant light.

"Although the Montis Abbey brothers were quite aware of the events outside their compound, they lived very separately during those times. But they did have reason to go to town on a regular basis."

"Why so?" Mark asked.

"The abbey's primary vocation, from its founding before the turn of the century, was penning calligraphy—the purpose of the scripting room." Pam nodded, remembering what he had said earlier. "They seldom composed original works, but always had a long list of patrons who required their tremendous skills. They were such patient men that even the most difficult and intricate writing became works of art under their quills. As their skills surpassed all others in the area, and as their reputation grew, more demanding projects were asked of them. When copies and printing of originals were required, they began to use the services of the Chatham Press in Lumby. At that time the Chatham Press was owned by—"

"William Beezer," Brooke interrupted, without thinking.

"Well, actually, his father, Woodrow Beezer, who had two young sons: William and his older brother, Benjamin, who would have been about eight at the time when the monks began using Chatham Press. Going there on a weekly basis to pick up work or drop off new pages, they usually saw the young boys.

"Although Woodrow Beezer was what most would call a religious man, he limited his conversations with the monks to the work at hand. It was, instead, young Benjamin who took the topic more seriously and frequently asked the brothers questions about their faith and about God. So it was no surprise to the brothers that when Benjamin became a young teen, he began visiting the abbey without his father's permission or knowledge.

"As his understanding and love for God grew, by the time he was fifteen he was quite sure that he wanted to commit his life to God, as had the brothers at Montis Abbey. Benjamin and William had terrible fights at that time, with William doing everything he could to keep his brother from joining Montis Abbey. He believed that once his brother entered the monastery, their relationship would never be the same; that he was, in a sense, losing his older brother to a God he didn't understand. He even told Benjamin that it would be cowardly for him to leave, because their family was close to financial ruin, having lost everything except for the press during the Depression. So Benjamin waited.

"It wasn't until a few years later, after the New Deal and relief programs had begun to turn around the economy of our country, that Benjamin saw an opportunity to join the abbey. In 1935 he entered Montis, right about the time that we had the orchard fire that destroyed most of our trees." Brother Matthew paused, trying to remember what he was told so long ago.

"Although his father was in disagreement with his eldest son's decision, he accepted Benjamin's calling and their attachment was never severed. In fact, it was said that his family members came to the abbey on occasion for Sunday mass. But William turned his back on his brother for the longest time."

"So, that's why Mr. Beezer is so angry?" Pam asked.

"No, not really, because over the years William and Benjamin became close once again, and saw each other frequently. In 1962, a few years after I had joined the community, and long before we even knew Brother Michael or Joshua, who were probably young boys themselves at the time," he said, smiling at both men, "Brother Benjamin was involved in a tragic accident. During one of the worst storms the valley had seen in a decade, three of us went up to secure the hives. The winds and rain were so strong, I had to grab branches and trunks to avoid being blown over. When we reached the hives we split up, and Brother Benjamin went to the far end of the field, by the woods. As he was strapping the hive, a large limb directly above him broke and fell on both him and the hive, which broke in half. The bees were agitated and stung Benjamin relentlessly. Brother Lawrence and I carried Benjamin as fast as we could down to the abbey's infirmary, but he was already in anaphylactic shock. Our abbot gave him an injection of epinephrine, but the bee

stings were too severe." He paused, visibly pained by the memory of that night. "He passed away before the doctor arrived from
Wheatley." He then quietly added, "He was only forty-five years
old. To die so young . . ." Tears appeared in his eyes, and everyone
was speechless.

Mark broke the silence, trying to ease Matthew's pain. "But it
sounds as if you did all you could."

"We did, but it wasn't enough. We knew that, William knew that,
and their father, then a very old man, knew that. The one time
William spoke to us was at Benjamin's funeral. He said we should
never have asked his brother to go out in such a storm for such a
senseless reason." He paused again, in reflection. "Now, after all
these years, I think perhaps William was right, but there was nothing we could do."

Brooke listened intently, trying to connect William, the younger
brother standing by Benjamin's grave in the prime of his life, to Mr.
Beezer the old man she had met, withered by anger and his own
inability to forgive.

After a light, casual dinner, the brothers had to leave for their
long drive back to the monastery, declining an offer by Mark and
Pam to spend the night at Montis. Likewise, Joshua left, saying he
had animals to feed and chores to do, but he promised he would
return the next weekend to assist where he could.

The following morning, Brother Matthew's story of William and
his brother Benjamin continued to weigh heavily on Brooke's mind.
She feared she was more similar to Mr. Beezer than not; both were
very intelligent, hard, judgmental people with a limited ability to forgive those who hurt them deeply. Brooke assumed that Mr. Beezer,
as she did, approached life fully guarded, and only had a small number of friends. Wanting to change for so long, but unsure how, Brooke
wrote and mailed a letter to the editor at *The Lumby Lines*.

During the following week Brooke was seldom seen, spending
most of her time working with various county officials and depart-
ments to get the necessary building permits issued. Additionally,

The Lumby Lines

Letter from the Editor:
The Town's Other Choice

BY BROOKE SHELLING   **MAY 29**

There are times when the human spirit becomes so strangled with anger that we are unable to see past the blame, unable to find the words that would allow us to begin to understand each other. We look at neighbors and see strangers, listen to voices and automatically distrust. There is no belief in the future because we are plagued by the past.

I have hope that we can rise above the noise and the discord, not necessarily by forgiving or forgetting, but by accepting man's imperfections and fragility. We are who we are, but we can decide to look forward and embrace the good within us all.

Having to rebuild that faith in ourselves and in each other is similar to our efforts at the Montis Inn. We are not simply replacing old stone with old stone, or laying wood on charred ashes, but instead carefully mending what was damaged and raising new beams.

We are keenly aware that the ripples from restoring Montis Abbey will touch many lives and possibly affect many generations, but we are taking great care to preserve what was and to shape what will be.

So, we would like to simply ask our friends and neighbors of Lumby to join the brothers of Montis Abbey, who have returned to offer their support, and share in this journey of discovery and recreation.

she met with several general contractors and selected the firm that would ultimately be responsible for transforming her blueprints into walls, roofs and floors. And finally, she found great pleasure in the long conversations she had with Joshua over the phone, occasionally lasting long past midnight.

Knowing that she was leaving in a few days to resume her life in Virginia, Mark and Pam were surprised to find Brooke planting a small garden on the south side of Taproot Lodge, which offered full, brilliant sunshine from morning to evening. She drove to Rocky Mount to buy at the farmers market young heirloom tomato plants, as well as small seedlings of zucchini, eggplant, melons and peppers.

"Am I taking you away from your work?" Brooke asked with a smile. She had arranged to meet Joshua for lunch before returning to Lumby.

"Not at all," he assured her. "Perhaps during your next visit I'll have a chance to show you Ross Orchards—it's really quite impressive."

"You seem to like it there."

"It's a good family business. The third generation has as much commitment as Zeb did eighty years ago when he tilled his first acre of land." As he talked about the orchards and his responsibilities there, Brooke saw for the first time a focus and intensity in Joshua's disposition, and she liked that. "They were kind enough to offer me a job when I first left Montis, and now they give me more flexibility and authority than I probably deserve," he said. Changing the subject, he asked, "Are you looking forward to going home?"

Brooke surveyed the colorful stands of the farmers market, the local residents smelling the ripeness of fruit, the children playing with the farm animals brought in for sale.

"I don't think so," she answered honestly.

"Do you have family in Virginia?" Joshua had not asked that question before. He had learned that Brooke was an intensely private and cautious person, and never wanted to challenge that comfortable distance between them.

"No. My parents divorced when I was ten. My brother was just leaving for college, and my mother, who wanted to be an artist, moved to France to live a very different life than what we could offer. So Dad and I carried on," she reminisced. "He was wonderful."

"When did he pass away?"

"Two days after my eighteenth birthday. He was still so young," she said sadly.

"Do you ever see your brother?"

"No. We talk twice a year at best, but he is much older than I am, and we never really had the opportunity to get to know each other. He and his family live in Maine now. He designs boats."

"And you, houses."

Her eyebrows came together as she considered what he had just said. "There is that similarity, I suppose."

"Was your father an architect?"

"No. He was a journalist, actually, for *The Washington Post.*"

They both took a minute to eat some of their lunch. Brooke felt comfortable with Joshua though their backgrounds were quite different. He was so honest, she felt she could trust him.

"Will someone be there to pick you up?" Joshua asked.

"No," Brooke answered with a frown. "There used to be someone to pick me up. He and I were together for six years. We started the architectural firm in Leesburg—life partners and business partners. It seemed ideal. But then he was offered an incredible opportunity in Japan."

It was impossible for Joshua to hide the interest he had in her story. "He left?"

"Yes, and I stayed. So," Brooke said, raising a glass of iced tea and returning to the original question, "I'll be taking a taxi home tomorrow. Alone."

Her ache was so deep sometimes, she was unsure how to heal herself. While in Lumby she had been thinking a lot about the purpose of her life, about the momentum and direction it had taken, and wondered if it was what it should be.

"So, do you consider Leesburg your home?" Joshua asked.

"I'm unsure. In truth, I feel a little lost right now, and I'm not sure where I belong," she continued, nervously playing with the food on her plate. "You know, I really envy those people who know what they're supposed to do in life. They have a purpose written on a slate at age ten or twelve, and each day all they have to do is navigate toward that end. How incredibly simple and efficient."

"Perhaps they might not see it that way," Joshua countered.

"How so?"

"Perhaps they feel shackled to something they feel is out of their control, a loss of freedom to explore different paths."

"Well, it must be a hell of a lot easier than for the poor souls like me whose destinies are kept hidden in some kind of cosmic game."

"Is it important to know your purpose in life?" he simply asked.

She thought hard about the question, moving her head slightly, considering different perspectives. "If I don't, I worry that I'll squander what's given to me. . . . It's important to know, so my life isn't wasted," Brooke finally answered.

"I don't think your life would be ever be wasted, Brooke. And I don't think we're limited to one purpose in life, or if we are, we need to walk different paths to realize it. We could be given an endless number of slates on which to write our own fate."

"Given by whom? God?"

"Whoever," Joshua answered. "If a person opts to use only one slate, so be it. But it seems we have such a greater chance of richness in our lives."

"How so?" Brooke asked.

"As I see it, on one of my new slates is being written my relationship with you, the Walkers, Montis Inn. On another was those years as Brother Joshua," he said fondly. "I think the difference between us is that you think the words are already written and are frustrated you can't read them, and I think we have to write them ourselves."

"I wouldn't know what to put down."

"You may have been doing it all along."

"Then why does everything seem to be an uphill battle?"

"You're cautious, and I think you may be fighting the current for no reason."

After lunch, while walking back to the car, they passed a small stand, and Brooke saw the perfect housewarming gift for Mark and Pam. That evening, Brooke gave her close friends the newest addition to the Montis Inn family: a little black Labrador puppy, which they named Clipper. The fact that Clipper was clearly misrepresented by the seller as being "housebroken" eluded Brooke, who was already on a flight back to Virginia the following morning when Mark stepped in some of Clipper's small accidents.

∽∾

TWELVE

Squawking

The Lumby Lines

Moose Milk to Nourish Town

BY SCOTT STEVENS   **JUNE 21**

In an effort to strengthen the sluggish produce
economy in Lumby, the Lumby Active Farmers
Association, LAFA, has voted to invest the club's
savings to buy one female moose from Red Rock
Ranch, Anchorage, Alaska, and begin processing
moose milk into moose cheese.

"It's pretty good if you eat it right out of the ice
box," David Hopwood, LAFA president, said in
an in-depth interview this afternoon. When asked
if there was a market for moose cheese, David
responded, "We're not sure about that, but if it's
an acquired taste thing, it might take a while to
catch on."

Moose milk contains 12–14% fat and 10–12%
protein. A moose takes up to two hours a day to
milk, and produces about two cups on a good
morning.
   The moose will be kept at Hopwood's Dairy Farm
out on Fulton Avenue. Anyone is welcome to come
by and visit.

Visitors who drive through Lumby with no reason to stop never
notice one of the town's prime oddities: many of the town's businesses reside on second floors. The locations of the stores as well
as their respective entrances are learned rather than found on any
map, even those printed by the Chatham Press. For that reason,
the residents of the town are healthier than most, having to climb
numerous staircases to complete simple tasks. But the quirkiness
of it all clearly outweighs the inconvenience of it all.

   The post office occupies the second floor of the police station,
with its own entrance on Farm to Market Road. Prior to taking per-
manent residence there, the Lumby P.O., which had to fight to be
assigned its own zip code, was originally located down the road in
The Feed Store, as were most services in town during the first part
of the century. From there, it moved to the back corner of Brad's
Hardware, where it stayed for twenty-two untroubled years until
space ran short as the store's inventory grew. Having no other place
to go, the post office returned to The Feed Store for a brief revis-
it, and then finally settled into its current location overlooking the
main intersection in town, well protected by those who occupy the
first floor.

   Its original home, The Feed Store, is arguably the oldest building
in town: a crooked wood structure that has weathered a hundred
years and two fires and sells most everything a farmer wants or
needs: horse and goat feed, hay, shavings, wood-burning stoves,

muck shovels, Wellington boots, fly strips, an assortment of young poultry and fowl, as well as, every so often, small livestock. The walls of The Feed Store are covered by yellowed public notices and bulletins from the early twenties onward: a small "Vote Harding" billboard is partially covered by a larger "Vote Coolidge" poster, someone advertising a new Model T Ford for $465, and Rob Johnson selling chickens—a dozen for a nickel. The walls not only encompass Lumby's history, but span much of our country's past as well, and one could spend hours just looking at all of the notes with the ink well faded, article clippings on browned newsprint and posters with curled, crusty edges.

Above the store's main barn, which holds all the feed, hay and livestock, is the town's only movie theater. Originally used as a makeshift vaudeville stage, and then converted into a loosely run casino, the space was finally reconstructed fifteen years ago to accommodate a forty-seven-seat theater with enough room in back for three rows of benches for those who could only afford to pay half price for a ticket.

The theater's location works well as long as the animals directly below remain quiet, but most residents would reluctantly admit that some movies have been ruined by an ill-timed bellowing moo or squawk, or the persistent clucking of chickens. Because of that, one always goes to the movies with a sense of apprehension, which might explain the theater's policy allowing its patrons to bring in both food and alcohol.

Back toward the center of town is one of Lumby's newer buildings: the small town hall. On its second floor is the local library, which at one time served, statistically, more canine than human visitors. The reason for this, although it's more a who than a what, was Charlotte Ross, the library's primary silent benefactor and possibly the town's most voracious reader.

Charlotte would visit the library daily, and on occasion, twice daily. Each morning shortly after the doors opened, Charlotte would slowly climb the stairs with a cup of Dickenson's coffee in one hand and three dog leashes attached to three small dogs in the other. Once in the library, she would take her usual seat at the large oak reading table well positioned against the north wall, where there are plenty of windows overlooking Main Street. For the following hour she would read several newspapers, always beginning with the *New York Times* and always ending with *The Washington Post*. On Mondays her routine would vary slightly as she added several weeklies, such as *Barron's* and *The Lumby Lines*, to her reading list.

If one asked Charlotte why she came to this place each morning, she would answer: the smell. She loved the smell of the library, the smell of old ink on old paper, of leather-bound books, of the shelves that have been varnished and polished with different oils over the years. It made her feel less old.

Equally as important, at the time the library allowed dogs. So when Charlotte visited, the librarian recorded, morning after morning, one person - three dogs, or on occasion, one person - four dogs when a small stray followed her inside. Likewise, most other visitors brought their pets, so it was easy to see how the final tally showed the unlikely dog to human visitor ratio, which clearly didn't rest well with the state administrators responsible for allocating funds for public libraries.

The Monday morning of the "Chile meeting," as it was called thereafter, started no differently. Charlotte sat in the library and turned the back pages of the *Post*.

"Good morning, Charlotte," Gabrielle said warmly as she walked up to her table and put her hand on the woman's thin shoulder.

"Oh, Gabrielle, how nice to see you. What brings you to the library today?"

"Chipotle."

"Excuse me?"

"I was asked to write a column for *The Lumby Lines* and needed to do some research on the chile pepper."

"Oh, very good for business," Charlotte said, nodding her head.

"Free advertising—nothing to sneeze at."

"No, but chipotle certainly is," Gabrielle joked. "I'm just about done here. How would you like to join me for a cup of coffee at the restaurant?"

Charlotte grinned broadly at that offer and lifted herself out of her chair, pulled together her dogs and belongings, and both women set off arm in arm. Walking down Main Street, they stopped in front of Wools and assessed the sale items in the window.

Wools was first built in 1936 as the smallest Woolworth's Five and Dime in the country, and it kept that status even after its major expansion in the early forties. Had it not been for the fact that one of F.W. Woolworth's senior executives owned a vacation home by Woodrow Lake and did his shopping in town, Lumby would never have been considered as a potential store location. But rules are broken, and although the store never showed a profit in its forty years, it served the town well. The residents of Lumby would always have fond memories of the formica lunch counter, the spinning stools, and best of all, the ice cream soda floats. When Woolworth finally closed six weeks to the day after the vacationing executive retired, the store was bought by a local resident, Orland Whistler, who shortened its name to Wools and began to sell only clothes.

It was easy to know the store's specials: one need only look at the people of Lumby, who one season wore red parkas and lined duck boots, and another, pink sweaters and yellow flip-flops. Excess inventory served the town well, and Wools, over the years, had become a profitable business.

As Charlotte and Gabrielle crossed the street, they saw William Beezer, hunched over, walking into the Chatham Press.

"So, has any of the ice melted between William and your husband?" Charlotte asked.

Gabrielle shook her head. "No, they never talk. It amazes me that they are so similar in some ways but extreme opposites in others. The few times I've suggested a reconciliation, Dennis just ignores it the way he does his father." She glanced back at the building. "The children and I see his mother and brother on occasion—visits that I'm sure William knows nothing about. She so loves playing with her youngest grandson."

They entered the restaurant and took their regular seats at the table in back. Charlotte asked, "And how is your oldest doing?"

"At odds with the world, especially us, right now. Brian is such a handful," she confessed, partially throwing up her arms.

"He'll eventually mature," Charlotte said encouragingly.

"You sound like Dennis. But he and his buddy, Terry McGuire, have a recklessness that just scares me."

At that moment, little Timmy came running through the door with his babysitter right behind. Once she saw that her young charge was in safe hands, sitting on his mom's lap, she waved and then left.

As Charlotte continued to sip her coffee, Gabrielle began cutting up fresh vegetables for the lunch meals, and the room began to smell of sweet onions and green peppers.

Gabrielle looked at Charlotte fondly. "I owe you a lot."

"For what?" Charlotte asked, looking up at her.

"You not only financed this restaurant, but you were one of the very few who truly welcomed me when we first arrived. Back then I stood out like a sore thumb, and it was painfully obvious that the townspeople didn't like outsiders."

"They still don't, but they're getting better." Charlotte put down her cup. "But it's really I who should thank you. The Green Chile has always shown a good profit."

"It's been fun."

"That's why you've been so successful," Charlotte said. "In fact, Gabrielle, I think it's time you become the sole owner."

"Oh, don't say that! I need your guidance. What would I ever do without you as my partner? I don't trust anyone else to test my crazy recipes. Further, I could never afford it."

"Money would not be an issue, I guarantee you that. And you'll always have my opinion. But I am old, and we need to be realistic

—we need to prepare," Charlotte said, spreading her thin hands out on the tablecloth.

"No, I don't want to talk about it," Gabrielle said firmly. She knew where the conversation was going, and the thought of someday not having Charlotte around was too much for her to bear. "The Green Chile is ours, and that's that." To further emphasize her point, Gabrielle slammed a large butcher knife down onto the chopping block, making a cracking sound that reverberated throughout the restaurant.

"We'll discuss it some more later," was all Charlotte said.

Two workers entered through the rear entrance and began helping Gabrielle in the kitchen. Rich hot aromas filled the air. The restaurant opened, and customers came in and took the front tables by the window.

"Speaking of your role as tester extraordinaire, would you let me know what you think of this?" Gabrielle placed a large dish in front of Charlotte. It smelled exquisite.

"Ummm. What is it?" Charlotte asked, eyeing the delicious-looking food.

"Buffalo and green chile chimichanga covered with a spiced mango sauce," she said proudly.

Looking over her shoulder, she saw Jimmy D walk in with Brad, who immediately noticed a loose hinge on the front door. "Gab, do you want me to fix that?"

"If you would, when it's convenient. Do you gentlemen want Coronas with limes today?"

"Perfect," Jimmy said, taking one of the front tables as well.

By twelve-thirty, the only Mexican eatery in town was filled once again with talking and laughter. More patrons came in, some paid their checks and left—a regular day all in all. Until a dump truck that had turned the corner from Farm to Market onto Old 41 back-fired three times and came to an abrupt, smoky stop directly in front of The Green Chile. The noise startled everyone, and soon the smell began to seep into the restaurant. From the bottom of the truck, black ooze trickled onto the asphalt.

"This is exactly what I was talking about," Brad said loudly, to be heard by all. "That dump truck is from Montis Abbey, and now it's going to screw up traffic all day and mess up our roads for weeks."

"It's not the abbey's fault," a man, who obviously knew Brad, voiced from the other side of the room. "Blame it on the hauler. He should've taken Mineral around town."

"The Montis folks should have told him that. It's their trash, and their responsibility for how it gets to the landfill," another man barked out, supporting Brad.

"They probably assumed that the driver wouldn't go through the center of town," Cantor said, having just walked in. He was followed by Mackenzie McGuire, who joined Charlotte at her table.

"Do you want some? A new recipe," Charlotte winked.

"And I heard they bought a bunch of lumber from Rocky Mount. They don't even bother going to Lumby Lumber," Brad told the crowd.

"Actually," Mackenzie interrupted, "I was the one who bought that lumber for them. Our own mill was out of six-by-sixes."

Outside, the crowd was still growing. Scott Stevens, who had been in the Chatham Press building when he heard the truck implode, walked around the truck asking the driver a series of questions and interviewing onlookers. By the time Simon Dixon arrived and put up flares, the spectators had grown to nearly fifty, many of whom had flowed into The Green Chile after the initial excitement abated.

Soon, a dozen more had joined the Montis debate. Gabrielle realized that an impromptu town meeting was taking place in her small restaurant.

The heated differences of opinion continued.

"And William Beezer's going to force them to stop work. They never even applied for a town business license," yet another man stated.

A few worried "ohs" were heard through the crowd.

"And I hear they don't have the building permits they need,"

Brad said accusingly.

"Mac, you're there every day. Is that true?" Jimmy asked.

"No, that's not true. They have all of their permits. In fact, they're consistently over building," she answered.

"What's that?" someone asked.

"Going beyond what the code requires," Mackenzie clarified.

"Well, that's a good thing!" someone else spoke out.

"So why is Beezer suing 'em?"

Scott Stevens, who had taken a seat in the corner when the crowd moved indoors, stood up. "Actually, he may not."

"How come?" Brad asked.

"It appears that the Walkers, the owners of the abbey, have done what's necessary as far as their restoration project. However, they'll have plenty to deal with from Mr. Beezer and the town council if they try to open an unlicensed business within the township of Lumby. Mr. Beezer said that bridge will be crossed soon enough."

More "ahs" from the crowd.

Charlotte stood up as if to go, but then turned and faced the group. "May I say one thing?" she said in her weak but determined voice. "I don't know the Walkers. Don't know if they were the right people to have bought Montis. But it wasn't ours to sell, so there you have it. What they do with their own property is their business. What matters to me is if they are good, honest folks who will care for our town and its residents as much as we do. And that's still to be seen. They've done me no harm . . . no good, but no harm either. So I think I'll wait a bit before passing judgment."

With that said, Charlotte sat down and continued eating the delicious chimichanga.

THIRTEEN

Passage

At seven the following Monday morning, Mackenzie was perched on the back steps of the abbey as Mark crossed the courtyard from the lodge. Terry sat next to her, drawing circles in the dirt with a long stick.

"I see you were busy this weekend," she said to Mark in a stern voice.

"Well, good morning, Mark," he said, as if having a lively conversation with himself. "And how was your weekend? Oh, fine, thank you, and yours? Oh, very good, thank you. Nice weather we're having, but I hear rain is coming."

Mac tried to keep a straight face watching Mark's antics. "All right," she finally conceded. "Good morning, Mark. How was your weekend? I see you were busy."

"Good morning, Mackenzie. Good morning, Terry. I had a terrific weekend."

"I noticed you framed up an interior wall on the second floor."

"Yesterday. I thought I would help out a little."

"Did you do that alone?" She raised her eyebrows.

"Me, myself and I," Mark said proudly.

"How nice," Mac said dryly. "Did it ever occur to you that there might be a slight problem because your wall ends in a framed-out window opening?"

Mark nodded his head, pointing his finger at the sky. "Strange you ask about that. I think you might have put the window too far over."

Mackenzie shook her head in feigned frustration. "Did you consider looking at the blueprints?"

"No, I couldn't find any, but I know that upstairs room is twelve by fifteen."

"It is, but it's fifteen by twelve. The wall you built should be over three feet to the right."

Mark thought about it for a minute. "Ahhhh. Well, that makes sense. We can just slide it over."

She turned to her son. "Terry, would you go up and start pulling nails from the bottom plate, please?" Then she gave Mark a further quizzical look. "And the door opening?"

"Exactly three by six foot eight—thirty-six inches wide, eighty inches high. I must have measured that thing four times."

"Measured what?"

"The door opening."

"So," she confirmed, "you used the door dimensions for the opening?"

"Yeah, and I put a header on top. Is there a problem?" he asked.

"A small one. The door frame is larger than the door," Mackenzie explained.

"Oh," Mark said in a low voice, his satisfaction draining quickly.

Mark looked so dejected that Mackenzie actually felt sorry for him. She had to admit that his heart was certainly in the right place even though his nails weren't.

"It was a good effort, though," she said, standing up. "You plumbed the wall nicely."

"Well, thank you," he said, perking up immediately.

"I'm down one worker today. Why don't you and I go adjust the opening and reset the wall," she said, "together."

꩜

Although good progress was being made, there had been other less-than-shining moments during the first few weeks of construction on the main building. Perhaps the reason was Mark's inexperience as a general contractor, or perhaps merely the general disorder that was to be expected when so many people converge in one small area.

But if fingers were to be pointed, one could rightfully point them at the cement truck that backed into the northwest corner of the community house, buckling the new post that had just been set the prior day, which cracked the beam that was placed overhead to support the half-burned roof trusses, which, now having no support, dropped like the deadweight they were, twenty-five feet to the ground, throwing ashes reminiscent of Mount Saint Helens. Pam thanked God that no one was injured while Mark was delighted that the accident, if one really insisted on using that word, offered a two-day jump on his schedule—no need to send anyone up on that part of the roof, because it was no longer there.

Or, a finger could be pointed at little Clipper, who, in his playful puppyness, pulled on the frayed end of a rope that just happened to be attached to the handle of a work bucket that toppled off the scaffolding and swung through the open window, hitting a loose two-by-four that, defying logic, fell back out the window and landed on the roof of Lumby's one and only police car, shattering the red and blue siren lights. Simon Dixon had stopped by for a cordial visit.

One final finger, of this three-finger hand of fate, could be pointed at Vinney's chicken, which when taken out of its crate to be fed some grain went absolutely berserk at the roar of the reciprocal saw. Mark estimated that the poultry mishap cost several thousand dollars and set the project back at least two days. Those who knew Mark well knew that it was best not to discuss the details of that particular incident.

꩜

In the early evenings, after the last car pulled away, Mark and Pam, with Clipper always underfoot, walked around the compound and through the buildings, which were eerily quiet after the commotion of the day. This was their favorite time together, to share in the wonder of what had been accomplished. They talked about the future, their lives at the inn, their changed priorities, and their fortune of having one another.

"You're quiet this evening. Is everything all right?" Mark asked, as they sat on the dirty floor in the main building, looking at the sky through the open roof.

"I'm relaxed," Pam smiled.

"That's nice to hear."

Clipper bolted through the door at full speed, made an exaggerated leap and landed on Mark's lap, and began crawling over his stretched-out legs.

"Clipper," Mark said in a low, corrective voice, but the attention only made the puppy more excited. Clipper scrambled off Mark's leg and pounced on his sneaker; it was a rare and cherished occasion that Clipper could play with them at his level.

Pam laughed as Clipper wrestled with the laces.

"Do you ever regret our decision not to adopt?" Pam asked.

"I occasionally think about it, but no, I've never regretted it. Why do you ask?"

"Maybe because the inn is so large and it feels empty right now."

"Don't worry, honey. Before you know it, it will be filled with friends and family, and their kids will be playing with our dogs, running through the orchard, picking more apples than they'll know what to do with."

"*Dogs?* We only have one."

"Well, I've been thinking about that," Mark said, trying to shake Clipper off his foot. "Maybe we should get another dog."

"Clipper would certainly enjoy that."

Hearing his name, the puppy pounced on Pam's lap, forcing her to roll backward in wonderful laughter, a laugh Mark never grew tired of.

൸

In the evening as Pam prepared dinner, Mark frequently went up to the orchards to work on his trees for an hour or two, although no real progress could be seen given the magnitude of the task. He had come to realize that the orchard was far too large for him to manage alone, and he had hired a firm from Wheatley that was to begin the following week.

Every few days he would also tend to the bees to the best of his cautious abilities, but desperately missed Brother Matthew's companionship and advice in this area. One of his greatest joys was when he brought a piece of raw honeycomb down to Pam for the first time, unstung.

One of his greatest curiosities was who was taking some of the plants from the marijuana field, tucked so far back and behind the bees that no one could possibly stray upon the field accidentally. Pam and Mark had talked about it, but had not decided what to do about the hemp, as they referred to it, as options were obviously limited. Perhaps as time went by, someone would take care of that problem for them.

At the end of June the Walkers had come to several conclusions: about two marijuana plants a day were being removed from the field; they very much missed Brooke; they wished the brothers would return; Clipper needed a four-legged, energetic companion; and Hank was looking forward to the Fourth of July celebrations. He had prepared himself by changing into—in the darkness of night—a full, well-tailored Uncle Sam's costume, with tall hat, white beard, and all. Duct-taped to his right wing was an American flag, and to his left, long sparklers.

The Lumby Lines

4th of July Celebration

BY CARRIE KERRY   **JUNE 28**

Volunteers are needed to help prepare for the 4th of July celebration events that are scheduled to be held at the Lumby Fairgrounds on Fairgrounds Road, promised to be bigger and better than ever.

The Quint Carnival will be arriving in town on July 2nd with rides and fair booths open to the public Friday July 2nd through Tuesday July 6th, 10a.m.-11 p.m. each night.

A petting zoo, clowns, pony rides, pig scramble, huckleberry pie-eating contest are scheduled to begin at 2p.m with fireworks starting around 9:30p.m. and lasting for seven minutes.

The newly inducted Mayor Toby, who received 43% of the town's vote last week, made no comment, but very much enjoyed the chewy bone given to him during the interview.

Lumby Police Department said that additional parking will be available on Maple Avenue and Tanager Street.

At Saint Cross Abbey, an hour's drive from Lumby, Brother Matthew put down *The Lumby Lines*, remembering times when some of the younger novices from Montis asked if they could attend the town's celebration. But that was years ago, and now he faced the same dire future that he had at his old monastery.

"You look troubled," Brother Michael said, walking into the annex.

"I am, Michael." Matthew gazed about the room that he had grown so fond of, which held so many memories for him. "Father Andrew has requested that I meet with the attorneys as well as the realtors so that we can make an informed decision regarding the sale of the abbey." On the word "sale" his voice broke.

Brother Michael sat heavily in the chair across from Matthew. "I didn't know it was that imminent." He shifted uncomfortably. "Perhaps I did, but I assumed that it would somehow be resolved . . . that we would be able to continue on."

"Walk with me?" Matthew offered, and they both went outside to a sparkling summer day. As they walked around the main chapel, Matthew looked at the glorious stained glass windows. Unlike the grandeur of Montis Abbey, Saint Cross resembled a quaint stone English church. Matthew thought the architectural lines at Saint Cross were more graceful than those at Montis, with round arched doorways and arched windows in all of the buildings.

To the right of the chapel wing, Matthew and Michael opened the wrought-iron gate and strolled through the common-grounds courtyard. The roses were in bloom and the garden's extraordinary color and fragrance carried throughout the abbey.

"I fear I have not been thankful enough," Matthew said contemplatively.

"For what?" Michael asked.

"For being given the opportunity to pray here," he said, gently fingering a rose while he bent over to appreciate the perfume.

"We have all been guilty of that, I'm afraid," Michael consoled.

At the west end of the garden, the monks walked through an arched breezeway that led to an internal courtyard surrounded on four sides by cloisters, open walkways with stone arched columns that supported the roof overhead. This is where Matthew came when he was deeply troubled. As with the other courtyard, these grounds were blooming with roses and ornamental trees that the abbot personally cultivated.

Matthew sat down on a stone bench and prayed. At times he

was angry at God, but on this particular day he felt very much at His mercy. Matthew tilted his head upward and let the sunshine drench his face.

"A glorious day," a familiar voice said.

"Yes, Father," Matthew heard Michael respond, but he did not open his eyes. He felt so very tired.

"Brother Michael, would you mind assisting me for a few minutes?" the abbot asked.

Michael looked back at Matthew and saw that he was deep in thought, or prayer, so he said nothing and followed Father Andrew inside.

A while later, Matthew joined them in the writing room. Father Andrew was standing in front of a large scroll that had been placed on the scribing table. The scroll was thirty-six inches high, and approximately three feet of its length of nine feet were showing. On the pale parchment paper were intricate writings and very small, fine drawings of different pen widths; black and gold leaf with red ink highlights glittered under the lights.

Staring at the scroll that he and the other monks had just finished, words rushed back to Matthew: the pointed apex, the serif, ascender and descender, the arm and the stem. Calligraphy had a complete language unto itself, and its vocabulary would be forever lost as the artist's pen was replaced by modern technology. Matthew was deeply saddened, for he knew that he was looking at one of the final calligraphic masterpieces that Saint Cross would ever create.

:∞:

With the Fourth of July a week away, Pam and Mark asked Brooke to fly out and join in the festivities.

"You really need to come back. We've made great progress," Mark said on the call to Brooke.

"So I heard. . . . The newspaper is calling it 'The Chicken Fiasco,'" Brooke teased.

"Okay," he conceded. "Not our finest foot forward, but it really is coming along. There's so much debris to clean up that a dumpster is being pulled from here every two or three days."

"Is it framed yet?"

"Almost. All of the exterior walls are up, except the south-facing bump-out. There was some concern about a five-foot section of the original footer, and the inspector thought that we should reinforce it. That's being done today, so the wall will go up tomorrow."

"How about the interior?"

"All of the load-bearing walls are in place, but none of the partitioned walls are up yet. By the way, we needed to make the library wall adjacent to the great room a two-by-six and not two-by-four," Mark said.

"Why so?" Brooke asked.

"The hand-hewn beam was mismeasured at the mill, and when it was craned into place, it extended two inches farther than your prints showed, so the county required it."

"Well, that's understandable," she said. They proceeded to talk about the construction work for another twenty minutes, comparing notes and making minor changes to the plans. After Mark and Brooke finished, Pam picked up the phone.

"The real reason we called," Pam explained, "was to see if you'd be interested in watching some fireworks over Lumby this weekend. The town is getting ready for a weekend-long celebration."

"I'd love to, but I can't," Brooke declined the offer. "I have two final client reviews coming up next week that I need to prepare for. My thoughts will be with you guys, though."

Pam heard in Brooke's voice an unfamiliar passiveness. The lack of her usual enthusiasm and energy made Pam concerned.

"Are you all right?" Pam asked.

"Just a little downcast, I suppose," Brooke answered. "I haven't been advertising and decided not to pursue a few bids when I returned, so I really have no jobs after I wrap up these two homes, and that's a bit depressing."

Pam wished she could offer a solution, but knew full well that her friend had to make those decisions for herself. "Why not use it as an opportunity to take a break? You're certainly invited to come and stay with us."

"I don't know if I could do that," Brooke said.

"Why not?" Pam asked.

"I don't know," Brook quietly said. "Seems I'm not sure about a lot of things these days."

After talking with Brooke, Pam and Mark also called Brother Matthew at Saint Cross Abbey, only to get the abbey's answering machine, so they left a message inviting the brother to Montis in July as well. Their final call made that night was to Joshua, in hopes that he would know of any littermates still available from Clipper's breeder.

That week preceding the Fourth saw several significant improvements at Montis Inn. The company Mark hired to manage the orchard brought in a crew of no less than two dozen workers who, over the course of three days, transformed the overgrown acreage into a paradise of immaculately trimmed trees springing from beautiful mounds of dark, fresh mulch.

Prior to their work, Mark had never noticed the exacting straightness of the rows, or the equidistant placement of each tree to the next. "Easier at harvest," one worker responded when Mark made mention. Also, he had never noticed the very extensive irrigation system that needed to be unearthed and repaired. The shed, across Farm to Market on the orchard side, had long been missing the control panel for the water management, but a new one was installed, allowing Mark to program the timing and the amount of water fed to his trees.

Although delighted with the progress, Mark had sadly realized over the course of the week that the orchard was no longer his private garden: it had become an enterprise unto itself, one that needed investment and would generate income if managed correctly. To retain a sense of belonging, he decided to assume complete responsibility for the sapling grove. He went out and bought his first dozen plum trees, as Brother Matthew had suggested he would want to do.

As the diseased and dead wood in the trees was pruned, so were the chapel's scarred remains of the fire, which were hauled away, one truckload after another. With clean cuts replacing the jagged burnt edges of lumber, the building now looked as though a skilled surgeon had amputated the back and top portions of the structure and rebuilt the side skeleton with timbered straight bones at right angles.

For Mark and Pam, one of the most memorable days of that summer was the Wednesday before the long holiday weekend, when, shortly before seven in the morning, four double-long flatbeds drove up Farm to Market Road carrying the roof trusses that had been manufactured south of Wheatley. Mark watched in awe as a towering crane, skyscraper high, was positioned in the middle of the road, and within minutes, began hoisting the fifty-foot trusses off the trucks and onto the hill across from the inn, which was the only accessible area large enough to accommodate such lengths of lumber.

After the delivery was complete, a crew of ten climbed the exterior walls and positioned themselves along the crossbeams and "sticks," as they referred to the ceiling frame. The crane lifted the first truss, secured by four thick straps, until the truss was upright, resting on the ground, allowing for the straps to be adjusted before being hoisted any higher. Then lifted another ten feet, the truss followed the swing of the crane toward the inn, gently listing and swaying as it moved over Farm to Market. As the crane arm swung over the driveway and moved closer to the inn, the truss was raised another thirty feet, and within seconds it hovered in midair, well above the framers.

The first truss was then slowly lowered toward the men, who caught it in gentle flight, positioned it, and secured it to the top plates. Releasing the straps, the crane arm was free to swing back toward the orchard to have another truss harnessed and dropped.

And so it was repeated again and again, with the trusses erected every two feet.

By five that evening, Montis had a roof structure, a frame on which the plywood, tar paper and shingles would be applied over the coming days. Within those few hours the building was once again given the depth, breadth and height that had been lost with the fire, and Mark and Pam were amazed by the volume of space inside their new inn.

ΩΩ

That same week Joshua came with a puppy in hand, a slightly larger yellow Lab littermate, which Mark and Pam named Cutter. So life was very good at Montis. The inn was framed, the orchard was producing fruit, and Clipper and Cutter were assisting by chewing on power cords, running off with tool belts almost too heavy for them to drag, and eating small scraps under the picnic table.

Pam especially appreciated these times, for she could separate herself, if only temporarily, from the worry that was always with her. She knew how fragile the balance was between happiness and tragedy, and how there are very few times in life when all of the levers were up: when the bills were paid, the dogs were fed, her husband and friends were healthy, and the tomatoes were ripe. But she also knew that in a split second one of those levers could trip, and adversity would rush in and flood their lives. That was one of the reasons she married Mark; he always unconditionally believed that the levers would stay up indefinitely, permanently. She so envied the freedom that that optimism gave him.

And it was the Fourth of July weekend, as fun and wondrous in Lumby as in any small town across the country.

The Lumby Lines

Sheriff's Complaints

SHERIFF SIMON DIXON   **JULY 3**

6:14a.m. A Lumby resident on Perimeter Road reported a canister of unknown contents, although smelling like day-old manure, was lying in the road.

9:42a.m. A caller reported finding her mail scattered in a field across the street from her home. Canada Geese pecking at the letters. Also, her mail-box had been painted green without her say so.

10:55a.m. Lee Bowland, 19, was arrested at Lumby Sporting Goods for making sexually obscene gestures at the bathing suit mannequin. No bond listed.

1:13p.m. Caller reported that he swerved to miss a moose on Priest Pass and wound up in the ditch.

3:33p.m. Todd Coleman, 20, of Rocky Mount, was arrested for being an intoxicated pedestrian. No bond listed.

6:02p.m. Car vs. mountain lion SR 541 west of Beaver Creek. Both survived.

7:17p.m. Terry McGuire and Brian Beezer, both 18, arrested for shooting trout in Goose Creek. Second offense. Bond was $200.

11:52p.m. Rick Deen reported the theft of his bike, which he thought he had used earlier, from in front of Wayside Bar.

JULY 4

12:51a.m. Lumby resident, identity withheld,

arrested for driving lawn mower through town while intoxicated.

8:41a.m. Allen Miller, age six, called to complain about his mom's oatmeal.

10:11a.m. LFD responded to caller who had fallen in potato storage silo and couldn't get out but cell phone was still working.

7:23p.m. Man reported that 48 homing pigeons released for July 4th celebration are still missing.

9:01p.m. LFD responded to call of sparks flying out of electrical control panel for firework show.

9:14p.m. LFD responded to small roof fire at 126 Fairground Road started by misfired firework missile.

9:16p.m. LFD responded to man whose arm was stuck in the Porta-Potty toilet at Fairgrounds.

11:30p.m. Police arrest Rocky Mount resident for sleeping in fountain. $140 bond.

JULY 5

12:41a.m. Steve Aiken, visitor from Westfield Village, reported sighting Martian space craft at Lovers Landing.

7:03a.m. Man reported feeling dizzy after smelling fungus on Canada geese dung in backyard.

10:21a.m. Owner of Lumby Hair Salon reported break-in. No damage or stolen property but two mannequin heads were super glued together in lip-lock position.

6:06p.m. Mrs. Hutchings reported small black bear going into neighbor's garage.

What Mark and Pam would always remember most from that weekend had little to do with the holiday celebrations, and more to do with an illegal entry that Mark felt Sheriff Dixon would understand if they had been caught in the act.

On Monday, the fifth of July, well before dawn while the town still slept off the prior night's festivities, Pam and Mark quietly drove up Farm to Market Road. Just before coming into Lumby, they turned off their car lights and pulled into the parking lot of the First Presbyterian Church.

Although they had always intended to become members as soon as their lives settled down, they had not yet talked to the minister. Nor had they even visited this church, which proved to be a significant disadvantage that morning. In the darkness before dawn, Mark and Pam walked around the chapel, first trying the primary doors, which were all locked, then the secondary doors.

"I thought churches were always open," Pam whispered.

"They must be giving God a break at night," Mark said.

Circling the chapel a second time, they began to check the windows. On the backside of the sanctuary, Mark fell into a window well that was hidden behind an enormous shrub.

"Jeez," he cried out as his shoulder glanced off the metal rim.

"Shhh," Pam quieted him. She looked around, waiting for a light to come on in the pastor's residence, but it remained dark.

"Try the window before you crawl out," Pam reminded him.

Although Mark would have never gone down into the well intentionally, it was good fortune that he stumbled into it because he found a large window unlocked. With gentle maneuvering, he made his way in, then took several minutes to locate the side entrance.

"This place is gorgeous," Mark said, holding the door open for Pam, Clipper and Cutter.

"How do you know? It's pitch-black inside."

"No, it's not. There are a couple of nightlights in the back of the chapel. Come see," he said excitedly, and led the way with the puppies acting very unlike themselves—remaining quiet and staying close by.

They walked to the front of the chapel, which was dimly lit as Mark had said. Pam opened the satchel she was carrying and took out several large candles, placing them on the steps leading up to the altar. Mark followed immediately behind and lit one after another. And then they waited.

As the gentle light of dawn began to illuminate the stained glass windows that surrounded them, Mark and Pam finally faced each other, took each other's hands, and in soft words repeated the vows that they had said to one another twenty years ago to the day and to the hour in a small Presbyterian church in Massachusetts.

ॐ

FOURTEEN

Journals

One morning at Montis, the phone rang at 5:45 a.m., waking both Mark and Pam.

"Sorry to be calling so early," Brooke said, "but the strangest thing just happened."

"What's that?" Pam asked, phone to ear, getting out of bed to let the puppies out for their morning business.

"Well, I just got a Fed Ex package delivered this morning."

"Okay," Pam said, looking at the clock and adding two hours for East Coast time. "And that's why you called?"

"Yes. But you would never believe what's in it," Brooke said excitedly.

"Tell all," she said, now more awake and curious.

"Two hundred-year-old handwritten journals," she said, her voice a little shaky.

"Not ordered through Amazon, I'm assuming," Pam chuckled.

"No, just the opposite, not ordered at all. And I have no idea who sent them. The return address was General Delivery in Lumby, but that's all."

Pam's ears pricked up at that. "Oh, that is weird. What are the journals?"

Brooke then remembered that she had never told Pam or Mark about the specifics of her attempt to find additional information on Montis Abbey, about the two entries she had found at the Wheatley Library, or about the two missing books.

"Well, both are leather-bound with 'Montis Abbey' engraved on the front."

"What?" Pam cried out.

Mark sat up in bed. "What's going on?"

"Hold on, I want Mark to pick up the other phone."

When Mark got on the line, Brooke continued. "One is quite large, about four hundred pages long, and it appears to be some kind of register or logbook, each line or two having a date on the left side followed by some writing. They look like descriptions and names. Oh, wait a minute," she said, thumbing through the journal. "Here's an actual ledger entry: $14.00 paid for labor in the orchard on September 18, 1939. Boy, this is amazing!" She paused, captivated with what she was reading. "Anyway, it begins with an entry for February 18, 1901, and ends with a note made on May 5, 1962."

Mark asked, "Who sent this to you?" and Brooke repeated what she had told Pam: she had no idea.

"What about the second?" Pam asked.

"It also has a leather cover, with 'Montis Abbey' engraved on the front but this one has a small, impressed crest as well." Looking through the first section, she continued. "It is more of a diary, long-handwritten, descriptive paragraphs about the abbey, the orchards, and what appear to be entries about their calligraphy jobs," she said, gently flipping the pages.

"Do you see anything about Brother Matthew?" Mark asked.

"Hold on, let me try to find it. When did he say he joined?"

"He said several years before Brother Benjamin died, so that would make it in the late fifties," Pam answered.

"Oh!" Brooke said excitedly. "Here it is," and she began reading directly from the journal: "Today we celebrated young Brother

Matthew taking his vows." She read on silently. "Yes, this is it. Wow!" she said in wonderment.

"What is it?" Mark asked.

"Oh, nothing specific. It's just that the journals are so old. This is just remarkable."

"God, I wish we could see them," Mark said.

"Look, let me go through these, and I'll give you a call back. I've got lots of work to wrap up, but I'll get to it over the next few days," Brooke promised.

"We'll be waiting," Pam responded.

"Oh, and one other thing. Would you fax me the real estate section from *The Lumby Lines* when you have a chance?" Brooke slipped in as an afterthought.

Pam was startled by her request. "Why so?"

Brooke answered tentatively, "I'm thinking about staying in Lumby for the rest of the summer, and thought I'd see if there were any interesting rentals."

"Brooke, don't be ridiculous," Mark said. "We only have a bazillion rooms here. You can have any one you want. In fact, we can give you an entire building."

Brooke laughed. "Well, thank you, but I want to give you guys some privacy, especially with so much commotion going on during the day. And I have a few projects I'm thinking about starting up."

Had she not known Brooke as well as she did, Pam might have been miffed by her rejection. "Well, you think about it, but we'll fax some pages over to you all the same."

"Thanks. Have you seen Joshua lately?" Brooke inquired, trying to sound casual.

"We see him every few days. He was here yesterday, in fact," Pam said brightly. "I think he would like to spend more time here, but he's been really busy at the orchard. Has he called you?" Pam asked, not wanting to pry but hopeful for her friend.

"We talk every three or four days," Brooke said, "but I feel something has changed. We don't seem as close as when I was in Lumby."

"That may be just Joshua feeling the distance, being uncertain about how you are feeling now that you're back home."

"Maybe," Brooke said unconvincingly. "One evening he seemed to slip and mention something about making a change in the near future, but he didn't want to discuss it any further. He backpedaled when I asked him about it." Brooke paused. "I do miss him, though."

"I know," Pam responded.

After hanging up, Mark walked back into the bedroom, where Pam was sitting in the window seat. "I wonder who sent them to her," Mark said, climbing back into bed.

"Well, I'm wondering who has had them for the last forty years, why they're showing up now, and why they were sent specifically to Brooke," she said, picking up *The Lumby Lines* and going over to the fax machine.

The Lumby Lines

Real Estate   July 6

Single car garage for rent to small car: Must share with tractor on blocks. $10/month. Call now 925-0746

Office for rent: Used to be Doc Gibbers old place before he passed. $120 per month, 2 month deposit. 925-3587

Garage for rent: Also used for storage so boxes stay. $12/mo. 925-5253

Parked RV in back: One bed, one bath with hookup. Quaint. $55 per month. 925-4439

House for sale: 18 Pine Street. Needs TLC but
has great potential. Electricity sometimes works.
Offered by Lumby Realty 925-5555

Certified piano teacher: Available to tutor your
child any age from 10-14. Experienced. Please
telephone 925-0174

Chicken coop good for 20 hens: One year lease.
$2/mo. 925-2985

**Delightful basement one very large room
apartment:** No windows but lots of light. Semi-
private entrance with semi-private bath on 3rd floor.
No appliances. Renter can replace carpet if desired.
925-6619

60×20 Barn: 4 stalls with hay loft. Negotiable.
North on Hunters Mill Rd. 925-4338

Location! Location! Nicely refinished 3/2 on
Mineral Street. Perfect for growing family. $82,900
Make offer. Call Joan Stokes at Main Street Realty
925-9292 and let the best realtor in town find your
dream home!

"She's going to be staying with us," Pam said confidently after
scanning the section, but Mark had already fallen back to sleep.

လၢသ

FIFTEEN

Cud

Construction progressed quickly with little incident and no accidents; the exterior studs were transformed into walls, and the roof
was decked out. Montis was now "in the dry," as the carpenters told
Pam and Mark, and that was a very good thing.

Within a matter of hours, the cast of characters changed as
if Montis had become a different show production. Mackenzie
McGuire and her framing crew, who had shared many weekday
breakfasts, every lunch and occasional dinners with Mark and
Pam over the past month, packed up their tools, bade farewell
and drove away, leaving Montis incredibly empty and quiet for a
midweek afternoon. With no activity, the puppies quickly became
bored, and wandered off to further explore the orchard.

Pam and Mark took the opportunity to walk through the rooms,
which appeared immense when they were just studs, but now
seemed claustrophobically enclosed because of the outside plywood shell. They knew that the appearance would change again
once the drywall was hung, and again after that once the trim and
painting were completed. Pam was fascinated at how one space, of
the exact same dimension, could look twice the size or half the size

at any point during construction.

"I'm getting nervous," Pam said in a quiet voice, as if she didn't want anyone to hear.

"Really?" Mark asked.

"Well, more of an excited nervous . . . like an excivous."

Mark laughed as he always did when Pam made up words.

"Why so?" he asked.

"It's getting close."

"It?"

"The completion. The inn."

"Oh, honey," Mark said, "I hate to disappoint you, but we are so not close to completion." He laughed. "Now, that's what you should be nervous about."

Pam then remembered how, when building the house in Falls Church, she thought it was all but complete when it was finally enclosed, but how, in reality, that was only the beginning of another phase, a more expensive phase: heating, plumbing and electric. Then Mark's words struck full force.

"Oh, God," she said.

"What?"

"It's so far away."

"You mean the completion, don't you?" Mark laughed.

"You're right. We're not even close to done." She shook her head. "And we're burning through money like it's a pile of leaves on a fall day."

"Hello?" someone called from the front door, as there was no doorbell, which was just fine, as there was no door either.

"We're in here," Mark called back from the great room on the first floor, looking through the interior studded walls toward the front door.

"Mark? It's Cantor. Where would you like us to park?" Cantor walked into the inn, slipping between the two-by-fours instead of walking around through the door opening. He was a small, agile, middle-aged man, with short, bushy black hair and huge hands.

Pam never understood if he was given that nickname because of his love for arias, or because of his own tenor voice that bellowed through the air ducts that he installed. Either way, his skills as a heating and air tradesman were highly recommended by so many in Wheatley that Mark sought him out shortly after buying the property.

"Anywhere other than the south side. The mason is having some stone delivered tomorrow and asked us to keep that area clear."

"No problem," Cantor said.

Within minutes the silence of Montis was broken by the Three Tenors singing "Funiculi," with Cantor singing every note. Clipper and Cutter, who had ventured into the far fields of the orchard, heard the music and came running. Within an hour, the first of the ductwork was being strapped in place.

∞

With the tradesmen working on the main building, Pam found peace in finishing the old library, which she had transformed into a beautiful multipurpose sitting room with a thick green area rug and several heavy upholstered chairs and leather sofas that one could sink into and spend the rest of the afternoon.

Pam refinished all of the bookshelves surrounding the windows, which were now curtained, and brought in two large antique library tables for the far end of the room, where they had laid the cables and electric lines for guests who had brought their laptops and wanted an Internet connection. A large television flanked the stone fireplace for those who wanted to watch the news or a good movie. A wonderful room, she thought as she stepped back and looked around.

Behind her, a weak knock on the open door was followed by an almost weaker "Excuse me?"

Pam turned to see a very old woman with brilliant silver hair loosely pulled up in a bun standing in the doorway.

"May I help you?" Pam asked, looking quite puzzled.

"Yes, I'm Charlotte Ross. I probably have no business here, but

Mackenzie McGuire mentioned that you may have a garden that could benefit from some compost."

Pam thought for a moment. "Oh, yes. That would be Brooke's garden by the side of the lodge. It's been badly neglected," Pam admitted, while trying to figure out who this strange but very polite woman was.

"Well, I have a tremendous amount at our orchard . . . really far more than we know what to do with. So perhaps, if you don't object, I can bring some by?" Charlotte offered.

Pam noticed the dirt under her nails and rightly assumed that the old woman was an avid gardener. "Yes, that would be appreciated." She paused, creating an awkward moment. "By the way, I'm Pam Walker," and gently shook her outstretched hand.

"How very nice to meet you. And what a wonderful library," Charlotte said, looking into the large room at all of the bookshelves. "Libraries are very special indeed."

"Yes, they are," Pam concurred.

Then as strangely as she appeared, Charlotte Ross left. But the following morning she returned sitting on the back of a pickup truck loaded with rich, dark compost. She and the driver spent most of the morning weeding and adding the organic matter to the dry soil. And under her capable hands, Brooke's garden was slowly transformed.

ﾛﾋﾗ

Mark and Pam had decided to finish the bedrooms in the old sleeping quarters as soon as possible, hoping that Brother Matthew, and perhaps Michael, would be returning that month. They asked the trim carpenters to come in for a few days, and the men finished all the rooms, adding molding and wainscoting, building bookshelves, restructuring closets and repairing drywall.

With four of the bedrooms, Pam decided to convert the adjacent bedrooms into private sitting rooms with a door connecting the two. So the doors from the hall to these converted rooms were framed up, enclosed, and drywalled. Finally, when all was completed, there were eight bedrooms: four with attached sitting rooms, all with private baths.

For three days, while the rooms were being repainted, Pam went furniture shopping in Wheatley and Rocky Mount. During the next week, trucks converged on Montis Inn, delivering rugs and runners, beds with wonderful wrought-iron and cherry headboards, and bureaus and vanities. On several evenings she worked well past midnight making beds, putting out fresh linens, and arranging books and artifacts on the shelves.

ကာ

Mark also had a well-established routine. He worked at the construction site until lunch and then, after a meal shared with the laborers, he went across the road into the orchards to work on his trees, weather permitting. The first days of each week were spent in the sapling field, which he called the Terrace because of its smaller size and the best views of Woodrow Lake. There he planted as many as two dozen young fruit trees a week, wrapping each one with protective wire so the deer wouldn't chew on the tender bark.

On most days Mark took Clipper and Cutter with him, where they displayed the unbridled joy of being puppies: to chase butterflies, dig holes, dig more holes, and sleep in the warm sun, round bellies rising and falling to their pants. One afternoon, while Mark planted cherry trees that had just been delivered from Rocky Mount, Cutter caught wind of something and took off to the edge of the woods. His barks, which were more like high-pitched squeaks, were nonetheless relentless. Clipper, although staying with Mark, also raised his fur and started growling. Mark leaned over to grab Clipper's collar and yelled at Cutter to get back.

Mark had read recent stories in *The Lumby Lines* about two mountain lions that had been sighted numerous times south of town. They were thought to be a pair, and they probably had a den somewhere between the lake and Lumby. He had seen tracks that could have been theirs once on the property, but that had been well over a month ago.

But there was something in the woods, and that something was big. Mark yelled at Cutter again, while Clipper frantically tried to free himself from Mark's grasp. From within the woods Mark heard a large piece of wood crack, loud enough to send Cutter running back to Mark, who nabbed his collar. With a dog in each hand, too heavy to pick them both up and run, Mark felt trapped. He flashed back to Brother Matthew's comment about how the monks would occasionally bring guns up in the fields to ward off bears and lions, and regretted not following up on the suggestion.

The dogs were going berserk, growling, cowering and pulling every which way to free themselves. Mark was squatting close to the ground, trembling, staring into the woods. He wanted to pick up the shovel to defend himself, but that would mean letting go of the dogs.

The noise in the woods got louder, breaking limbs. Mark struggled to see, but the brush along the edge was just too thick. The animal or animals were large and getting closer; Mark saw the top of a fallen tree shift by the weight of something stepping on it. That was it. Mark let go of Cutter, picked up Clipper, and started to run as fast as he could in the opposite direction.

Moo.

In his panic he thought he heard a low, fierce growl. Mark's heart was racing. He was disoriented. He turned around quickly enough to look but not slow his run. He then stumbled over some gardening tools and hit the ground with Clipper flying in the air.

Moo.

He recovered, looked around again, and almost stopped breathing. A Guernsey cow sauntered into the clearing not far from where he had been working. Mark, kneeling on the ground, felt his heart drop back into his chest. Heart attack at the tender age of forty-four, he thought.

Clipper and Cutter, seeing the animal was not a predator, started running circles around the slow-moving bovine, trying to catch its swaying tail. The only thing the cow was interested in was chewing her cud. After a minute of recovery and laughter, Mark got up and walked over to the beast. A worn, frayed rope was tied around her neck, but there were no branding marks. That didn't mean anything. But then again, maybe it did, because Mark knew absolutely nothing about cows.

Mark did remember an article he had read about "free range" states where cattle had the right of way on all roads. The article told of a man who hit a large steer, his wife dying in the accident, and then, to add salt to the wound, the man had to reimburse the farmer for the cow. So, this unfortunate fellow was out one car (totaled), one wife (deceased), and two thousand dollars (prize steer).

Moo.

Mark took off his belt, attached it to the rope already around the cow's neck, and escorted the unwelcome visitor down to Montis Abbey, having absolutely no idea what he was going to do with the cow once there. Medium-rare hamburgers for all, he thought.

"Bertha!" one of the workers called out while Mark was walking across Farm to Market Road. Bertha? Mark looked at the animal in tow.

"Do you know this cow?" Mark asked.

"Yeah, she belongs to that Mcnear fellow with the big farm off Killdrop Road. She just won best in show for Guernseys at the fairground last week. See the circle of brown hair on her forehead? That's how I know. She's the one who beat my Josie May," he said.

"Didn't know your wife was entered," one of the workers on the roof yelled out, to which everyone broke out in laughter and catcalls.

Moo.

The Walkers checked *The Lumby Lines*, expecting to see a story about Bertha, but only saw one interesting article, which they faxed to Brooke.

The Lumby Lines

Fork River Festival

BY CARRIE KERRY   **JULY 12**

Volunteers are needed to help prepare for the 8th annual Fork River Festival scheduled for Saturday, August 21st, rain or shine. The Festival will have the same format as last year's because it was so successful:

8:00a.m. Breakfast and dry-land raft design competition at Kelly's Bend on the Fork River. To remind our readers, during this first competition, the panel will only be judging the appearance of the raft, and not sea-worthiness.

11:45a.m. Dry-land raft awards announced.

12:00p.m. BBQ lunch at the same location provided by Jimmy D's.

1:00-4:00p.m. Raft race. Boats will enter at Kelly's Bend and proceed down to the finish line at the entrance to Woodrow Lake. This year there will be a staggered start, due to the pileup of all the rafts last year. Entrants will be given their start times by Mr. Dickenson during lunch.

5:00p.m. Family-style dinner at Shelburne Beach.

Mayor Toby will be participating this year. Lumby
Police Department said that parking will be
available on the dirt access road to Kelly's Bend
as well as the public parking area by Shelburne
Beach. Competition rules and raft specifications are
available at Lumby Sporting Goods.

Immediately below the article was an invitation of sorts:

THE MONTIS INN

Would like to invite our neighbors of Lumby
for dessert and coffee after the Fork River Festival

Good luck to all competitors

Mark looked at Pam and said, "Well, this is a nice surprise, but
didn't you want to first talk with me about it?"

"Mark, I had nothing to do with it," she said, and they both
stared at the paper in utter bewilderment.

SIXTEEN

Motivation

"I had forgotten how university campuses empty out during summer break," Dennis Beezer said as they walked back to the car. In the empty quad only a handful of students were lying on the grass reading.

"What?" Joshua asked absently, absorbed in riffling through a large pile of papers that he was carrying.

"The campus is empty," Dennis repeated.

"I think I'm missing one of the prerequisite reading lists."

"I doubt that. We were in there for two hours and she seemed quite thorough."

"Ah, here it is," Joshua said, holding it up victoriously. Looking up, he commented how empty the campus looked. Dennis laughed. "I really appreciate you coming along. It would have taken me an hour just to find the registration building."

"It was my pleasure," Dennis said. "And for what it's worth, I think you're going to do just great." It really pleased Dennis to be helping out as Joshua began this new period in his life. They had been the closest of friends for fifteen years and had seen each other through thick and thin, and this was definitely the thick.

They had originally met shortly after Dennis moved his family from Mexico. Just before "the evacuation," as he and Gabrielle called it, Dennis had placed several calls to Lumby, and during one such conversation with a realtor, he had learned of a very small cottage for rent on Deer Trail Lane. Although it was owned by Montis Abbey, it was quite removed from the compound and had its own entrance—a perfect place to bide their time as they settled into their new life in the Northwest.

After Dennis and Gabrielle moved in, they would regularly see several of the monks from the monastery. The most frequent visitor was Brother Joshua, a young novice who had joined Montis the prior year and was assigned the chore of maintaining the graveyard and cottage grounds. A few years younger than Dennis, Joshua had a strong spirit and focus that Dennis very much admired. During the spring months of that first year, Dennis and Joshua became friends as they jointly maintained the gardens and lawn around the cabin, and both men came to trust each other's honesty and opinions. That friendship grew over the following years, and the two became like brothers.

Dennis continued. "You've been preparing for this for a long time. It must feel good to finally be registered as a graduate student."

Joshua nodded. "Well, my classes don't begin until January, but it does feel good." He looked down at the heavy stack of papers on his lap. "Intimidating but good."

"One step at a time," Dennis said supportively. "Hey, do you mind if we stop by my office for one minute before heading up to Saint Cross? I need to pick up some papers."

"Not at all. They're not expecting us for another few hours anyway."

While Joshua waited in the car, he began to wade through the pre-course materials. A few minutes later, Dennis walked out of the office and, getting back into the car, handed him a manila envelope. "This is slightly bizarre."

"What's that?" Joshua asked.

"Well, about two weeks ago Scott Stevens applied for a job at the *Sentinel.* Two days later, I find that sitting on my desk." He nodded at the envelope. "No stamp, no return address, and no one in the office saw who dropped it off."

Joshua glanced at the headline of the article, dated four months prior. "*Corrupt Reporting Practices at the Wheatley Sentinel,* by Scott Stevens."

Joshua shook his head as he finished reading the article. "This is so slanderous it's almost funny."

"Almost, but not quite."

"It sounds like you should be tarred and feathered before being thrown in jail," Joshua chuckled.

"I know it's ludicrous, but the hairs on my neck went up the first time I read it," Dennis said, checking his speedometer. Heading out of town, they were now approaching a stretch of road notorious for speed traps.

"So, I assume good old Scott Stevens won't be getting a job offer from you anytime soon?"

"No. But the unfortunate circumstance is that, other than the article being a fictitious piece of crap, he's a pretty good writer. I've known him for a long time, and I swear that boy is his own worst enemy. He pulls idiotic stunts and sabotages his best efforts."

"I'm surprised you sound as empathetic as you do given the poison ink he used to write this."

"He's young and stupid," Dennis said with a shrug.

"Yes, but we all have to grow up and take responsibility for our actions."

"Agreed."

"So, who do you think sent this to you?" Joshua asked in a more mysterious voice.

Dennis thought for a moment. "I don't know. I was trying to figure out who might have had access to it: perhaps someone at *The Lumby Lines* if he actually had the gall to submit it. Probably one of his colleagues."

"Or William?" Joshua proposed.

Dennis laughed. "Oh, wouldn't that be a sick twist? Why on earth would my father, who I haven't talked to since returning to Lumby, feed me that article?"

Joshua considered the question. "Three possible reasons: first, he's trying to protect you."

"Impossible—that would never occur to him. Next," he said, waving his hand as if to bring on another answer.

"Second, self-interest. . . . He doesn't want Scott to leave."

"Self-interest sounds like my father, but Scott isn't *that* good. Next," he said, waving his hand again.

"Third," Joshua paused, and said more softly, "to intentionally hurt you."

"Ah, that sounds more like it. As sad as it is for me to admit it, if it was my father, that would be his motive." Though Dennis said this jocularly, he soon fell silent, mulling over how they could have become so estranged.

William Beezer was a man of stringent control, over himself as well as others in his life. The recipient of much of his exacting nature was his eldest son, Dennis, who was a smart but scrawny young boy capable of developing his own clever defenses against his father's heavy-handed reign.

Although Dennis did as expected and excelled in academics during his youth, he knew he was a constant disappointment to his father in the area of athletics. Dennis lacked two necessary attributes: a strong body, as he was slow to mature, and a competitive ruthlessness, which he never did acquire, contrary to his father's best plans.

To encourage Dennis to think strategically, William Beezer engaged his young charge in chess for ten years of Sunday mornings; move after move, match after match, until Dennis excelled in the game. Clearly, it was chess, and the fact that William sprinkled his son's summer reading list with such classics as *The Art of War*, *The Prince* and a knee-high stack of legal books that gave

Dennis strong tactical thinking. "You must always know the ground on which you stand," was one of Dennis's most significant lessons.

During his senior year in high school, Dennis agreed to a verbal contract offered by his father: he was to attend Stanford University, major in journalism and sustain an A average. In return, his father would finance his education, his summer internships, and pay for enough return trips to Lumby to ensure William's upper hand in his son's development.

What was never discussed was William's "painfully self-evident" assumption that Dennis would return to Lumby shortly after graduation to begin his career at *The Lumby Lines*, and then, a few years later, move into a management position at the Chatham Press.

Two obstacles stood between William and that well-conceived plan: first, Dennis never intended to work for his father, and second, he met and shortly thereafter married Gabrielle Carillo.

Thinking of his wife, Dennis asked Joshua, "So, how is your love life, if I may be so direct?"

Joshua was, as usual, forthright. "I'd like you and Gabrielle to meet Brooke as soon as she returns to Lumby."

"Well, this is momentous," Dennis teased.

"Over a chicken enchilada at The Green Chile, not a formal state dinner," Joshua said, minimizing the significance of his suggestion.

Dennis sensed his friend's nervousness. "We certainly would enjoy that," was all he said.

Joshua looked out his side window at the mountains in the foreground. "I really like her, Dennis. She's someone I could see spending the rest of my life with. She's beautiful, smart and caring and has a dry sense of humor I would never tire from. But . . ."

"But what?"

"But she'll only be here for a month or so and then she'll return to Virginia at the end of the summer."

Dennis added that to the picture that was forming. "How does she feel about you?"

"I don't know. She's very guarded with her emotions. I think she may feel the same, but neither of us will discuss it. I don't want to force her into a conversation she's not ready to have." Dennis didn't respond but waited for Joshua to continue. "A long-distance relationship that has no hope of reuniting at some point seems a little futile."

"Does she know that you've been accepted at the university?"

"No, I haven't told her yet. I'm afraid that would just about end the little we have between us."

"If she's anything like you've described, I would expect her to be very happy for you."

"She would be, so much so that she wouldn't do anything that would interfere with my goal . . . even if that meant forgoing our relationship."

Dennis nodded. "She seems like a keeper to me."

"Oh, that she is," Joshua said with a faint smile on his face.

"So, will she be here for the raft race?"

"I think so. She's supposed to be flying in next week."

"Great," Dennis said, humor peppering his voice. "Then she can see how well you handle utter humiliation when we leave you in our wake."

"I doubt that seriously," Joshua responded. "If you remember, I've beaten you nine out of the last twelve years."

"Oh, but you have absolutely no idea what awaits you on the river. We've been designing our raft for three months now—even took the plans to a hull expert in Rocky Mount. I'll give you one friendly word of advice: be prepared."

"Actually, that's two words," Joshua jokingly corrected him. "But you're really putting the fear of God in me—I'm shaking in my boots." He began shaking his legs just as they pulled up to Saint Cross monastery.

Brother Matthew was in the courtyard when he heard the laughter from the car. "Oh, so nice to see you two," he said, approaching Dennis and Joshua as they got out and stretched.

Joshua noticed that his old friend looked unusually tired and very troubled, and he wondered why.

"The grounds look beautiful," Dennis remarked.

"Yes, we are trying to prepare the property," Matthew responded.

"For what?" Joshua asked.

"I'll explain soon enough," Matthew said, dodging the question.

They passed through the archway and into the interior courtyard, where they strolled through the cloisters.

"This is one of the most extraordinary places I've ever seen," Dennis said, taking in the large courtyard surrounded by the stone arched walkways. He had only been to Saint Cross a few other times, and he was awed during each visit. "It's as if one becomes totally disconnected from the outside world."

"It must be a wonderful place to meditate," Joshua concurred.

"The other day I was thinking how very different Montis was," Matthew said. "This abbey is more intimate . . . smaller. But I am equally fond of both." That reminded him of something, and he turned to Joshua. "I appreciate you offering to pick up the papers that the Walkers need to support their application for historical landmark status. I would have delivered them myself, but we are very busy right now." His voice weakened and trailed off.

Brother Michael came up from behind. "Well, this is a nice surprise," he said, shaking hands with the visitors. "Will you be staying the afternoon?"

"No, I'm afraid not. We just came by for a few minutes."

"If you would excuse me, I'll go in and get that folder," Matthew said.

As Matthew slowly walked away, his shoulders heavily bent, Joshua turned to Michael. "Is Matthew well? He looks very frail."

"This has been difficult for all of us, but I think it's taken more of a personal toll on him."

"What has?"

Michael winced, realizing that Joshua had not been told, and he was unsure how to continue.

"Brother Michael, what is it?" Joshua insisted, growing fearful.

Michael began hesitantly. "The work that has always sustained us is no longer in demand, and the limited requests that come in are too few and far between. Our funds are almost depleted and we have no recourse." He dropped his head. "It appears we will have to sell the abbey at the end of the summer."

ෂඛ

SEVENTEEN

Cottage

The Lumby Lines

Sheriff's Complaints

SHERIFF SIMON DIXON   **JULY 14**

9:42p.m. Received complaint from Osborn Group Home that 10 gallons of gas were stolen from their van.

10:22p.m. Lumby man reported steer had gotten out of pasture in Mcnear Meadows-Killdrop Road area. Gate and trees felled and missing.

10:49p.m. Patron of Jimmy D's on Old 41 reported several kids driving up and down Mineral St. dragging large elm behind their pickup.

11:53p.m. EMS responded to 18 Berry Lane where a 63-year old woman was having trouble breathing.

JULY 15

1:14a.m. Deer damages Chevrolet, Fork River area.

2:18a.m. LFD responded to pickup truck fire west bank of Beaver Creek. Occupants attempting to dry seats. Access blocked by large elm spanning streambed, attached to pickup.

2:43a.m. Terry McGuire and Brian Beezer, both of Lumby, brought in for questioning.

When Brooke called that evening, they had much to catch up on. They told her about the progress on the buildings, the cow, the Fork River Festival and the anonymous invitation sent out to the town by the inn.

Brooke, in turn, began to tell them about the journals.

"They're fascinating. I can't wait for you to see them next week."

"Is that when you'll be arriving?" Pam asked.

"Yeah, I think so," she answered. "But I need to tell you guys something pretty important. This afternoon, when I was going through the last few pages of the first journal, tightly stuck into the binding on the second-to-last page was a check."

"An old check?" Mark asked.

"No, don't think that's the case here," she said a little strangely. "It's a cashier's check."

"For what?" Mark asked.

"More like 'to whom,'" Brooke corrected him. "The check's made out to the Montis Inn."

There were several beats of dead silence. "You've got to be kidding," Pam said.

"No, and it's dated last month."

What on earth is going on? Mark thought. "For how much?"

"I don't quite know how to say this without sounding crazy,"

Brooke said. "But it's made out for fifty thousand dollars."

This time the silence on the phone was total.

"Are you guys there?" Brooke asked.

"Yeah," Mark responded shakily.

Brooke told them a few other interesting things about the books, that there were repeated entries about a "stone cottage" and several financial entries she couldn't understand even when comparing the logbook to the diary. But Mark and Pam remained mute for the rest of the call, in complete bafflement at what Brooke had told them.

{∞}

Brother Matthew arrived shortly thereafter, in the late morning while Mark and Joshua were restacking stone for the mason, who had begun laying the back wall.

"Just wonderful progress," Matthew said, approaching the two men.

"Oh, Matthew, I'm so glad you're here," Mark said, standing and stretching his sore back.

Then he noticed Matthew was carrying a small bag. "Will you be staying with us for a while?"

"For a few days, if it's not too much of an imposition."

Worry lines had replaced his good-natured smile, and he looked older than the last time they were together.

"No, absolutely not, the bees would appreciate it. I think they think I'm doing them all a disservice. Here, you must be tired after the long drive. Let me show you to your room. It's a little different than the last time you slept here," Mark said, leading the way to the sleeping quarters.

"My heavens," Brother Matthew said when he walked into his guest quarters. "You've done such a marvelous job, I barely recognize it."

"Well, Pam did all the work in the back buildings," Mark confessed. "Please make yourself at home. I have about an hour's more work to do, but Pam is in the lodge if you would like to go over and have a cup of tea. There's fresh honey over there, too," he added with a broad smile.

Dinner that evening was a celebration: sirloin steak (not Bertha, as Mark assured Pam) and fresh vegetables from the farmers market. Mark, Pam, Joshua and Matthew shared wine, walked around the compound, strolled through the orchard, which had been transformed since Brother Matthew's last visit, and shared more wine.

Pam and Mark continued to ask all the questions that they had thought of since his last visit, and Matthew patiently obliged. The Walkers told Matthew and Joshua about the journals and the check Brooke had found. Matthew said he vaguely remembered several monastery journals lying around, and the abbot making entries into leather-bound books, but couldn't recall ever reading them himself.

"Brooke said that a stone cottage was mentioned several times in the logbook," Mark said, once back at the lodge.

"Yes, that would be the cottage on the east side of the property," Matthew answered.

"What cottage?" Pam asked, and went to get the plat map, being certain that there wasn't any building on the property other than those at the compound and the one cold-storage shed across the road.

"There is a cottage in the northeast corner of the property that could, many years ago, be accessed from Deer Trail Lane, a small dirt road that runs parallel to Farm to Market Road."

"I see Deer Trail, but there is no building marked on the plat," Pam said, studying the surveyor's map spread out on the dining room table.

"Well, it should be right about there," Joshua confirmed, and pointed to the upper-right corner of the property line, which would place it past the cemetery that they saw during Matthew's first visit to Montis.

∞

The following morning, Mark, Pam and Joshua, who had also spent the night in the sleeping quarters, went to the cottage while

Brother Matthew remained alone for prayer and contemplation. On the way to the cottage, they unintentionally took the same path to the cemetery. Walking into the clearing, they found the cemetery quite changed. Someone had come in and manicured the small field, the grass was mowed, weeds along the edge cut back, and each gravestone edged. Joshua noticed that even the stones that had been knocked over had been uprighted and reset in the soil.

"You guys did a great job cleaning this up," Joshua said, with obvious appreciation.

Mark looked mystified. "Actually, we didn't. We didn't know anyone had come back here since Brother Matthew showed it to us last month."

"Well, someone's been here and they did a lot of work," Pam ventured, giving Mark a quizzical look.

They continued on for a few minutes more. The dense woods were difficult to walk through, making it impossible to see anything beyond a short distance, including the small house, which was surrounded by trees that hugged the walls and roof. Perhaps in winter the cottage could be made out through the bare limbs, but Pam thought even that was unlikely.

"This would be a storybook cottage if the trees were cleared from around the house," Pam said, almost in awe of the thought of what it could be.

"The trees' roots must be tearing up the foundation," Mark said, with Joshua agreeing.

The outside footprint of the cottage was no larger than thirty feet by thirty feet, but the height suggested a second floor inside. Joshua led the way to the front, where they could see an overgrown gravel road leading away in the opposite direction.

"That goes for about a third of a mile, maybe even half a mile, and then connects with Deer Trail Lane," Joshua explained. "Many years ago, a good friend of mine lived in the cottage with his wife when they first moved to Lumby, so I used to spend a fair amount of time here when I was at the abbey."

"But that can't be all our land?" Pam asked, remembering what she had seen on the plat.

"No," Joshua answered, "it's not. We have, well, you have an easement through two properties. I'm sure there wouldn't be any issue if you cleaned it up; the properties that have given the easements have never been used, and the owners are really nice folks. In fact, one of them lives in Rocky Mount."

They proceeded to the front stoop. The cabin's two most obvious features were the walls' massive pieces of stone that must have required several men to dry-stack, and the front door: a four-inch-thick, hand-hewn piece of oak on large wrought-iron hinges, with a curved top. Nice touch, Pam thought.

The inside of the cottage, although empty, was enchanting if one could overlook the dust and spiderwebs. From the front door, they walked into a comfortable-size living room with a large wood stove and a bathroom to the left. Close to the entrance was a staircase leading to an upstairs loft. At the far end of the living room was a small kitchen with ample cabinets. To the right of that, a door led into a bedroom. The windows were small but well placed to maximize the sun during the summer. Overall, it was a charming cottage.

Pam took hold of Mark's hand. "Are you thinking what I'm thinking?"

"If you're thinking of Brooke, we're thinking the same," Mark said, squeezing back.

Joshua perked up at hearing Brooke's name mentioned. "I don't follow," he tried to say nonchalantly.

He explained about their conversation with Brooke about her desire to find a rental for the remainder of the summer.

"Is it too isolated for her?" Joshua asked with a concerned expression.

"Oh, I don't think so," Pam said. "She's very private, very much a hermit. I think she would love it. But if she's coming next Tuesday, that only leaves four days to clean it up."

"Mountains can be moved in sooner time," Joshua said, winking at Mark, who nodded in concurrence.

ՀՕՀ

And he was correct. By the time Joshua left to pick up Brooke, who was still unaware of the accommodations her friends had prepared, the cottage was not only immaculately cleaned, but had been furnished in an enchanting country style. The yard surrounding the small house had been cleared of trees and the drive-way had been skimmed and regraveled.

Joshua arrived at the airport several hours in advance and bided his time reading one of the local papers. When the announcement was made that the plane from Washington had landed, Joshua jumped up and went directly to the gate. In nervous anticipation, he began pacing the floor, thinking how he was going to greet her, and then rethinking how he was going to greet her. He had intentionally not bought roses—well, he had, but then decided that would be too significant a gesture and left them in his car.

He was so lost in thought, his eyes intently focused on the ground, that he didn't notice Brooke, who had deboarded and was standing ten feet away from him, watching in amusement.

"Are you looking for friends down there?" he heard her ask.

He looked up. "Brooke!" he exclaimed. Spontaneously he hugged her, which was followed by a long kiss, just as spontaneous. So much for well-made plans. "It's wonderful to see you," he said.

"I've missed you a lot," she said, stepping back and putting a hand on his cheek. "You look wonderful."

"So do you," he said, embracing her tightly. And she wanted to stay there, in his arms, a little longer.

After getting caught up during the drive from Rocky Mount to Lumby, Joshua casually said, "By the way, I think Mark and Pam found a place for you to rent."

"Oh, that's wonderful! I really didn't want to impose on them. They've already done so much for me." Brooke noticed the smile on his face. "Have you seen it?" she asked.

To which Joshua chuckled, thinking of the ten- and twelve-hour days he had spent working on the cottage since showing it to Mark and Pam the previous week. "Yeah," he said.

"Well, is it nice?"

"Old," he said, shaking his head, adding a slight frown.

"Oh," she said, some of the excitement draining from her voice.

As Joshua turned onto Deer Trail Lane, Brooke asked if this was where her house was.

"Yeah, somewhere around here, I think."

A few miles down, Joshua slowed and turned into the driveway. Brooke immediately noticed the large rural delivery mailbox—18 Deer Trail Lane on the front of the box, and "B. Shelling" on the side. She smiled, knowing that it was Pam's idea.

They drove down the long, winding driveway, and Brooke suddenly saw, through a break in the brush and trees, the cottage and her two friends sitting on the front stoop.

She opened the car door before Joshua came to a complete stop. "I love it," she screamed, and ran over to hug her friends. "Who owns it?"

"You do," Pam said to a very perplexed Brooke. "Well, we do, but we're giving it to you. Well, actually there's really nothing to give, since this house, as far as the county is concerned, doesn't exist. So here are keys to the best nothing you can ever have," Pam said, and embraced her best friend again.

Brooke walked into the cottage, and immediately knew she was home.

ᗏᗋ

EIGHTEEN

Donativum

It took Brooke only minutes to unpack. It took more time to freshen up after a full day of travel, although she did so as quickly as possible, knowing that Joshua was waiting in the living room. As she walked about the cottage, she deeply appreciated the time, effort and expense her friends had taken to make her feel at home. The living room furniture, consisting of a sofa and two chairs, was overstuffed and tremendously comfortable, and the bedroom was equally inviting with a quilt-covered queen-size bed, an antique bureau and a matching vanity. The dining table was large enough to seat four comfortably, and Pam had stocked the cabinets, drawers and refrigerator with utensils and food. Mark and Joshua had carried a rolltop desk up into the loft and placed next to that several chairs bought in Wheatley. Brooke cherished every inch of it like no other house in which she had ever lived.

Joshua fidgeted in one of the overstuffed chairs, not knowing quite what to do. They were both feeling a little awkward. Looking down at the coffee table, Joshua saw a fine way to break the silence: he began reading *The Lumby Lines* articles out loud to get them

caught up with local town news. As he read, he heard Brooke laugh
from whichever room she was in at the time.

The Lumby Lines

No Chickens Here

BY SCOTT STEVENS   **JULY 18**

The town of Lumby is still feeling the aftereffects
of the poultry truck incident at the corner of
Fairgrounds and Hunts Mill Roads last Thursday
when one hundred chickens were given their
freedom from broken crates that slid off a flatbed
trailer. Although approximately eighty chickens
were immediately captured, twenty escapees are
still on the loose.

In an effort to curtail those to-be-fryers, the
Lumby Police set numerous traps throughout the
Fairgrounds.

However, the police have reported that after
three days, all they found in the traps were several
chicken rotisseries from Dickenson's, two rubber
chickens, three furry stuffed chickens, one "very
nice ceramic rooster" and one live Canada goose.
All items are being held as evidence except for the
rotisserie chicken, which the police department had
for lunch.

"Clearly, the people of Lumby like these chickens
and aren't afraid to stand behind them," Sheriff
Simon Dixon said. He did not elaborate on how the
police would respond.

The state's poultry farms range from one acre to 55 acres, and produce almost one million eggs per year, twenty million broilers, thirty thousand fowl, and a lot of acidic compost.

Before leaving for dinner, Brooke turned on several lamps and took a heavily wrapped package from her suitcase.

"Do you want me to carry that?" Joshua offered.

"If you don't mind. They're awfully heavy."

"Can I ask what it is?"

"Ah," she said in a hesitant tone. "A secret for this evening."

Joshua wanted to walk her over to the inn, to give her the opportunity to become acquainted with the back path to and from her cottage. Although it had been cleared over the last few days, it was still rough enough that one could easily lose one's footing, or one's way, in the dark.

Because of the narrowness of the clearing, Joshua walked ahead of Brooke. She noticed the saplings that had been cut and piled with other trimmed brush, and the tree limbs that had been removed to make the path passable.

"I'm assuming you had a hand in making all of this possible?" Brooke asked.

"Only a small hand," Joshua smiled.

"Somehow I doubt that. But, thank you," she said, putting her hand on his shoulder, directly in front of her. She only kept her hand there for a few seconds before, feeling the contact had lasted too long, she removed it.

As they came to the cemetery, Brooke stopped and peered through the dusky clearing. "The grass has grown so much since I've been gone."

"It was you who cleaned it up?" Joshua asked.

"A small hand," she teased him. "I really didn't have enough time to do it justice though; it had been neglected for so many years. But I'll work on it over the next few weeks."

Brooke looked back at the path they had just traveled. "I'm surprised that I didn't notice that before. Was it here all along?" she asked.

"Yes, but the path hadn't been used for at least ten years, so it was so heavily overgrown you would have never known it was there," Joshua explained.

Brooke scrutinized the woods again, trying to see her cottage. She finally decided it was no longer visible.

They continued toward the inn.

"Are you happy to be back?"

"Very," she said. She wanted to tell him more, to tell him she missed him, to tell him that he was one of the reasons she had to return to Lumby. But she was too tired, and too cautious. He had a whole life out here that she really knew nothing about.

"And you?" she asked.

He put his head down and kept on walking. "Yes, it's wonderful that you're here. But, in truth, it's hard."

"How so?"

He stopped and looked into her eyes. "I'm already preparing for you to leave again."

"I'm sorry," she said. Of course he wouldn't commit if she was going to leave him behind again.

Looking ahead at the inn, he added in a lighter tone, "Perhaps we can go to the lake on Saturday?"

"That would be nice," Brooke smiled.

∞

Pam prepared a feast that night to celebrate the reunion of good friends. Brother Matthew conversed with Pam while Brooke, Joshua and Mark walked from building to building explaining, inspecting and evaluating.

Upon returning to the lodge, Brooke said to Pam, "I'm amazed at how much progress you've made while I've been gone. This is just remarkable."

"The orchard is in better condition than it has been in twenty years," Brother Matthew concurred. "You really have done Montis Abbey honor."

Mark and Pam felt very proud hearing those words from Matthew. Although they never sought his approval, they always knew that if they were on the right track, he would be in agreement.

"Brother Matthew, did Mark and Pam tell you about the journals I received in Virginia?" Brooke asked.

"Yes, but I'm afraid I have very little insight to offer. Did you bring them with you?"

"I did," she answered, taking the package from the side table and carefully unwrapping it. Before laying the journals down, Brooke turned to the back page of the larger journal and gently pulled out the cashier's check.

"I assume this is for you guys," she said, handing the check to Mark.

He took the check gingerly and turned it over several times, looking at it from every angle. "I have no idea what to make of this," he said, passing it to his wife.

"I really don't feel comfortable doing anything with it until we know what or who is behind it," Pam said, with her guard up.

"Perhaps it's a simple gift that should be received with an open heart," Matthew said.

Pam gave the kind monk sitting at her dining table a penetrating look. "Did you send this to us, Brother Matthew?"

Matthew laughed. "Oh, no. I would if it was available, but unfortunately, we have no money to offer."

Brooke looked at Joshua. "Did *you?*"

He laughed harder than Matthew. "Ah, right," he answered facetiously.

"Well, that takes care of everyone we know of who cares as much for Montis Inn as we do. Why don't we just sit on it for a while?" Mark suggested.

"Agreed," Pam said.

Brooke laid the journals on the table. When Matthew saw them, he ran his hands over the first, feeling the etched words "Montis Abbey" on the leather.

"Ah, yes," he said, closing his eyes, trying to remember so long ago. "I vaguely remember seeing books such as these, but I think there were many over the years, not just two."

"I think you're right," Brooke concurred, "because one journal appears to be a diary, but it only covers 1937 through 1947, and then again from 1957 through 1962. So, I would assume other journals covered the time before, in between, and after."

Brother Matthew picked up the smaller of the two journals and carefully began to skim through the pages, frequently bringing the book very close to his face, studying it intensely. After several minutes he said, "I think this first section, up until 1947, was written by Brother Simon."

"Why do you think that, Matthew?" Joshua asked, his curiosity piqued.

"Because all the other brothers seem to be referenced in one way or another, either about chores, or illnesses, or travels away from the monastery. So, I'm assuming the author, the 'I,' is the only one not mentioned by name: Simon."

"And do you think that's true for the second section?" Joshua asked.

"No, Simon passed away in the late forties, certainly no later than 1950. And that may be why the writing stopped, perhaps he was too ill to continue. But this second section," Matthew said with a smile, "was definitely written by Brother Benjamin. Do you see the spirals he makes as dots on top of the i's? He always did that, even in his calligraphy, although it was technically wrong." Brother Matthew laughed softly as he remembered back. "We always used to tease him for that, or perhaps chide him more for his desire to have a style of his own."

"Is that bad, to want recognition?" Brooke asked, standing over his shoulder.

"It is not why one becomes a monk, Brooke," Matthew answered, looking up at her with a smile.

She patted his shoulder. He was such an honorable man. "Brother Matthew, maybe you can help me understand something. I noticed that beginning in 1937, there were repeated entries made each month through August of 1966." She paused, opening the journal to reference one of the pages. "It says 'Donativum Talio Incendium—IC' followed by an amount, which seemed to be very substantial for that period. Do you know what that means?"

"Well, 'Donativum' is 'donation' or 'offering,' 'Talio' means 'retribution,' and 'Incendium' is 'fire,'" Brother Matthew explained. "And 'IC' is an abbreviation we used frequently; it stands for 'Incomperus Collator,' which loosely translates to 'unknown giver.'"

"An anonymous donor?" Pam asked.

"Yes, exactly," Matthew said.

"So," Brooke continued, "these ledger entries were for anonymous donations received as restitution for a fire?"

"That's what it would appear to be, but I don't remember any of the brothers ever discussing that," Matthew responded.

"Was there a fire at Montis, other than the one last year?" Mark asked.

"There were two that I'm aware of," Matthew explained. "One in the mid-thirties, when most of the orchard was destroyed, and the other in the late sixties, when the annex roof was struck by lightning. We lost most of that building."

"Ah, that's why the annex has a different architectural style from the rest of the sleeping quarters?" Brooke asked, thinking about all of the windows and fine trim in the annex.

"Exactly," Matthew answered.

"So, the fire the journal entries refer to was the orchard fire?" Pam asked.

Matthew nodded his head in agreement. "I think that's what I would assume as well."

"I also noticed that the smaller journal, the diary, was written in English, but the larger was written in both Latin and English. Do you know why that would be?" Brooke asked.

"For centuries Latin was used, so probably some of the older brothers kept with tradition while many of the novices, not knowing Latin when they entered into the monastery, recorded in English."

"Brother Matthew," Pam said, "would you mind terribly if we kept the journals for another week?"

"Mind? I'm a little confused," Brother Matthew said.

"Well, these journals belong to the monks of Montis Abbey. But, if you have no objections, Mark and I would really like a chance to look through them and see if there's any information that may help in our restoration efforts. They also may offer some information that could support our landmark status application."

"That's very kind of you to offer them, but I feel differently," Brother Matthew said. "I believe that these journals belong to Montis; they are part of its history."

"We appreciate that," Mark said to Matthew. "But before making any decisions, perhaps you would like to discuss it with the other brothers."

He didn't take long to consider the idea. "I believe they would feel as I do, but thank you for the offer."

It was getting late, and Brooke was the first to tire because of the long travel day and jet lag. After saying good night, Brooke left with Joshua, who insisted on escorting her home. Walking through the woods, he offered her his hand. When they got close to the cottage, she saw the lights burning through the windows. They were stained glass, which she hadn't noticed before. The colors in the glass, though, were all light tones and hues so as not to reduce the sun coming in during the day.

"Would you like to come in for coffee?" Brooke asked as they approached the front of the cottage.

"It's awfully late. I really should be going."

There was then an awkward pause that lasted longer than either ever thought possible.

"Thanks again for picking me up at the airport," she said to break the silence.

"It's good to see you again," he said, taking her hand. At that point Joshua finally leaned over and gave Brooke a nervous, dry kiss on the lips to which Brooke didn't fully respond given the abruptness of it all. Joshua quickly turned away and walked over to his car.

Before getting in, he turned back to Brooke. "I've only had two relationships since leaving the abbey, and both imploded without any warning, so I suppose I'm not very insightful about things like this." He paused, trying to find the right words. "So, after you set your own course and decide where you're going, if you could share that with me, it would help."

Brooke wanted to tell him that he was a significant part of her course, but couldn't. "I will," was all she could say.

After his car's lights disappeared down the drive, Brooke had the first real opportunity to look at the cottage. She hadn't noticed all the details when they first came in: the hand-hewn beams in the ceilings, another small stained glass window in the bathroom, and a door off her bedroom that led to a stone patio in the back. She discovered, too, that Mark had installed a small satellite TV for her to watch the morning news, which they knew she enjoyed. She opened the woodstove, and even though it hadn't been used in years, it still smelled of winter. Her sleep that night, under the quilts, in her stone cottage, was one of the most restful in her adult life.

NINETEEN

Captain

The following morning Hank all but screamed out his intentions for the Fork River Festival raft race. Due to the reserved personality that gave him such wide appeal, he kept his comments to himself. Since this was one of those rare life experiences that one actually had to see to believe, the good townspeople of Lumby, who were commuting down to Wheatley on Farm to Market Road, honked in appreciation when they saw Hank. Again, being modest, Hank opted not to give a gesture in reply.

That morning Pam and Mark awoke to car horns: a quick beep every few minutes, interspersed with an occasional longer blast. Thinking that it was both too early and too loud to be the construction workers, Mark dressed and went out to investigate.

Hank was, as always, waiting patiently in front of Montis Inn. But now he was standing front and center on a raft, commanding a five-foot-long by equally wide float whose deck was well over two feet off the ground. The raft's hull was made of two bright yellow pontoons with plastic drums duct-taped in between. Stretched across the top, and loosely secured to the outside hulls of each pontoon, was chicken wire forming a ship's deck. Centered on the deck was a pale yellow cracked toilet bowl serving as the captain's chair.

Too early in the morning, and too far from reality, Mark stood in amazement before walking up to the raft for a closer look. Stapled to the front of what appeared to be a running board was the noble craft's nameplate: "Stars and Stripes Too." Mark assumed that either Hank's float had become the next-generation ship to the famous America's Cup winner, or Hank was just feeling very patriotic at the time of the christening. Below the nameplate, and flapping in the breeze, was Hank's raft race application.

FORK RIVER RAFT RACE

ENTRANT: *Stars and Stripes Too*

LENGTH: *Limit waived for no specific reason*

HEIGHT: *Probably within regulations*

WEIGHT: *No one will get a hernia lifting it into the water*

HULL CONSTRUCTION: *Mostly borrowed with permission*

DECK CONSTRUCTION: *Metal chicken wire, borrowed without permission*

PROPULSION: *Paddle wheel and flamingo power*

Paddle wheel? Mark was stumped. Getting on all fours in front of the raft and looking underneath, he saw a strange contraption between the pontoons that looked like the upper part of a gigantic egg-beater, with three plastic paddle blades attached.

Then, trying to determine exactly where it came up through the deck, Mark crawled over to the side of the raft, and finally realized that the main shaft rod came up through the toilet. Standing up and stretching enough to look down into the toilet, he did indeed see two bicycle pedals, which made absolute sense as both of Hank's skinny legs could easily fit into the Kohler toilet. Overall, Mark was mighty impressed with the engineering that went into the raft race entry.

Hank was watching Mark with a wary eye, not wanting his design to be copied. Hank stood on the deck, in front of the captain's seat toilet bowl, wearing his yachting clothes: topsiders, khaki pants and a dark blue polo shirt, which was mostly covered by a fluorescent orange life vest certified for 250 pounds—good enough for Hank, who was the most proficient swimmer among his friends. Around his neck were a name tag, a pair of miniature binoculars, and a whistle to be used if things went awry on the river.

Mark went back to finish reading the application, now interested to see what classes Hank had entered. The stamped application form read: "Entry fees paid for: One-man raft race, American Heritage Class (Dry-land), $5.00; Committee's Choice (Dry-land), $5.00"; and handwritten on the next line, "Fowl Class (Wet or Dry), Priceless." He must have used a Mastercard, Mark assumed.

A line of cars, previously held up by a slow-moving tractor in front of them, passed in procession, all honking at Hank. Mark just smiled and waved back, as any slightly embarrassed parent would. Yet it gave him an idea. He would have to talk with Joshua to see what he thought.

∽

After breakfast, Mark asked Brother Matthew if he would like to walk through the orchard prior to his drive back to Saint Cross Abbey. Mark had several questions about the harvests, the first of which was scheduled for the following week, assuming favorable weather. So, with Cutter and Clipper underfoot, the two friends walked across Farm to Market Road, with Matthew making note of Hank's new status. Stopping at the shed, the men discussed the new irrigation control unit within, which had been recently installed. Walking up the hill, they talked at great length about the timing and frequency of harvesting, as well as the selling of the crops.

Picking up an apple and taking a small bite, Matthew smiled. "I miss this. There's really no better taste in the world," he said, with which Mark concurred. Matthew advised that Pam and Mark gather their own fruit prior to the laborers coming in.

"I don't understand," Mark asked. "There's plenty of fruit."

"Oh, but they're not all the same," Matthew explained.

"Agreed. There are peaches and apples and pears."

"Oh, my!" Matthew laughed. "But," he continued more seriously, "there are not only different varieties for each fruit, but there are very different tastes within each variety. Here, let me show you." Matthew slowly looked around and went to one tree, and pulled an apple off. "A Jonathan," he said, holding the apple up in the palm of his hand. "A wonderful sample: deep red, meaty, slightly tart and very versatile." He then walked some distance away, crossing over eight rows, smelling the leaves, looking at the soil, and picked another that looked, to Mark, identical to the first.

Walking back, Matthew held the second up, saying, "Another Jonathan, the same fruit," to which Mark nodded his head.

"Oh, but they're not at all the same. Here, taste," and he gave Mark the first apple. "Really concentrate on the taste—the sugar, the tartness, the texture. Now taste this," and gave Mark the second apple.

To Mark's surprise, the second apple was as different as if it was another variety altogether. It was sweeter, less tart, but also less crisp.

"That's amazing. Is one just riper than the other?" Mark asked.

"No, they're just about the same ripeness. But the trees are very different; they have different soil, different drainage, different exposure and sun," Matthew explained. "Even the breezes off the lake through the orchard will affect the fruits of individual trees. So you and Pam will come to choose certain trees over the seasons, those trees that produce the finest of each variety. It's one of the wonderful rewards of living here."

"Were the abbey's personal trees marked?"

"Yes, but those marks are probably long gone," Matthew answered, looking around to see if he could identify one.

"On a few trees I've seen a faded X just below the first branch. Would that be it?" Mark asked.

"Yes, exactly. But some orchard owners use tape or flags, which are equally as effective. Again, you need to find your own favorites among the trees," Matthew advised.

They continued to walk through the orchard, passing the pears and nectarines. They discussed at length the saplings Mark had planted, when best to transplant them in the main orchard, and how to protect them from the deer.

After crossing through the Darwin plum grove, Mark, Matthew and the puppies, who were wrestling a limb much larger and heavier than the two combined, walked through the small clearing into the beeyard or, as Mark referred to it, the bee field. With some embarrassment, he admitted that he had not spent any time on the bees, and feared that damage had been done due to his neglect.

"Don't be so hard on yourself, Mark," Matthew said. "You and Pam have done a tremendous job restoring Montis. Perhaps I can make a suggestion: you may want to consider hiring a beekeeper for the first few seasons, more for you than for the bees. There's a tremendous amount to be learned. And his costs would be covered by the sale of the honey."

"That's a great idea. Can you recommend someone?" Mark asked.

"There was a very good man, Chuck Bryson, who used to live up in the mountains west of the lake. He was incredibly knowledgeable, and helped us for twenty or more years, basically taught us all we knew about bees. I haven't talked with him for a long time, but it may be worth seeing if he's available to lend a hand."

Walking around the back side of the beeyard, Matthew added that Chuck was the only person apart from the brothers and the doctor who was aware of the marijuana growing in the adjacent field.

"Speaking of which," Mark said, "there appears to be someone who's harvesting our hemp crop on a regular basis. Did you ever have that problem?"

Matthew shook his head. "No, to the best of our knowledge, no one knew about it when we were here. Maybe some boys have stumbled upon it while hunting?"

"I don't know. There's never any sign of trespassing, and whoever is taking it is just ripping out the stems versus cutting them with a blade."

"It's a mystery," Matthew agreed.

Walking back down through the orchard, Matthew grew noticeably quieter.

"I am unsure when I'll be returning, Mark," he said at last.

"Is something wrong, Matthew?" Mark asked.

"Yes, perhaps."

"What is it?" Mark asked out of concern.

"Two weeks ago, the monks at Saint Cross agreed to close the monastery. We can no longer sustain ourselves. The Church has significantly decreased its subsidy, and other contributions have slowed with the economy. The little income we have from the small community isn't enough to keep the abbey going." Matthew paused. "Unfortunately, the buildings are in disrepair, and two of the brothers are ill and are in need of medical assistance. We think that the best option is to sell the monastery and join another, larger abbey on the West Coast."

"I'm so sorry to hear that," Mark said, genuinely upset. "Are there no other options?"

"None that we can see. Donations seem only to be short-term solutions, just postponing the inevitable. We don't have a real income-producing business, since the demand for our writing has been replaced with computer graphics and newer technologies."

Mark decided not to probe any further, seeing that Matthew was shaken by the situation. Neither Mark nor Matthew knew how to continue the discussion, so they walked back to the lodge in silence.

When the men returned, Pam was setting out lunch on the picnic table while Brooke was entertaining herself by reading the paper.

The Lumby Lines

Sheriff's Complaints

SHERIFF SIMON DIXON   **JULY 28**

3:18a.m. Deer vs. car. Saturn totaled, as was deer.

5:41a.m. EMS responded to call to resuscitate Jersey cow that had electrocuted itself on downed wire in field. Cow lived.

7:04a.m. Two unidentified Lumby residents arrested for chaining themselves to elm tree at corner of Grant and Main. Protestors remained naked until police arrived. No bond listed.

7:05a.m. John Morris reported three medium-size dogs trying to down a moose calf. He shot at them and they ran off. Calf appears ok.

8:19a.m. Reverend Olson reported one bullet hole in bathroom window at Holy Episcopal.

9:39a.m. Suzette at S&T's reported someone stole a flower bulb. It could have been a large squirrel.

11:11a.m. A caller on Cherry Street reported that a large tropical-looking parrot just landed on her roof and is pecking at her satellite dish, if someone says it's missing.

11:13a.m. Same caller reported that bird is now across the street at the Herbert house.

1:18p.m. Mcnear reported that two of his cows had been taken out of the barn and were missing.

3:27p.m. Woman reported that a car in front of Dickenson's has too many bumper stickers on it.

5:09p.m. Sally Mae called to report that Toby was missing. He went out last night and hasn't been seen again. The town mayor is missing in action.

7:57p.m. EMS responded to caller who had shoved his personal part through a fence hole and was bitten by a dog on the other side.

"Did you read the article about the potbelly pig being named executor and benefactor for some fellow's will who passed away in his sleep the other night?" Mark asked, walking up to Brooke.

"No, but somehow that just doesn't surprise me," she said. "But there are lots of ads and a few comments on the raft festival coming up. I didn't see any mention of the party to be thrown at Montis after the festival. Did you ever find out who submitted that invitation?" Brooke asked.

"No," Pam said. "I'll go to the Chatham Press and ask about it next time I'm in town. But in truth, I suppose the idea has sort of grown on us," she said, looking at Mark. "And now we're actually looking forward to it. This may be a good opportunity to open the doors and have the town over to see the restoration."

"It will also be a good chance to share in some of the harvest. We're planning on having the children go up in the orchard to pick their own apples," Mark added.

"A wonderful gesture," Matthew confirmed.

After lunch, Mark, Pam and Brooke said goodbye to Matthew. Only Mark knew that it might be a long time before all of them would be together again.

ගඟ

TWENTY

Supers

Chuck Bryson was an easy man to find, and an easier man to like. As Brother Matthew had hoped, he still lived in the foothills of the mountains outside Wheatley. He came over the day after Mark called him, apologizing that he couldn't come sooner, but he needed to "tend to some wandering goats." Parking in front of Montis Inn, Chuck got out and introduced himself in his plain way of speaking. He was a very tall, lean man in his late sixties, with thick gray hair to his shoulders and an easy, timeworn smile.

"Ah, yes. I remember now. Langstroth hives, very good. And how many supers did you say there were?" Chuck asked, reaching back into his car.

Mark cocked his head and looked at him in bewilderment, not knowing what to say without looking like the complete idiot that he was on the subject of bees. "I'm sorry?"

"Well, fine enough. Let's go have a look, then. Could you lend a hand, please," he said as he began taking equipment out of his car and emptying it into Mark's outstretched arms.

"Very good. We're off, then," he said, walking across the road. As Mark followed, so did Clipper and Cutter.

"Ah, wonderful puppies," Chuck said, leaning over and rubbing their backs. "But not on this excursion. Best they stay behind."

So Mark, arms still full of equipment, ran them back to the lodge, and then rejoined Chuck, who was already marching through the orchard. Mark was out of breath when he finally caught up, but Chuck's pace left him no chance to rest.

"So, Chuck, have you lived here long?" Mark asked as they made their brisk way through the trees.

"Born and raised," Chuck responded with a smile.

"And have you always been a beekeeper?"

"No, taught at U.C. Berkeley for about twenty years."

"Entomology?"

"Quantum physics, but the bees came in very handy for demonstrations," he laughed.

Quantum physics? Mark thought. When they reached the top of the knoll, Chuck stopped and surveyed the site.

"It's been many years," he said. "How are my old friends from the abbey?"

"All are well, and Brother Matthew sends his regards."

"Oh, very good," he said.

Although Chuck wasn't running, his long strides made it impossible for Mark to walk comfortably beside him, so he decided to follow at a slow jog.

"I assume this is your first, then?" Chuck asked.

"My first beehive?" Mark asked. "Yes."

"Well, you actually have several beehives making up one apiary, or beeyard."

"Ah," Mark said, remembering those same words from Brother Matthew.

Once Chuck entered the bee field, as Mark called it, he slowed his pace noticeably. With Mark close behind, Chuck advanced to the center of the meadow and placed his equipment down, indicating to Mark to do the same. He then picked up one of two helmets and placed it on Mark's head.

"The right clothes are very important," Chuck explained. "The veil will protect your head and neck. And bee gloves," he continued as he handed Mark a pair, "are just that."

With the two men clothed, Chuck picked up the remaining articles lying on the grass. "A hive tool, used to separate the different parts of the hive and to remove the frames," Chuck explained, holding up what looked like a short, flat crowbar.

"And a smoker," he continued. "Very important, indeed. Consists of a firepot and bellows so smoke can be puffed into the colony."

"Does that sedate them?" Mark asked.

"It calms them," Chuck answered. "Let's take a look," he said, and walked over to the beehive on his far left. "There are several layers," Chuck said, pointing to each section as he explained. "On the top are the covers—two of them." He lowered his hand, pointing to a larger section. "One or more supers, spelled s-u-p-e-r, which gives the worker bees storage space for the honey they collect. They are often half the depth of the hive body. Then below that, the hive body, which can vary from five to ten inches deep depending on its use. Then finally the bottom board and the hive stand."

Chuck was so thorough in his discussion that Mark had no need to ask questions.

After smoking the hive and waiting a few minutes, Chuck carefully lifted the outer and inner covers, and Mark watched as Chuck gently brushed away the lethargic bees and separated the large layers of the hive, inspecting the supers and the frames within the hive. "To hold the beeswax combs," he said, holding up one of the wooden frames. He worked smoothly and continuously, with very few bees flying around him. He closely inspected the hive and then, just as attentively, reassembled it.

"Aren't we going to take any honey?" Mark asked.

"Tomorrow will be a good day for that," Chuck answered.

"Okay." He hesitated before making a request. "About tomorrow, if you have no objections, I believe Joshua would like to join

us. He would have been here today, but he had other commitments at work."

"Would that be Brother Joshua?" Chuck asked.

"Well, yes, but no. Same person, but he left the order several
years ago."

"Oh, it will be a delight to see him again. How very good."

Once the hive top was put in place, Chuck reached down and
with a large magic marker wrote "#1." He then took out a notebook
from his white coveralls and began writing, pausing every few minutes, and writing again. Mark was at a loss as to what Chuck saw
that would constitute four pages of notes, but he felt very confident that he and his bees were now in excellent hands.

Chuck, with Mark watching intently, systematically examined
each of the remaining hives in the field, marking each and then
writing several pages of notes. As he worked, he casually repeated
what he was doing, so by the last hive Mark understood the funda-
mental components of a Langstroth hive.

"Wonderful," Chuck said as he backed away from the apiary,
removing his veil and gloves. "Let's return tomorrow. We'll need to
extrude and repair. Will be great fun." With that, he started to walk
down through the orchard, with Mark once again jogging behind.

"Looks like you'll have more apples than you'll know what to do
with," Chuck said with a smile as they walked through the rows of
trees. "What plans do you have for the fruit?"

"None as of yet," Mark admitted.

"Ah, well, best you line things up now. The time you harvest will
depend on who you sell to."

"I don't follow," Mark said.

"Some buyers will want the fruit early, before it's ripe. Others
may have you wait a week or two."

"Ah, I see," Mark said, concerned that he had not thought
through this part of the apple business.

"I hear you're making great progress on the abbey," Chuck
commented, seeing the compound in full view with half a dozen

tradesmen's vans parked outside.

"We are," Mark concurred. "If it hadn't been for the fire damage, we would be done by now."

"That was so unfortunate. Such young boys to do such a terrible thing," Chuck said, shaking his head.

"What?" Mark said with a start. "We thought it was an accident."

Chuck was unsure what to say, but certainly regretted the comment that he made. He wasn't one to gossip or discuss town rumors. "It's really not my place to say."

Mark looked at Chuck directly. "Do you know something about the fire?"

Chuck answered with a vague wave. "Only what I heard. It's so regrettable that it was never solved."

"I don't understand," Mark said. They were both standing at the bottom of the orchard.

Chuck regarded the construction at Montis and again shook his head. "It was rumored that two boys from Lumby set the fire," Chuck explained. "Maybe out of boredom, probably out of viciousness, or both. No one knows. No one had the chance to get to the truth."

"Why not?"

"Because one of the boys was Brian Beezer."

"Who is . . . ?" Mark pried further.

"Dennis Beezer's son. William Beezer's grandson."

This new information whirled around Mark just as the bees had. "But why weren't the police involved?"

"Simon Dixon was involved. He did all he could without losing his badge. But when Brian was finally questioned, his family offered a full account of his whereabouts that night—quite different from those who saw him in town a few hours prior to the fire."

"And so it was dropped?"

"At the owner's request, yes," Chuck said.

"Why would the owners of Montis not want to get to the bottom of it?"

"No one knew. They just assumed that William Beezer was somehow involved," Chuck said, still gazing at the old stone abbey. "So unfortunate. It was such a beautiful building."

"And it still is. Please come in and see how it's taking shape," Mark offered.

TWENTY-ONE
Outrigging

"You've been staring at those plans for an hour," Gabrielle said as she walked into the living room.

Dennis, who was seated at the large table with a full-size blueprint of a raft design spread out before him, grunted. "It's not a simple structure."

"It's a raft," she said dryly.

"Yes, but a complex one," he said, shaking his index finger upward.

Gabrielle rolled her eyes. "So when are you actually going to start building this schooner?"

"This morning," he answered triumphantly. "I've asked Brian to help out, as well as Terry McGuire. He and his mom should be coming over shortly."

"Aft, I see. Terry's involvement wouldn't have anything to do with Mackenzie being a great carpenter, would it?"

He bristled at this suggestion. "No, not at all. I'm fully capable of—"

"Cutting off your own finger," she inserted.

Dennis sat upright. "I don't understand why you always underestimate my woodworking skills," he protested.

"Because your projects always seem to involve a quick trip to the emergency room," she teased him.

"Twice," he corrected her.

"This year, yes. But three times last year." She went over and kissed him on the cheek. "But I still love you. Just please be careful."

"Not to worry," he said jovially. "The raft will build itself."

"Whatever you say, honey."

An hour later, with enough wood to build an outhouse spread across their front yard, a nail had not yet been hammered. Mackenzie and Dennis were still sitting on the front porch discussing the movement of the rudder, which would be hindered if the current design was used. They turned the prints upside down and then right side up, hoping a new perspective would shed light on a solution.

"I got it!" Mac finally said. "If we just separate those two-by-fours by eight inches, I think there would be enough span for the rudder."

Dennis studied the plans and thought about what Mac had suggested and then nodded. "Agreed." He got up and opened the front door. "Boys, we're ready for you," he yelled inside. "Time's a'wastin'."

He and Mackenzie began to lay out the wood for the decking, with Gabrielle pulling together the tools. Soon Dennis called out to the boys again.

"They probably have their headsets on," Mackenzie said after another few minutes passed.

"They probably are a little lazy," he countered, and then in a much louder voice yelled out, "Final warning, gentlemen."

Brian lethargically walked outside with Terry directly behind. "Do we really have to?" he whined.

"If you're in the race, you help build the raft—that was our deal," his father said. He started handing out directions, which they reluctantly began to follow.

When Mackenzie saw that the men were well under way, she

walked over and sat next to Gabrielle, who had pulled up several lawn chairs.

"So what do you think?" Gabrielle asked with significant apprehension.

"I think it actually might float," Mac answered. "It will be heavy, so it will ride low in the water, but I think it will be really stable."

"Oh, that's a relief."

"But, then again, I know absolutely nothing about boats. The thing might sink as soon as it hits the water," Mac shrugged.

"Well, that's not encouraging!"

"Don't worry," she said, patting Gabrielle's arm. "Terry's a poor swimmer, and I wouldn't let him participate if I thought it was dangerous."

"Will you be in the race?"

"No, Terry has a major issue with his mother being there—very uncool, he said. So I promised that I would stay on shore."

"Too bad. I was hoping you would be my husband's voice of reason out on the water." Mac laughed. "He takes this so seriously, and this year I think Joshua is egging him on all the more."

"Friendly competition of testosterone levels, I call it."

"Watch it, Dad!" Brian yelled out. "You just drilled through my boot!"

"Any blood?" Dennis asked without stopping.

"I don't think so," Brian said, but then added more forcefully, "but there could've been."

"Good, let's continue."

"Mr. Beezer, can I make a suggestion?"

"Sure, Terry, what is it?"

The teenager put one hand on Dennis's wrist and the other on the drill. "If you angle your drill this way"—and he moved both wrist and drill at the same time—"you'll almost always get a perfect forty-five-degree entry."

Dennis tried it, and then took another screw and tried it again.

"Well, that's very good, Terry," he said excitedly. "I never knew that. Thanks a lot." For the first time that day Terry smiled.

Watching the men's major struggles and minor triumphs, Gabrielle and Mac passed time with idle conversation. "So, are you going to the Montis Inn party after the race?" Gabrielle asked.

"Probably not. I think that would just worsen everyone's perception."

Gabrielle looked at her quizzically. "I don't follow."

"The folks who oppose the Walkers think that I'm on their side."

"I didn't know there were *sides.*"

"I didn't either until I said that the Walkers weren't as heinous as some people had suggested. I think since then I've been labeled a 'yuppie lover.' Isn't that just ludicrous?" She was frustrated and paused to calm herself. "So, I'm just keeping my distance."

Brian yelled out again. "God, Dad! What are you doing? You just sawed through the tiller!"

Mackenzie jumped up. "I'll be back," she called over her shoulder and raced over to the makeshift boatyard.

Mac picked up the plans and handed them to her son. "Terry, take the prints and you and Brian go build the stanchion and outrigger over there."

Dennis looked at her in surprise. "Can he really do that?" he asked softly as the boys walked away.

"Better than either of us, I guarantee it," Mac said confidently. "He thinks it would be a crime if people actually knew he was good at something. And I'm sure he enjoys working with his hands." She paused, looking at her son. "But he astonishes me sometimes. He can construct anything out of anything . . . very much like his father."

The memories of those years flashed in her eyes, and Dennis asked cautiously, "Do you ever hear from him?"

"No, that ship's long set sail," she said bitterly. "We got a call about three years ago when Rick was unemployed and down on his luck in California."

"I'm sorry."

"Me too. Actually, I'm sorry for Terry—no son deserves that from his father." She desperately wanted to change the subject. "Here, help me lift this, and let's get this deck finished."

At one-thirty, Gabrielle brought out lunch for the workers. Brian and Terry filled their plates and quickly went inside.

"God forbid they spend any time with us," Gabrielle said, hearing the front door slam.

"Honey, don't take it personally. They're boys."

"They're legal adults," Gabrielle corrected him.

Mackenzie chimed in. "You know, what concerns me more than being shunned is Terry's blatant avoidance of any responsibility. That and his bad attitude toward almost everything."

"I can't agree more," Gabrielle said, serving up the plates.

"Ahoy!" a voice called out.

Everyone turned and saw Joshua walking up the driveway, waving.

"Come to illegally photograph the competition, or are you just here to steal our plans?" Dennis said in a sinister tone.

"Dennis, how could you say that to a man of God?" Joshua innocently asked.

"Excuse me?" Dennis laughed. "Wasn't that eons ago? And if you still have a rapport with your maker, you should start praying now because there is no chance you'll win this year."

Joshua looked over at the front yard. The deck was finished and resting on two large pontoons. Likewise, the boys had completed the outrigging and had attached it to the hull. "It actually looks Viking," Joshua said. "Too bad you'll lose all that wood when it sinks."

Gabrielle looked apprehensively at Mackenzie, who just shook her head.

ʚᏻ

TWENTY-TWO

Possibilities

Brooke had tended her garden daily since returning, and with the added benefit of local advice and compost both supplied by Charlotte Ross, the garden was growing in great abundance. With so many vegetables at hand, she invited Joshua, Pam and Mark to her first dinner. She prepared chilled tomato soup, salad, corn, and several plates of different mixed vegetables all from her garden, while Joshua barbecued chicken on a grill he had brought over from his house.

"To good friends," Pam toasted, noticing that Brooke was more dressed up than usual.

"To this cottage," Brooke added.

Over dinner, while the others ate, Mark recounted in detail the conversation he had had with Brother Matthew about the financial crisis at Saint Cross Abbey.

"So, have they already finalized the sale of the abbey?" Joshua asked.

"No, I don't think so," Mark answered. "It seems the brothers just agreed among themselves a few weeks ago. It was obvious that Matthew was still struggling with the idea."

"I don't fully understand," Pam said. "If it's a simple issue of cash flow, why don't they do something about it?"

"I don't think they know how," Joshua said.

"There's really not a lot to know."

"That's all second nature to you, Pam," Mark said, "but the rest of us have to blunder our way through."

"These men have never had to start a new business; I don't think they would know where to begin," Joshua added.

"I agree with Joshua," Brooke said. "For those of us not strong in business, what you suggest is daunting."

"So why not help them?" Pam suggested.

"Matthew said donations would just prolong the inevitable," Mark reminded her.

"No, not give them money," Pam explained, wheels already turning in her mind. "We can be their business advisers."

"I don't quite follow," said Joshua, who was the least familiar with Pam's background in starting up new companies.

"We can identify business opportunities for them—ways in which they could make the income they need to be self-sustaining. And we can help them through the steps of starting a new enterprise."

"Such as?" Brooke asked.

"I have no idea," Pam said, getting up to fill everyone's wineglass. "Joshua, could you tell us about how monastic money is handled?"

Joshua gave a helpless expression. "I never was directly involved at Montis, but I can assure you that it was always difficult. We received a subsidy from the Church, but communities are expected to generate the funds they need to pay their way."

"Did Matthew mention what work they're now doing at the abbey?" Brooke asked Mark.

"I got the sense that the brothers who joined Saint Cross from Montis Abbey tried to continue with calligraphy, but he said their skills have been replaced by computer graphics."

"And the others?" Brooke asked.

"He didn't say."

Joshua then added, "Matthew told me that the monks of Saint Cross have, for the last sixty years, specialized in iconography."

"Iconography?" Mark asked.

"Icon painting, icon conservation and restoration, wall paintings, work like that," Joshua explained.

Pam thought for a minute. "So going from Montis to Saint Cross wasn't a huge leap. . . ."

"Of skill and expertise? No. Both monasteries dealt with the arts in some form."

"And is there a demand for iconography now?" Brooke asked.

"It probably had a similar fate as calligraphic writing," Joshua presumed.

Pam sat forward in her chair, listening intently. "What do some of the other monasteries do?"

Joshua gave it a moment's thought. "Many make food: cakes, breads, even specialty chocolates. Some produce gourmet coffee and teas and of course wine. Several sell religious and Gregorian chant recordings."

"Can the monks of Saint Cross sing?" Brooke asked.

"If the Montis brothers are a representative sample, I would say definitely not," Joshua chuckled, shaking his head.

Pam was struck by something else he had said. "The foods and coffees; are they sold only at the monasteries?"

"No. Actually, some are sold internationally. The Internet has changed everything. A small community that once sold only in the back of their chapel now can fill an order in Russia."

"Do any make clothes?" Pam asked, again trying to think through different options the brothers might have.

"Some convert the raw wools into yarns, but I really don't know about that," Joshua answered tentatively.

"How about writing a book?" Mark proposed.

"It's a great idea, but I think it would take too long," Brooke chimed in. "Taylor and I wrote an architectural book, and it was fourteen months from final draft to getting our first royalty payment. And that was after twelve months of writing it."

"Oh, yeah, I had forgotten you guys did that—that was a great book," Pam commented. "We need something that offers a turnaround time of four to six weeks."

"How about cheeses or some dairy product?" Mark suggested.

"That's an interesting possibility," Brooke said.

"There maybe a logistical issue," Joshua said, discouraged. "Saint Cross Abbey doesn't own a lot of land, so the brothers would either have to buy the milk or lease the land for their own herd."

"Leaving us a fallback plan of cakes and breads?" Mark asked.

Pam shook her head, her eyebrows narrowed in concentration. "I think that market is too saturated. Before leaving the firm a few months ago, my last client hired us to do some market research on baby boom buying patterns. My client was planning on opening a chain of gourmet specialty stores along the East Coast and wanted to know what was selling."

"And what did you find?" Brooke asked.

"Bar none, jarred products were showing tremendous growth, with profit margins two and three times better than other food products."

"Jarred products like dried figs and olive oil?" Joshua asked.

"Yes, but we specifically looked at syrups, jams and sauces."

"What about jams?" Mark asked. "Chuck Bryson just mentioned how extraordinary the Montis jams were decades ago."

Pam was doubtful about that possibility. "Well, we certainly have all the fruit they would need, but when we did our research in March, it showed an overproduction in that market; there were almost too many entrants for the demand of high-end preserves. I think it would be hard to grab enough market share from already well-positioned companies."

"How about syrups or sauces?" Mark continued.

"Boy, I love a homemade sauce," Brooke said, reminiscing. "When I was young, whenever I got sick, my mother used to make a rum sauce for me. It's one of the few nice memories I have of her before she left us," she said, frowning slightly. "Lying in bed, I would hear her chopping up the apples, and a few minutes later, our house would smell of melting butter that turned into a rich aroma of applesauce. Also, I could smell the rum as soon as she poured it in the pan."

They all stared at Brooke.

"What's wrong?" She looked around, startled by everyone's expressions. "What did I say?"

"A rum sauce?" Pam asked.

"Yeah, but I've never seen it in any shop. I guess it was something that was passed down from my grandmother."

"Do you know the recipe?" Pam inquired.

"Oh, no. That was almost forty years ago."

"Well," Pam started, "you may resent your mom for leaving you and your father, but she may have just given the brothers of Saint Cross something no one could have ever imagined: a viable business."

"Pam," Mark said excitedly, "do you remember seeing anything in your research about rum sauces?"

"No, but that's a good thing. We may be able to create a new product, and a new market."

"If there's nothing being sold like it, how do we know that it will sell?" Joshua asked.

"Fair question," Pam answered. "We'll do a comparative analysis: select a few products of similar usage and price, and use their numbers to forecast sales."

Pam, who had spent her professional life defining new companies and saving failing businesses from bankruptcy, became energized and, at midnight, when she and Mark returned to the lodge, Pam got on her computer and began constructing a business plan for the monks of Saint Cross.

∽∾∽

"Well hello, stranger," said a familiar voice over the phone after Pam had been on hold for a few minutes. "I heard you moved out

West, joined a monastery and became a nun."

Pam started laughing. "Oh, that's too funny. The rumors are only partially true—we did move out West, but my husband and I actually bought a monastery, not joined one."

"My God, why did you do that?" he asked.

"We're converting it into a historic inn. A little different from the work I was doing in Washington."

"That's an understatement. I hope you're not calling for some construction advice."

"No, but thanks for taking my unexpected call. Evan, I need your help," and for the next ten minutes, Pam told her old business associate about Saint Cross, the brothers and a potential new product.

"You own the best marketing company in D.C. Can you ask one or two of your folks to look at the business plan we wrote up for the brothers and let me know if we're on target?"

"If you email it to me today, I'll work on it myself, but it will take a day or two."

"That would be great."

"Why don't you call me at five tomorrow afternoon? I should have something for you then."

"I owe you one. Thanks very much, Evan."

Pam also called suppliers of rum and sugar, equipment manufacturers to discuss fruit presses and boilers, business associates to discuss sales methods, and past colleagues to test out some of her assumptions.

That night she was again up until three a.m. doing market research, product research, and by the time she called Evan back, she felt confident that they would agree the monks might just hit pay dirt with fruit-flavored rum sauces.

"We revised your numbers some. Look at what we just faxed you, on page two," Evan told Pam.

"You increased the second-year forecast?" Pam was stunned.

"We think that once your product gets traction, there's no limit to the number of sales channels you could have. There are no direct competitors out there, so we consider it a new product in an emerging market."

"That's great," Pam said.

"The only hole in your business plan is regarding FDA regulations."

"How so?"

"If the monks will be using this plan to obtain financing, you need to include a section on FDA labeling requirements: naming of food conventions, product identification, label positioning, nutrient claims, even type size."

"Easily done," Pam responded, making a note on page seven of her copy.

"Other than that," Evan took a deep breath, "we think you may have found a diamond, assuming you can keep operating expenses in check. And if Saint Cross ever decides to form a public corporation, let me know—I'd like to buy some of their shares."

Her next call was to Brother Matthew to schedule a time to meet with the monastic community and outline her strategy.

ΣΟℭ

The following day, Brooke and Joshua ventured into town to pick up a couple of Fork River Festival raft race applications at Lumby Sporting Goods. Although Brooke thought Joshua was taking the raft race more seriously than the event deserved, she appreciated the fact that he had a running feud with one of his friends and wanted to sustain his winning record.

The store, which Brooke had never been in before, was one of the last remaining old-time establishments of its kind, passed down from father to son and then again to son.

As Brooke walked in, she first noticed, and then immediately heard, the wide-planked pine floors, so worn and warped over the years that the creaking underfoot was almost deafening. Also, all of the countertops, cabinets and shelves were made of heavy oak and glowed richly from the countless layers of varnish that had been applied over the decades. Three counter-height cabinets kept guns under secure lock and key behind thick, irregular blown-glass panes. On top sat a hand-cranked cash register.

As Brooke and Joshua walked through the store looking for pamphlets on the raft race, Brooke noticed that the owner of Lumby Sporting Goods didn't let the name of the store limit the type of merchandise he sold. In addition to fishing, hunting and camping equipment, the store also stocked most items found in a small town hardware store: gardening equipment and seed, hardware, plumbing fixtures, and a very limited selection of tile—one design, one size, one color. The store also served as a small pharmacy and grocery shop—the true one-stop shopping opportunity right there in Lumby. And finally, most important to all, it rented videos.

Not finding the applications on the counter, they stood in line while two other customers were paying their bills and talking with the cashier about the best dry fly size to use for the rainbow trout in Long Lake Creek, which Joshua listened to with some interest. Brooke caught up on local news in *The Lumby Lines* lying on the counter.

The Lumby Lines

What's News Around Town

By Scott Stevens   **August 9**

A busy week in our sleepy town of Lumby.
    Last Tuesday, the Lumby Active Farmers Association, LAFA, accepted a UPS COD shipment from Anchorage for one Alaskan moose bought by the Association as the foundation milker

to start its moose cheese business. Although the animal was certified to be in outstanding health by Dr. Campbell, the moose was in fact an elk, and the elk was in fact a male, as guessed by two Association members after seeing three-foot antlers. A no-return policy leaves the elk with LAFA for the time being.

The honorable Mayor Toby has been confirmed as deceased due to injuries sustained from an animal fight. "He appears to have been attacked by a large mountain lion," Dr. Campbell said after examining the body. Services for Toby will be held at Sally Mae's house after the donkey basketball game next Thursday.

A mayoral revote to fill the empty position will be scheduled during the next week. Assuming that prior candidates are still interested, Jimmy Daniels, of Jimmy D's, and Hannah Jones, of Pine Street, will be on the ballot.

As the town readies itself for the Fork River Festival, numerous people have complained about missing boat parts and yard debris. The police would like to remind all participants that they are responsible for legally acquiring their own raft materials.

The Montis Inn has applied for reinstatement as a National Historic Landmark with the National Park Service, U.S. Department of the Interior. If accepted, the Montis Inn will be the only historic landmark in Lumby, and one of only 2,300 in the entire country.

Chickens are still on the loose at the Fairgrounds, and are steadily gaining popularity. Of the nine remaining escapees, seven have been named, and now have commemorative plaques hanging in a long row on the south-side chain-link fence.

And, on a sad note, Joy, The Lumby Lines horoscope and weather contributor extraordinaire for the last eighteen years, will be retiring next month. Bye, Joy!

"Hey Joshua." The man behind the counter smiled broadly. "Been a while, stranger. How's life treating you in Rocky Mount?"

"Good, thanks," he answered. Turning to Brooke, who was standing behind him, "Joel, this is Brooke Shelling. Brooke, Joel, who's the owner of this great store."

"Nice to meet you, ma'am," Joel said in a charming way, tilting his head slightly.

Brooke was enamored by his manners. "Well, thank you. And your store is just wonderful. I've never quite seen anything like it."

"Well, thank you, ma'am. We do our best. So what brings you two in from the heat?"

"We need a few applications," Joshua answered.

"For the raft race, of course," he said, digging through papers in one of the top drawers. "The Almanac predicts heavy rains the week before, so you best build her heavy but high this year. And rumor has it that Dennis has a craft that will take the bite out of any rattlesnake."

Joshua laughed. "Just rumor," was all he said.

With several brochures in hand, Brooke and Joshua walked down Main Street to their next stop, The Feed Store, which was to be followed by a visit to Brad's Hardware. Joshua explained that every few years, raft plans were sold "under the table," and if so, he might be interested in previewing one or two them.

"Stolen plans?" Brooke asked in amazement.

"Not stolen, exactly. Just borrowed from the captains of prior winning rafts."

"Well, Joshua," she said seductively, leaning over to whisper in his ear, "you can captain my raft anytime."

He then stopped and, putting his arm around her, gave her a long, warm kiss that was noticed by many in town, including Gabrielle Beezer, who happened to be cleaning the front windows of her restaurant, and William Beezer, who was staring out the window of his second-floor office at the Chatham Press.

ಞಞ

Sauced

Mark and Pam were preparing to leave for Saint Cross Abbey just as the fruit pickers arrived. During the following few days the orchard would host a dozen migrant workers who went from row to row, farm to farm, season to season, harvesting just about anything that was in or above the ground. With Matthew's concurrence, Mark had decided against using the heavy harvesters that could cover three rows at a time, opting instead for the traditional method of hand-picking using open-top picking ladders. Harvesting was well under way when Mark and Pam pulled out of their driveway with three bushel baskets of various fruit to take to the monks.

After an hour's drive to Saint Cross Abbey, after the tour Matthew gave, and after the introductions, Pam and Mark were cordially brought into a large dining room with a center table long enough to seat two dozen brothers. Everyone gathered around the table, eager to hear what the two had to say.

"From Brother Matthew," Pam began, "we understand that Saint Cross Abbey has all but lost its main source of income, and that the abbey will need to close unless there's a significant change in finances." The monks, all watching Pam intently, nodded their heads in agreement. "Well, last week Joshua helped us understand the basics of monastery economics, and I think we may have come up with a new business that could allow Saint Cross Abbey to be self-sustaining."

"Doing what?" the abbot asked. "Our skills are very specific."

"Well, let me explain," Pam answered. "As some of you know, Montis Inn has a good supply of fruits: apples, peaches, pears, cherries, nectarines and plums. Having recently bought the property, we don't have any contracts to sell our produce, so we're flexible as to where it goes and, for the first few years at least, what price it goes for. Mark and I think it should come here, initially as a donation, and then sold to you at a significant discount once Saint Cross Abbey is in the black."

"But what would we do with fruit?" Brother Michael asked.

"This is where product demand and creative marketing come into play. We think, based upon all of the research we pulled together, that Saint Cross Abbey should," she paused, swallowing, "make flavored sauces. Specifically, rum sauces."

With those words, one could hear a pin drop. Pam looked around the room and saw two dozen sincere but very confused faces, with some jaws wide open.

"I know it may sound a little far-fetched," Mark added, also noticing the expression on everyone's faces. "But this might actually work."

Pam continued, "Our idea is for you to receive the harvest from our orchard, as well as the honey from our hives, and you process it with simple ingredients and make a product line of old-fashioned, organic rum sauces under the brand name: Saint Cross Rum Sauce, using a sketch of the monastery on the label."

Pam tried to get them to envision the product. Waving her hands like a banner, she said, "Imagine, on the shelves of niche organic stores and upper-end specialty shops, these wonderful, blown-glass mason jars filled with thick rum sauce of different tastes and colors, all of them made with natural ingredients. And the jars would have the same parchment label, with an ink sketch of the monastery, and in old font written at the top 'Saint Cross Rum Sauce' and on the bottom 'Produced with care by the monks of Saint Cross Abbey'."

A positive murmur began to be heard among the monks.

"The company I used to work for ran some informal marketing surveys on this last week, and they think that it could be a huge success. The sales of monastic products are climbing, consumers are looking for more organic foods and are willing to pay premium prices for higher-quality items. There are no large companies that currently produce a line of rum sauces, although fruit sauces will be a little more competitive. And companies like Whole Foods and Williams-Sonoma would love the opportunity to put a unique product like this on their shelves. So the idea would be to start small and local, but to grow quickly for national distribution."

One of the brothers pointed out, "But we know nothing about processing fruits or making rum sauce."

Mark and Pam smiled at each other. "Well, that's one of the nice things about this plan: it's simple," she said. "The recipes are very easy, using only a few ingredients such as eggs, butter, sugar, and of course rum. And the equipment that you'll need to process the fruit won't break the bank."

"But, unfortunately," another brother commented, "there is no bank to break. We really don't have any cash to buy even the cheapest of equipment."

"That's the second part of our plan," Mark explained. "As Brother Matthew knows, we received an anonymous check several months ago. Not knowing who it was from, or why it was sent to us, we haven't cashed it. So, we have signed it over to Saint Cross Abbey for you to use as your start-up money."

"That's too much to offer," Brother Matthew protested.

"We don't think so," Pam responded warmly. "All of this seems very right to us."

"Saint Cross Rum Sauce. A very catchy name," one brother said.

"But isn't this exploiting our religious calling?" the abbot asked, frowning at the other monks.

"I don't think so," Brother Matthew said. "I think that most, if not all, of the Orders that produce food use their monastic names."

"Yes," another brother added. "I would go so far as to say that some may even use it to increase their sales."

It was clear to Mark and Pam that the brothers had a lot to discuss among themselves. After answering several other questions, and offering further details to their idea, they placed the business plan, which Pam had printed off her computer, and the cashier's check on the table.

"We hope you take us up on the offer," Mark said, shaking Matthew's hand.

The following morning, Matthew called the Walkers and told them that the committee had gratefully accepted their offer. Saint Cross Rum Sauce, which would later become the Saint Cross Sauce Company, was officially launched. That same day Mark and Pam sent over to the monastery a dozen baskets of each fruit for the brothers to start testing and improving upon different recipes, and developing the methods they would use to process the fruit.

:∞:

When the Pavarotti arias stopped at Montis Inn, Pam knew that another change of cast in the main building was nigh. Cantor and his men had completed the heating and air systems, ultimately laying more than a quarter mile of ductwork and installing three commercial-grade systems, each the size of a small car, in the basement of the main building directly below what would have been the altar and main crucifix.

Mark and Pam's only compromise in this area concerned a smaller sitting room in the far southwest corner of the second floor, which offered the most expansive views of Woodrow Lake and the surrounding mountains. Although they had originally planned to convert that into their master bedroom, retrofitting enough infrastructure to heat the room, given the room's exposure to the winds off the lake, would have required more time and expense than the adjacent rooms combined.

But Cantor was gracious enough to bring out a reputable chimney sweep, Graham, the longtime owner of Ashes to Ashes Inc., to ensure the small fireplace in that room was safe and usable, and confirm that it would at least offer enough heat on cold winter days for the room to be used as it was originally intended, as an afternoon reading room, when the sun flooded through the windows.

The other fireplaces were in varying degrees of disrepair, and they jointly developed a plan that would allow all fireplaces to pass inspection and be operational by winter. Unfortunately, Ashes to Ashes was just one more of those six- to ten-thousand-dollar unexpected expenses that were causing havoc with the budget and driving their costs to be double what was originally estimated for the restoration.

"It will be fine," Pam always reassured her husband on those few occasions he found courage enough to ask her about their finances. Mark was always unsure if it was fine, or if his wife was just protecting him and carrying an unspoken burden alone. He convinced himself that it was the prior. Pam always wondered if her husband actually cared about the details, or just wanted to be reassured that his dream would come to fruition. She assumed the latter.

Also arriving at Montis on Cantor's heels were the plumber and then the electrician, who were each scheduled to stay slightly over one week. As was the case with the chimneys, the plumber advised that a well man be brought in as soon as possible, that very afternoon if it could be arranged. Although there was adequate water going to the lodge and back buildings from a dedicated well behind the dining room, Earl was quite sure that the original well that serviced the main building, located between the chapel and the annex, was either totally dry or too shallow to support the needs of the inn. Earl also advised that a septic company be called in without delay.

Another unexpected twelve thousand dollars, followed by a soft voice saying, "It will be fine."

ɷ

That evening, Pam and Mark, accompanied by Brooke and Joshua, addressed the very serious business of the Fork River raft race. Hank, already well prepared, kept a close eye on the budding competition.

The four decided to have a strategy session over dinner with one or two bottles of wine, depending upon how easily the strategy developed itself.

"Okay," Brooke said, pulling out the guidelines and applications from her shirt pocket. "There will be three races," she began to read. "One-man, two-man, and as-many-as-you-can-get-on."

"Would you want to enter the two-man or the crowd?" Joshua asked.

"It's our first year," Mark said. "Joshua, you're the expert—you've done this before. So, if you don't object, I vote we go it together."

Joshua nodded. "I think that's a great idea."

"Agreed," Pam said, and Brooke nodded in agreement as well. "What else does it say?"

Brooke glanced at Joshua, but he was content to let her explain the requirements to her friends. "In the spirit of the race, and to encourage ingenuity and creativity, all rafts must be man-made to qualify. Commercially manufactured hulls are not allowed, and all rafts must be self-propelled via oars, paddle wheels, poles, body parts, or any combination thereof," she read.

"How about inner tubes?" Mark interrupted, looking at Joshua for guidance.

Brooke scanned the guidelines. "Yes, but only if they are used as a hull flotation device with a deck, and not as the raft itself. What's a PFD?"

"A personal flotation device. A life jacket," Joshua answered.

"Ah," Brooke said. "Well, they're required." She continued reading. "All rafts will be inspected prior to launching and may be disqualified for any number of reasons by the River Master. All decisions and/or rulings made by the River Master are final."

"Who's the River Master?" Pam asked.

"Probably Hank," Joshua joked.

"He can't be. . . . He's in the race," Mark said, before realizing how stupid that sounded. To cure his problems he poured himself another glass of wine.

"Are there any size limitations?" Mark asked, recovering himself.

"None that I see," Brooke answered. "Oh, wait. Sorry, here it is. Each raft must be at least three feet wide, four feet long, one foot high from the waterline, and must be able to support the total weight of all crewmembers. The weight of the raft, without crew-members, can't exceed five hundred pounds."

"Anything else?" Pam asked.

"Yeah, just one, and leave it to Lumby," Brooke said, laughing. "Fancy dress, though not obligatory, is very much appreciated."

"Well, I needed a tux anyway," Mark said, leaning sideways to kiss his wife.

Over dinner the four discussed design options, what could and could not be used as a hull, deck material, and propulsion. Since Joshua had made several rafts for races in prior years, the three looked to him for guidance. By the end of the evening, the consensus was that Hank's design was actually very good, but improvements could be made on the materials: they would use two sealed drums as the pontoons, with three three-foot-diameter heavy rubber inner tubes in between the drums for flotation, all tied together with marine rope. The decking would be canvas over heavy mesh, both stretched on a PVC frame and attached to the drums. Joshua strongly advocated a rudder, so one was added in between the second and third inner tubes. The details were loose, but the diagrams were quite impressive.

ↄ◌ↄ

As the date of the race loomed, Mark and Joshua spent most daylight hours behind the annex constructing the raft. Brooke made several trips to Wheatley for materials not sold in Lumby, and for those items not sold in Wheatley, Joshua brought them back from

Rocky Mount. Meanwhile, Pam was busy preparing for the Montis Inn feast, unsure if ten or five hundred would come after the festival. But when she needed to take a break, she sat back and enjoyed the raft-building show.

TWENTY-FOUR

Tastings

"Don't worry, Brooke, they're my closest friends. I'm sure they'll be as enchanted by you as I am," Joshua said reassuringly as they drove into Lumby.

It was a beautiful summer day, and Gabrielle was sweeping the walk in front of the restaurant as they pulled up and parked on Main Street.

"Gabrielle!" Joshua smiled, jumping out and giving her a warm embrace. "I'd like you to meet Brooke Shelling. Brooke, Gabrielle Beezer."

"It's so nice to finally meet you," Gabrielle said, shaking her hand. "Please come in."

As Brooke walked into The Green Chile, she was enwrapped with rich aromas. "It smells so wonderful," Brooke exclaimed. "I've heard tremendous reviews of your cooking."

"Well, thank you. We enjoy it." Gabrielle led them to a front table.

"Joshua tells me that you are the owner?"

Gabrielle jokingly twisted Joshua's ear. "He lied in part. I am the co-owner with Charlotte Ross."

"Oh, what a delightful woman!" Brooke said in admiration.

"She has been patiently teaching me the finer arts of gardening."

"You couldn't get a better teacher on the subject," Gabrielle said.

"She's just amazing. I only wish I'm as healthy and as active at her age."

"Me too," Gabrielle concurred.

"Hi, I'm Dennis Beezer," he said, walking up to the table and shaking Brooke's hand. "Sorry for being a little late, but the glue slowed down traffic on Farm to Market."

Joshua looked puzzled. "The glue?"

"Yeah, a truck carrying processed epoxy jackknifed just north of Wheatley when it veered away from a moose and calf that were crossing the road. The container split open and glue poured out on the asphalt. With the cars moving so slowly around the accident, the tires became covered with the superglue and everything came to a sticky standstill."

Brooke laughed. "Another exposé opportunity for Scott Stevens, no doubt."

"Oh, do you know Scott?" Dennis asked.

"No, I've never met him, but I see his name in *The Lumby Lines* each week. I understand that you're also in newspapers?"

"Yes, the *Wheatley Sentinel*."

"I'm sorry, I haven't had a chance to read it yet," Brooke admitted with some embarrassment.

"We'll be sure to fix that," he winked.

"So Joshua told us that you are living in the Montis cottage?" Gabrielle asked.

Brooke smiled. "Yes, and it's a delight."

"We lived there fifteen years ago," Gabrielle said.

Brooke looked at her hosts in surprise. "Oh, I didn't know that."

"Yes, when we first moved to Lumby from Boca Del Rio. We stayed there for almost a year. In fact, that's how we came to know Joshua," Gabrielle explained. "It's very small, but it holds such good memories for us."

Dennis leaned over and kissed his wife on the cheek. "It does, indeed."

Brooke looked at Joshua and smiled. "It is charming."

"And Montis is so amazing. What your friends are doing is quite admirable," Gabrielle commented.

"Well, some would call it crazy, but they're making good progress. They're very committed to authentically restoring the abbey."

"And you are their architect?" Dennis asked, unable to suppress his investigative nature.

"To the best of my abilities, yes. But in truth, I have no experience with hundred-year-old chapels, so I would say my contribution is pretty limited."

"Joshua told us that you have an architectural practice in Virginia?" Gabrielle asked.

"That sounds far more substantive than what it is right now. But yes, I have a small firm in Leesburg."

Dennis leaned forward, finding the opportunity to ask the one question he wanted to know. "So, when will you be returning home?"

Brooke fell back slightly, almost unnoticeably. The question caught her off guard. "I don't exactly know," she started to say. She looked at Joshua, who was watching her closely. "I don't know," she repeated and looked downward.

Sensing that he had pushed too far, Dennis asked in a much lighter tone, "But you will be at the raft race?"

She greeted the change of subject with relief. "I wouldn't miss it for the world. Joshua told me that you have a flawed raft," she laughed.

Dennis gave his friend the evil eye. "If he could be so lucky."

Gabrielle leaned over to Brooke. "We really need to talk. Perhaps between the two of us we can knock some sense into these stubborn sailors." Brooke laughed some more.

After lunch, the four stood outside the restaurant and chatted. Gabrielle liked Brooke and suggested they have dinner one night over at their house. Dennis was more cautious, concerned that Joshua would be in too deep when Brooke finally tired of Lumby and returned to Virginia.

Joshua waved to a man who was walking on the other side of the street.

"Would you like to meet Mark Walker?" Joshua offered.

"Perhaps later," Dennis said quickly. "We really need to be going," and escorted his wife back into The Green Chile after good-byes were said.

Joshua stared as Dennis went inside abruptly. He remembered that Mackenzie had mentioned that the townspeople were intentionally keeping their distance from the "East Coasters," as they called them, but Joshua was amazed to think that Dennis could be one of them.

∽∞∾

The following days were a blur to all involved in the Saint Cross business initiative. The monks showed great enthusiasm for the project, always staying one step ahead of their outside support. With Mark and Pam's assistance, the brothers at Saint Cross reconfigured two rooms adjacent to the kitchen to serve as a medium-scale rum sauce-processing center.

The first room, which was originally a cold-storage pantry, was set up to preprocess the fruit: washing, grading, peeling, and pulping. As stainless steel processing equipment was delivered, Mark and a few of his laborers from Montis worked side by side with the brothers to build frames, redirect plumbing, which was now one of Mark's favorite hobbies, and move electrical outlets. Even Cantor was called in for a few days to assist with a commercial air system that was needed to keep several of the rooms chilled.

Since the monastery already had a large commercial kitchen, only slight rearrangements were necessary to accommodate areas for jar sterilization and the anticipated volume of sauces to be made. Finally, the large community room next to the kitchen was rearranged to accommodate the canning, cooling, sealing and shipping of the rum sauce. Sofas and chairs were replaced by hundreds of boxes for empty mason jars, boxes containing thousands of labels, and boxes that contained boxes that the brothers would use for shipping and delivery. The production line, if one was to call it that, contained the newest technologies and offered the cost savings and efficiencies that would carry the monastery well into the coming decades, assuming the sauce was a success.

Additionally, the brothers met with various farmers in the area to sell, or give away, the fruit byproducts that would not be used in the sauce, and coordinated the delivery of large quantities of rum, which raised more than a few eyebrows in their small town. To be able to use the year's harvest, the Saint Cross Rum Sauce was rolled out at breakneck speed.

When Brooke and Joshua walked into the lodge one afternoon, they found Mark, Pam and Brother Matthew carefully scrutinizing a dozen rum sauce jar labels designed by a small firm in Wheatley and driven up to Montis that very morning.

"I think my second choice would be this one," Matthew said, holding up a label that had a slightly simpler design than most of the others. "Perhaps it looks more humble," he added.

"Humble rum," Joshua joked, and went over and shook Matthew's hand. "I hear that the new business is up and running. Congratulations."

Matthew gave a broad smile, trying to hold back the happiness he felt about the future of Saint Cross Abbey. "Well, thank you, Joshua. We are still working out some small problems, and haven't sold anything yet, but we may be very close, I think. It's just amazing how far we've come in two weeks when we started with nothing. I can't thank you all enough."

"No thanks necessary," Mark responded. "It's helped us out as well, truly."

"So, what do you guys think of these?" Pam asked Brooke and Joshua, rearranging the labels on the dining room table.

Brooke took a long look and finally said, "These two are my favorites," and pointed out two similar designs with different color combinations.

Joshua added, "Yes, I also like that one," pointing to the first label Brooke had selected. She gave him such a sparkling smile that Pam's curiosity went on full alert.

"Great," Pam said, eyeing Brooke. "That's the one the three of us first picked out twenty minutes ago."

"So, is that it?" Matthew asked.

"Why don't you take the label back to Saint Cross Abbey tomorrow to make sure the abbot and brothers agree?" Pam suggested. "If so, we can call the printers."

"So," Mark said, clapping his hands, "on to the sampling."

Brother Matthew took from a box by his feet nine medium-size glasses, each with plastic wrap on top, sealed with a rubber band. "I was concerned that they would spill on the drive over."

"Now can we try?" Joshua asked, winking at Brooke.

"Hold on," Pam said, taking several plates from the cabinet. "I made a few different cakes and bought some ice cream to sample with." She passed the first two plates to Brooke and Joshua.

Sitting down, each person first tasted each of the sauces by itself, and discussed their likes and dislikes. The apple and peach rum sauces were absolutely delicious, and proclaimed a smashing success. Moving on to the others, Pam and Brooke felt that the rum overpowered the pears, whereas the men thought it was a perfect balance. And everyone agreed more sugar was needed for the plum sauce, but the nectarine was outstanding. For the next hour they tasted the various rum sauces on four different cakes and with three different ice creams.

"I'm not sure if I'm drunk or just stuffed," Joshua said at last, pushing back his chair.

"Probably just full," Matthew responded. "Most of the alcohol evaporates in the cooking process."

"Well, that just sobered me up," Joshua laughed.

"This cake," Brooke said, pointing to one of the many yellow cakes on the table, "is delicious with the peach sauce. Is it your recipe?"

"My mother's," Pam said, licking a spoon.

"It's such a great pairing. Too bad we can't send the recipe out with the sauce."

Silence. They all looked at each other.

"What a great idea," Pam said, going into the bedroom to get the one sample they had of the glass mason jar that was going to be used.

Putting it on the table, Brooke said, "Why couldn't we put a cake recipe on the back of the label?"

"Not enough space," Pam advised, knowing the labeling that would be required by the FDA.

"Will the jars be individually packaged in boxes?" Joshua asked.

"No," Mark answered.

"Well, couldn't we print the recipe on a small card and attach it to the jar?" Brooke suggested.

Pam nodded her head, thinking. "How about having a band at the neck of the jar?"

"A rubber band?" Mark asked.

She smirked. "A nice elastic band, perhaps in gold or green to match the color on the label, and we can punch a small hole in the corner of the recipe card. It would look like a miniature leaflet or tag attached to the neck of the jar."

"What a wonderful idea," Matthew said. "Would you mind if we begin with this recipe?"

"I think my mom would be more than honored," Pam said.

"Oh, very good," Matthew said. "Because I'm in agreement with Brooke—it's just delicious!"

∽∾

The following week, the monks of Saint Cross Abbey used *The Lumby Lines* to quietly introduce their new product, with the unspoken thought that both the paper and the town were so small that if a mistake was made, few would notice.

℘

TWENTY-FIVE

Sinking

Four days prior to the raft race, the rain began, and it continued to pour for three days after that. The eleven inches of rain that fell on Lumby that week had several effects. First, it was excuse enough for *The Lumby Lines* to print a special edition.

𝔗𝔥𝔢 𝔏𝔲𝔪𝔟𝔶 𝔏𝔦𝔫𝔢𝔰

Special Edition
Come Hell or High Water

BY CARRIE KERRY   AUGUST 20

The torrential rains that have stayed with us for the last four days have left Lumby waterlogged, but the weather report shows all likelihood of the storm clearing out this evening.

Sam Friedman, Lumby's Park Manager, reported that at least one hundred wood ducks have invaded the newly formed lake at the Fairgrounds, and are wreaking havoc for the chickens that have taken up residence there. Additionally, he said that Porta-Potty #2 has floated away, and the roof on Porta-Potty #5 has collapsed.

The Lumby Landfill is also suffering adverse effects from the rain, with a major landslide occurring last night on the north hill. The police have asked all residents to stop using it as a toboggan run, as the sleds are deepening the trenches.

Several residents are blaming the rains on the government cloud-seeding program. "This just isn't normal, and Ruth Ann saw a couple of airplanes up there, and they looked like they were dropping something out the windows," said an unidentified patron at Jimmy D's.

Whether the weather is from Mother Nature or the CIA, we should start drying out tomorrow, just in time for the Fork River Festival. See you all there!

The downpour brought about several other changes. The second harvest of the Montis orchard had to be moved back eight days, the drywall for the inn's main building couldn't be delivered, honey collection for the monks was postponed until Chuck Bryson felt the bees were dry, and the Fork River rose to flood levels, running higher and faster than most folks in Lumby could ever remember. But by the morning of the festival, the rafts were complete, Hank and his float had disappeared, and the sun finally broke through and promised a stunningly beautiful day.

With the mud, Cutter and Clipper (who insisted on helping) and the broken trailer axle, the loading of the raft at Montis Inn precariously teetered between hilarious and disastrous. Mark had to call four of the workers to hoist the raft onto the trailer, which immediately collapsed. One of the workers offered his flatbed, and within an hour the raft was questionably secured and traveling down Farm to Market Road.

Getting to Kelly's Bend on the Fork River proved to be more treacherous. The rain had converted the dirt access road into a mud channel, making it impassable for either truck or trailer. So the River Master, Sal Gentile, who was also the proprietor of Lumby Liquors, decided to put the backs of the good men of Lumby to work, and had the volunteers create two lines, shoulder to shoulder, the length of the access road. For nearly an hour, each float was passed down the line, man to man, float after float, until all twenty-nine entries were resting by the swollen banks of the Fork River for the dry-land competition.

Although Joshua repeatedly looked around for Dennis, it wasn't until the rafts were at the river's edge that he saw his friend standing next to a very formidable-looking craft.

"Quite impressive," Joshua said, slapping Dennis on the back.

"There she be—*The Neptune*," Dennis said proudly, raising his arm. He was wearing an elaborate Viking costume. Brian and Terry, in jeans and pretending not to know him, were sitting on the deck with headphones on. Gabrielle, who looked very much like a Viking's wife, and Mackenzie were talking with friends some distance away.

"I just wanted to wish you good luck," Joshua said.

Dennis clasped him by the arm. "Be safe out there. I've never seen the river this high or this fast."

"Nor I."

"Accepted," Sal yelled out, after walking around and surveying the first raft.

Joshua tried to peek through the crowd to see which raft Sal was inspecting. "I need to get back. We're about to be judged."

"See you after the race. I'll be waiting for you on the lake," Dennis laughed.

Ten minutes later, "Accepted, but will be disqualified if you don't put duct tape on the exposed metal before the start of the race." Sal continued to go down the line of rafts, only disqualifying one two-man entry for illegal use of materials.

Sal walked up to Mark and Joshua's raft, introduced himself, and began the inspection. Walking twice around the boat, if one could call it that, all he said was, "Disqualified," and began to move on to the next entry.

"Disqualified?" Mark asked.

"Disqualified," Sal repeated.

"Why?" Mark asked, louder than he intended.

"No name," Sal answered.

"No name?" Mark asked.

"No name," Sal repeated, on the edge of annoyance.

"But there is no regulation about a name," Joshua contended.

"Was last year," Sal said, with his back now turned.

In no more than six seconds, Mark pulled a magic marker from Joshua's shirt pocket, accidently ripping the fabric, and wrote something on the PVC deck frame on the right side of the raft.

"Perhaps you overlooked it—it's on the deck piping," Mark said, catching up to Sal, who had begun inspecting the next raft.

"Where?" he asked.

"On the starboard frame," Mark said.

"Raft name?"

"*Lazy Bones II.*"

"Accepted," Sal acknowledged, and updated his list.

Although their raft participated in two of the dry-land competitions, to no one's surprise, *Lazy Bones II* lost by a very wide margin. The rafts that won were amazing works of creative genius. The American Heritage Award went to a monstrous float that had a six-foot-tall replica of the Statue of Liberty on the deck, which also served as the sail mast. The Committee's Choice Award, with Sal being "the committee," was given to the raft entered by Jimmy D's, Sal's highest-volume customer and the sponsor for this year's barbecue lunch. No surprise and no argument after everyone tasted the ribs and chicken wings, even if the wings had come from the fairground poultry fiasco.

In prior years many wore costumes during the dry-land competition, but this year everything was too muddy. After lunch, people started to disappear into the woods and reemerged a few minutes later in full attire. So, too, did Mark and Joshua. Mark changed into an ancient tuxedo Pam had found at the Nearly New shop, while Joshua opted for the formal castaway look: no shirt, shredded shorts, sneakers and a blue necktie.

Pam and Brooke, who had stayed at Montis Inn during the dry-land competition to prepare the coffee and dessert that would be served that evening, arrived in full dress well before their scheduled launch. Brooke wore work boots, a white-sheet toga and a ratty belt made out of heavy rope that appeared to have been borrowed from the stonemason. Pam opted for a denim skirt and a cotton top. All four of their costumes were on the boringly conservative side compared to some of those who were preparing to float the river.

The first floats in the river were the one-man rafts, which included five entries. All were not much larger than minimum size, three feet by four feet, with two being little more than a board placed on a heavy rubber inner tube. When the mariners began to push their rafts off the shore and into the water, the trouble began. The river's current was so strong and so swift that the first raft was literally swept away with the owner still on the shore. Sal Gentile, who was overseeing the start of the race, radioed down to his assistant, presumably at the mouth of Woodrow Lake, telling him that the first raft was "unmanned and moving at quite the clip."

The other four entrants, not wanting to repeat the trial and error of the first, recruited volunteers to tether the raft until the gun.

Bang! And they were off, gaining tremendous speed just ten yards offshore. The second raft, not using the inner tube technology, but instead opting for lighter-weight, less expensive styrofoam, broke apart within the first minute. A rescue line was thrown to the captain at the first bend, pulling him from the turbulent current.

Within two minutes the rafts were well out of sight and Sal, through his twenty-year-old megaphone, advised the two-man skippers to prepare their crafts. One by one, the seven rafts, larger and appearing more structurally sound than the one-man, were hoisted into the river. Before the starting gun sounded, one raft took on so much water on top that the additional weight caused its flotation to crack and, to the dismay of the owner, the raft sank three feet down, three feet offshore. Another raft, the last in line, literally flipped end over end when hit by a wave surge, and landed on the raft next to it, causing no damage to the flippee, but considerable havoc to the flipper. At this point in the race, more debris than intact rafts was being ferried down toward Woodrow Lake.

Bang! The lines were dropped, and the furious paddling began. Once the rafts were caught in the river's current, however, the riders immediately realized that no amount of paddling could increase their speed. The objective changed from propelling the boats to stabilizing them, or just hanging on for dear life. By the first bend, five boats were still floating, although one had lost a crewmember, resulting in immediate disqualification.

Sal had arranged the seventeen as-many-as-you-can-get-on rafts for a staggered start, with three heats of six, six and five rafts.

Lazy Bones II was in the first group, and well positioned, being farthest downstream and well away from the next boat entering the water. Several people helped Mark and Joshua slide the raft into the water. Mark was almost swept under the raft when he took one step too many away from the shore while trying to swing the front end of the boat into position. With some effort, and the help of eight other people to hold the raft, Pam, Brooke, Joshua and Mark boarded. Immediately the river's bucking dropped them to their knees.

Joshua turned around. Four boats upriver was *The Neptune*, with Dennis well balanced on its deck. Although the raft lay low in the water due to its weight, it looked to be far better balanced than many of the others, which, although tethered, were being violently tossed by the current.

"I had no idea it was going to be this rough," Pam said, a little shaken.

"It should get smoother once we get on the river," Mark said.

"We're already on the river," Brooke protested slightly.

"We'll be fine," Joshua assured her, putting his arm through hers.

The wait seemed endless, but then, Bang! and the volunteers threw the lines onto the raft. For a few seconds the raft didn't move. Mark, thinking that the added weight of all four crewmembers had dug the raft into the sand, stood up and was about to step off when the raft suddenly surged forward. Had Pam not grabbed his arm, Mark would have been left behind, disqualifying *Lazy Bones II*. As their raft shot off, Joshua saw Dennis wave at him as *The Neptune* rushed past. Joshua noticed that both boys were sitting safely on the deck, and thought he saw Terry McGuire tighten his life vest and start to wrap the rope around his waist, but *Lazy Bones II* lurched forward again.

The acceleration of the raft was so startling that Mark told Pam and Brooke, "Lie flat on the deck!" He and Joshua attempted to control the raft by using a small rudder and two long oars. The rudder broke two hundred yards into the race. Passing the first bend was a blur, with Mark thinking gloomily that they still had four miles to go before the calm of Woodrow Lake. They were quickly coming up on *The Neptune*, which appeared to be slowed by its bulky weight.

Joshua, turning to see where the other rafts were, saw two approaching from the left side. "Watch out!" Mark and Joshua looked at each other with an unspoken understanding that winning took a distant second to finishing the race intact and with the four of them uninjured.

As they rounded the bend, though, the river broadened and the current slowed, making the ride more manageable. Pam and Brooke sat up and, taking their own oars, began to help with the raft's navigation. The new tactic, Mark yelled to be heard over the rush of the water, was to stay out of everyone's way.

Two rafts on their left appeared to be keeping clear. Mark and Joshua tried to steer to the right side of the river, but were swept into deeper waters by the strong current. The raft closest to *Lazy Bones II* was the Heritage Award winner, which had already lost the top of the Statue of Liberty and was heading directly for some trees that extended well over the water. There were no less than eight crew members, all dressed in Civil War uniforms, on the deck trying to control the unwieldy raft.

Dennis, steering *The Neptune*, was in a dead heat with *Lazy Bones II*, keeping a steady speed in the center of the river. Brian was managing the rudder, and Terry was still seated on the deck. Slightly in front of them, but closer to the far bank, was a log raft with four Robinson Crusoe-looking mates on board; three of the men Mark recognized from the construction site.

The rafts began to pick up speed as the river narrowed between high, straight banks on each side. Going through the gulch seemed almost suicidal. Joshua had told Mark that this was the worst part of the course, tricky even when the water was at its normal level.

Lazy Bones II was the first raft through the gulch, careening radically but staying level enough not to flip. Within fifteen seconds it was followed by the Crusoe log raft, which looked to have tremendous drag underneath and was torquing in all directions. The logs were beginning to pull away from each other and rope was snapping like thread. *The Neptune* was close on their heels, but still a safe distance behind. Unfortunately, within seconds, the log raft broke apart, sending the crew into the water. Two of its logs crashed into the front of *The Neptune* with such force that Dennis and Brian were also thrown into the river, with wood and logs shattering around them.

Joshua frantically searched for Dennis among the raft pieces, now free of body weight and moving much faster. He saw Dennis's head bob up as well as Brian's. Also in the water were the Crusoe crewmembers, twisting as the life vests kept their heads above water. All were accounted for . . . all but one.

Joshua looked around for Terry McGuire. *The Neptune* had shattered into two main sections, and Terry was on neither. Joshua panicked when he saw an empty life vest float past *Lazy Bones II*. He looked back at the largest piece remaining of his friend's raft and then scanned the water, thinking that Terry might be holding on for dear life. That's when he spotted the boy being dragged fifteen feet behind the raft by a rope he had tied around his waist.

Lazy Bones II had caught a slightly slower current next to the bank, so within seconds, the drowning boy, whom the others did not see, was parallel to them in the river. Joshua, reacting without thinking, dove in. Brooke yelled out, thinking that Joshua had fallen overboard, but then she saw that he was frantically trying to swim to a large piece of raft that was rushing past them. Mark spotted an arm jerk up from behind the broken raft, and suddenly realized what Joshua was doing. Mark yelled at Pam to try to get the raft to shore, and dove in after Joshua.

Pam and Brooke watched helplessly while trying to land the raft. Neither Dennis nor Brian Beezer witnessed any of this, as they were already far ahead, their bodies being tossed by the fierce current.

Joshua finally made it to Terry's side and lifted the boy's head above water. Yet he couldn't untie the rope, which had swollen with water and was taut from the force of the drag. Joshua, relying on his life vest, rolled on his back, and held onto the same rope that was tied to the boy. He stretched his legs out in front of him to fend off the shattered raft that was pulling them downstream and then tried to buoy Terry on his stomach. Just when his strength was about to give out, he felt Mark grab his arm. Clinging to the both of them, Mark desperately hacked at the rope with a pocketknife he had pulled from his tuxedo pants.

It took Mark no more than twenty seconds to cut the rope, but Joshua, with the boy on his chest, was swallowing tremendous amounts of water. He couldn't find enough air to get into his burning lungs. The sky was beginning to darken, and for a moment Joshua thought it was sunset and that they had been on the river all afternoon.

He then felt the rope snap, and the three of them were freed from the devilish pull of the raft. Mark took Terry's limp body so Joshua could raise his chest and get desperately needed air. Joshua started to cough violently, and Mark saw water and blood spurt from his mouth. After the seizure ended, Joshua put his hand on Mark's shoulder, and the two kicked with all of their strength to the riverbank.

By this time, Dennis had made it to shore with his son and had run upstream. He jumped back into the river to pull Joshua out while others helped Terry and Mark. When Terry was finally brought to dry ground, he rolled on his side, violently vomiting water and blood and moaning in pain. Within minutes, Mackenzie and Gabrielle, who had seen the accident from the riverbank, were by their sides.

Everything that followed that afternoon was a blur to both Mark and Joshua. Mark, as he told Pam later, remembered the incident in silent, still photographs: Terry's body lying on the ground with his arm bloodied from a compound fracture, the tormented look on the face of his mother, Mackenzie, the lettering of the ambulance, Pam leaning over to kiss him.

He also remembered Mackenzie coming up to both Joshua and him and kissing them on the cheek, thanking them for saving the life of her only son. And small Charlotte Ross putting a blanket over his shoulders.

Joshua recalled those things as well. But he would also carry in his memory album Dennis Beezer extending a hand to Mark and almost carrying him to the ambulance. When Dennis returned, he said their race rivalry was over and that Joshua had won. Finally, Joshua would keep in his heart forever the expression in Brooke's eyes as she looked down at him. In that moment, after such a horrendous experience, Joshua knew he loved her.

TWENTY-SIX
Gathering

After the doctor tended to both Joshua and Mark at the river, Pam drove the four back to Montis, exhausted, grateful, blessed. Pulling into the driveway, Pam and Brooke noticed that Hank had returned, now dressed in debonair maître d's attire, holding a serving tray with a bottle of wine, four empty wineglasses and one filled mason jar. At his feet was a case of wine and a case of Saint Cross Rum Sauce.

"Do you think Matthew did that?" Pam asked.

"I don't think so," Brooke said hesitantly. "But who else has the rum sauce?"

"No one that I'm aware of."

The men sat silently in the back seat, their eyes closed, although neither was sleeping; they were listening and smiling. The same thoughts crossed both of their minds: life is precious, and it's good to be home again. As soon as they went into the lodge, Mark and Joshua went to their rooms to rest until company arrived.

In the meantime, the women finished the preparations for that evening's party. Brooke cut the pies and cakes that had been delivered that afternoon.

"The cakes are done. What's next?"

"There are several gallons of cut fresh fruit in the refrigerator of the main kitchen. If you could transfer that to the large serving bowls, that would be great." Pam looked around. "And then I think the only thing to be done is make the coffee."

"Do you have any idea how many folks will be coming this evening?"

"No idea. It might only be a few of the contractors and their families."

"Or an entire town?"

Pam shook her head and laughed. "Oh, I seriously doubt that. Working around the construction site, I've overheard some talk. It seems we're still very much considered outsiders—and probably will be for years."

Brooke shrugged her shoulders. "Perhaps that's the price one pays for living in such a small town."

"And if it is, that's all right. We so love it here." Pam paused. "But it would be nice if . . ."

After a few seconds Brooke leaned forward, waiting for Pam to finish her thought. "Yes?"

"Nothing," she said, and then quickly changed the subject. "I'll walk over to the dining room with you."

Just as Pam and Brooke walked through the front door of the lodge, a large flatbed trailer came to a stop by the main building. *Lazy Bones II* rocked precariously on top. Seeing the raft again sent a chill up Pam's spine.

Dennis Beezer stepped out from the driver's side. She didn't recognize the teenager who sat quietly in the passenger seat.

"Hi, Pam," Dennis said, walking up and extending his hand. "I'm Dennis Beezer. We met briefly this afternoon."

"Yes, I think so," Pam said, trying to remember him in all the chaos after the accident.

"Hey, Dennis," Brooke said.

"Hi, Brooke. I didn't think you'd mind if we dropped by. They wanted the rafts out of the water by the end of day, and I thought we'd bring your boat over for you."

"That's really nice of you," Pam said. "We left as soon as the doctor looked at Mark and Joshua. We didn't even think about the raft."

"Where would you like us to put it?" Dennis asked.

"If it wasn't for the drums, I'd say burn it in the Lumby landfill. But," she looked around for a discreet dumping site, "if you could back around and put it behind the lodge, that would be great."

The three walked back to the truck. "Quite the accident today," Dennis said. "I've never seen anything like it in fifteen years of the race."

"Is Terry McGuire all right?" Pam asked.

"Yeah, he'll be in the hospital for a few days. A badly broken arm and some cracked ribs, but I heard he'll be fine. But I don't know if the same can be said for his mother, Mackenzie."

"She seems like a strong woman. We were able to get to know her while she worked on the abbey. But it must have been incredibly hard for her to see her son in such danger," Pam sympathized.

"The whole thing was such a nightmare." Brooke gave a shudder.

"Stupid that he tied that rope around his waist," Dennis said, shaking his head. "Had I seen him do it, I would have told him to untie it immediately."

"Dennis, don't blame yourself. He made a mistake," Brooke said kindly.

He responded with an appreciative smile. "How are Joshua and your husband?" he asked.

Pam glanced back at the lodge. "Asleep, but fine."

"To think that your raft was almost disqualified. I hate to consider what would have happened if you guys weren't on the river when you were," Dennis said.

"Something we'll never have to know, thank God," Pam said. A lever never flipped.

"Never have to know what?" a voice questioned from the other side of the truck, behind the raft.

Turning, they all watched a man walk around the flatbed, stopping to take a few photographs of *Lazy Bones II*.

"What brings you here?" Dennis asked, putting himself between Scott and the women.

"Just wanted to meet the river warriors, and ask a few questions for my articles," he said in a casual, friendly manner.

"Pam, this is Scott Stevens from *The Lumby Lines*," Dennis said.

"Yes, I've seen your name in the paper."

"And you must be Brooke Shelling?" Scott asked.

"I am," Brooke answered coolly.

Dennis, who was substantially larger than Scott, walked over and put his arm around Scott's shoulder. "Well, since you're here, Scott, you can volunteer to help us with the raft."

"Sure enough," Scott answered, as if he actually had the option to refuse.

After the flatbed was repositioned, Brian stepped out of the truck. "What can I do to help, Dad?" he asked.

Dennis proudly looked at his son. "Thanks for offering, Brian," he said.

After the five wrestled with dry-docking *Lazy Bones II* behind the lodge, Dennis confirmed the evening activities with Pam and asked if he and his wife could help in any preparations. Only after Pam assured him there wasn't anything left to do did they leave to rejoin Gabrielle and the others back at Woodrow Lake.

"So, what can we do for you?" Pam politely asked Scott, who was still hanging around, uninvited.

"I was hoping to meet," Scott looked at a notepad he had pulled from his shirt pocket, "Mark Walker and Joshua Turner."

"Neither is available right now," Brooke said firmly.

"I'm assuming they're all right after the accident?"

"They're both fine," Pam answered, "but they're tending to preparations for tonight, so this probably isn't a very good time. Perhaps you could stop by later?"

"Thanks for the invitation. I'll do that," Scott said with a smile.

"But since I have you here, would you like to comment on the party you'll be hosting here at Montis this evening?"

"Speaking of which," Pam maintained a gracious smile, "we've got so much to do before our guests arrive. Why don't we talk this evening?"

"Say no more," Scott said, raising his arms as if to surrender. "I'll see you tonight."

∞

Mark and Joshua awoke in the late afternoon, shortly before cars began to arrive at Montis Inn. Although the party wasn't to begin until after sunset, word had gotten around that the children were invited to pick apples, so parents with children of all ages came early and went into the orchards to share the delight of picking apples.

Sitting on the front porch, Mark watched a young boy with short dark brown hair play with Clipper and Cutter across the street. The boy had found an apple on the ground and was using it to play fetch. Unfortunately, after Clipper retrieved it, and after Cutter attempted to take it away, there was little left over other than a small, slimy, broken-up piece of core. Mark was laughing as Joshua and Brooke sat down on the front steps. The boy was giggling so hard, he fell over and became an immediate licking target for the puppies, who began to indiscriminately jump all over him, making the boy giggle that much harder.

"Kids and puppies—a perfect match," Mark said as an idle comment.

"Did you and Pam ever consider having children?" Joshua asked casually.

"That just wasn't an option for us," Mark answered but offered no further explanation.

"Nor for me, at least while I was at Montis. It's definitely something our abbot would never have understood," Joshua laughed.

They continued to watch the boy, who had gotten up and was running between the trees being chased by Clipper. Cutter had stayed behind to eat the last of the apple.

"Timmy," a woman's voice called.

Mark then noticed, for the first time, a striking woman with long, almost black hair and a dark complexion sitting at the bottom of the hill between the boy and Farm to Market Road.

"Timmy, it's time to go," she repeated.

The boy stopped and changed direction, running down to his mother with both dogs on his heels. When he finally reached her, out of breath but still giggling, she took his hand, walked him to the side of the road, and stopped to look both ways. With no cars in sight, they crossed and walked up the path to the main house.

"Good evening," the woman said, still holding on to her youngest son's hand. Mark was at a loss for who she was. "We met briefly by the river today," she said warmly. "I'm Gabrielle Beezer."

"Oh, I'm sorry," Joshua said, forgetting his manners. "Mark, this is Gabrielle, Dennis's wife. Gabrielle, Mark Walker."

"Ah, yes," Mark said. "Joshua has mentioned you and your husband many times. It's nice to finally meet you. We've enjoyed watching your son play."

"He had a wonderful time," Gabrielle said, gazing fondly at the young boy.

"Can I take the puppies home if you don't want them?" Timmy asked Mark, trying to bend over to pet one of them, but still firmly in his mother's grasp.

"Well, they're pretty used to their dog beds inside, so I think they'd be a little homesick. But you can come by to see them anytime you want," Mark offered as a consolation.

"Okay," little Timmy said.

"I wanted to thank you for having us over. Your inn is just beautiful."

"Well, thank you. I'm glad you were able to come," Mark said cordially.

"Look, Mommy," Timmy said, pulling on his mother's arm. "It's Dad."

Dennis was getting out of their car, waving at a small group gathered over by the library.

"Can I go see him?" Timmy asked, trying to pull out of his mother's hold.

"All right, but run in a straight line," she said. Timmy and the puppies ran off again, with his mother watching until he was safe with his father.

"My other son, Brian, should be coming down from the orchard with some friends shortly," she said, looking back up at the fields. "I hope they don't take advantage of your generosity and walk away with half the harvest."

Mark dismissed the notion. "I don't think that's possible—there are a lot of apples up there."

"They brought large trash bags," Gabrielle confessed under her breath, to which everyone laughed.

"Enterprising young men," Brooke said.

"That's an understatement. Please remember that when he tries to sell you your own newspaper that he just stole from your own mailbox."

"Teenage boys are a handful at times," Mark said encouragingly.

"Good afternoon," Dennis said, being pulled to the porch by Timmy. "Mark, I don't know if we were actually introduced at the river, but I'm Dennis Beezer." He shook Mark's hand warmly.

"Very nice to finally meet you as well. Pam told me that you dropped off our raft this afternoon—thanks very much."

"We're tremendously grateful that you saved Terry McGuire. I don't know what Mackenzie would have ever done if . . ." Gabrielle said.

It was a subject better left alone. Instead, Mark asked, "Can I show you around?"

"Unfortunately, we need to get home," Gabrielle said. "A babysitter will be coming by in an hour or so. Perhaps we can take you up on your offer when we return this evening, if you're not too busy. We just stopped by to see if you needed anything for tonight."

Mark, seeing Cutter and Clipper playing ferocious tug-of-war with a wicker basket someone had left on the porch, said with a chuckle, "Dog tranquilizers would be greatly appreciated."

∞

As the sun set, Pam and Mark began lighting the lanterns they had staked around the compound and turning on the lights in the main building. To the delight of Pam and Brooke, Mark and Joshua had strung long lines of small white Christmas lights along the front gable and roofline of the inn. Montis looked like a fairytale chateau.

The townspeople began to arrive shortly thereafter, and within an hour, a hundred and fifty people were strolling through the compound, many still in their costumes from the day's main event. They admired the roses and flower gardens. They meandered through the back buildings and into the main inn, which was still in the process of final restoration but finished enough for those to appreciate all of its charm. Several couples took blankets up into the orchard and enjoyed the sights and sounds from a distance.

Mark and Pam sat at the picnic table on the front porch, greeting people as they arrived, while Brooke and Joshua assisted by overseeing coffee and dessert.

"Well, if it isn't Sheriff Dixon," Mark said, smiling. He was introduced to Simon's wife, Anna, an attractive woman with reddish-brown hair and dark brown eyes that appeared to lighten when she smiled. Simon had frequently spoken of her during their "after-incident" conversations, and Mark could now see that Simon's description was very accurate.

"We haven't gotten an emergency call from Montis in several weeks. We were concerned that your restoration efforts had stopped altogether," Simon teased.

"Thanks for saving him so many times," Pam said, patting her husband on the leg.

"Well, no dead bodies yet," Mark quipped.

"I heard you came pretty close to being one yourself today," Simon said.

"Best forgotten," Mark said, wanting to change the subject.

The sheriff would have none of it. "Mark, you and Joshua did something extraordinary. You should know how much the town appreciates it."

"Anyone would have done the same."

"I don't think so," Simon said. "You showed us all something today."

Jimmy D, with Brad close behind, walked up and slapped Simon on the shoulder.

"Is he causing you any trouble?" Jimmy asked Mark.

Simon laughed. "I think you know Jimmy?"

"Yes, good seeing you again. I'm glad you could come tonight," Pam said courteously.

Simon continued with the introductions. "And this is Brad Harper."

"Ah, yes. Brad's Hardware," Mark made the connection. "You have a great store."

"Well, thanks. Have seen you in there a few times. . . . Sorry I've been unable to make the introduction," he said in embarrassment, knowing full well how many times Mark had been in his store and how he had deliberately avoided the "East Coaster." "But come by when you're up to it, and I'll give you the full tour. There are a few back rooms with products that most customers don't know about—you'll really enjoy looking around. And we need to set you up with a business discount."

"I'll certainly take you up on that," Mark smiled broadly.

"Well, we didn't mean to interrupt," Jimmy said, backing away. "We just wanted to shake your hand and officially welcome you to our town."

∞

"What a wonderful party," Russell Harris said, walking up to Pam and Mark, who had found a few minutes to themselves. "It's been quite some time since I last saw you. How have you been?"

"Well, thanks," Mark answered. Turning, he saw Brooke and

Joshua approach. "Let me introduce you to our good friends, Brooke Shelling and Joshua Turner. Guys, this is Russell Harris, our attorney who handled the purchase of Montis."

"Nice meeting you," Russell said, shaking their hands. Turning back to Mark and Pam, he continued. "It's just amazing what you've done. It looks spectacular."

"Thanks," Pam said. "We hope to open the inn for the holidays. Please have a seat and join us."

Russell sat at the end of the table. "Have you recovered from today's heroics?"

"Not fully, but almost," Mark said, and then veered off that subject. "I read in *The Lumby Lines* that you're the attorney representing the potbelly pig that was named executor and benefactor in someone's will. Very interesting clientele you have."

Russell laughed. "Well, I don't know if I'm actually representing Seymour, but, yes, I'm the lucky one overseeing the case."

"Good use of an education, no doubt?" Brooke said.

"Well, they never specifically prepared me for this one."

"Are you the only attorney in Lumby?" Mark asked.

"Ours is the only law firm," he answered. "So between my partner and me, we touch upon a lot of the legal proceedings in town."

"I'm curious. Can a pig actually inherit an estate?" Brooke asked.

He answered with a broad smile. "In our state, yes, with a trustee. However, it can't act as executor, so those are issues we're working through now."

"Ah," Brooke said. "People do strange things."

"Strange in appearance, at least," Russell said.

"What do you mean?"

"Well, I've seen a lot of cases where wills and final letters of instruction appear totally bizarre, but once I understood the background or the reasoning behind the choices that the people made, it becomes quite logical. Usually, last requests are well thought out."

After several more minutes of conversation, Russell bade them good night, and Mark and Pam rejoined the crowd in the courtyard, making new acquaintances and catching up with the people who worked at Montis daily. Everyone was genuinely concerned about Joshua and Mark, and expressed their gratitude for the two men's heroic rescue.

While Mark and Pam were talking to Cantor, Mark noticed an old man walking toward the back of the annex, away from the crowd. The reason he took notice was that the man, before disappearing behind the building, stopped, turned as if to make sure he wasn't being watched and then stepped into the darkness. Feeling uneasy, Mark began to follow, but was held by Cantor, who insisted on introducing him to a few townsfolk. By the time Mark broke loose and was able to circle around the annex several minutes later, no one was there.

Mark rejoined his wife just as Charlotte Ross shuffled up to them.

"Delightful party," she said. "How nice it was for you to invite the town to Montis. And everyone has come! Not only did you save the life of a boy, but you brought an entire town together. We are so, so grateful," she almost whispered, patting Mark's hand.

"Well, thank you," Mark said gently.

"And what you have done for Montis. This is such a special place." As she looked around, the Christmas lights reflected in her old eyes.

"Have you been here before?" Pam asked, as taken by Charlotte as the first time she met her.

"I used to play here almost every Sunday of my childhood," she spoke slowly, reminiscing. "When we first came, the abbey had just been built. It would take over an hour for us to come from Rocky Mount by buggy. The monastic family was very cloistered then, but they allowed my parents to worship here. Children weren't invited into the chapel, so I sat up on that hill and listened to the Gregorian chants."

A gentleman several years her junior walked up and kissed Charlotte gently on her cheek.

"I thought you were lost," she teased him. "This is my husband, Zak Taylor. Zak, these are the Walkers, Pam and Mark."

"We heard you recently got married. Congratulations," Pam said.

"Silly at our age perhaps, but it's nice to have someone by your side," Zak said. "It's wonderful what you've done here. Charlotte has always spoken so fondly of the abbey. At one point last year I thought she was going to get out her checkbook and buy Montis just to have it tended to."

"Well, it's been a wonderful experience," Mark said, and then turning to Charlotte, added, "And I hear you've made quite a contribution to Brooke's garden."

"Oh, she's such a delightful person. She reminds me of myself at her age. Is she here?" Charlotte asked.

"Yes, in the lodge. Please, just go in," Pam offered.

"Thank you," Zak said, and the two walked off, arm in arm supporting each other, in search of Brooke.

Finally they were alone.

"Are you all right?" Pam asked her husband.

"Yes, why do you ask?"

"Because your hands are shaking."

"I suppose I'm cold and a little tired—it's been a long day."

As she was leaning over to kiss him, she saw, over Mark's shoulder, Scott Stevens walking toward them.

"Oh, God," she groaned, almost to herself.

"What's wrong?" Mark asked.

"Nothing, why don't we go to the lodge?" she suggested. She then watched Dennis walk up behind Scott, put his hand on Scott's arm and divert him to the opposite side of the compound. As Dennis turned back to Pam, she mouthed thank you, and he smiled.

After delivering Scott to a remote corner of the party, Dennis returned to talk to Mark and Pam.

"I finally had the opportunity to walk through the main building and the annex. What you've done is extraordinary," Dennis said. "The last time I saw the chapel was the day after the fire." He stared at the building, where there was once a charred scar.

Seeing his discomfort, Mark said, "We've enjoyed every step of the restoration."

"Hello," Mackenzie said, walking up to them.

Everyone was surprised to see her. "Mac! What are you doing here?" Dennis asked.

"Visiting hours just ended and Terry will sleep through the night. I wanted to come by and say thank you." Tears came to her eyes as she reached over and put her hand on Mark's arm. "I'll never be able to repay you and Joshua."

Mark hugged her. "I'm sorry, I was so terrified," she cried softly. "Are you all right?"

"Yes, we're fine," he reassured her. "And Terry is fine."

"I came so close to losing him today," she said as Mark released her.

"But you didn't."

Mackenzie wiped the tears away. "I've never seen so many people from Lumby in one place," she said, looking around, trying to smile.

"And I think we've met each one of them," Mark laughed. "Everyone has just been wonderful."

"I think that's what they're saying of you and Joshua," Dennis countered. Moving to Mackenzie's side, he offered, "Why don't we find Gabrielle and we can drive you home? You must be exhausted."

"I would appreciate that." She turned to Mark. "Please tell Joshua how grateful I am for what you two did." And tears again filled her eyes.

"And the same from me," Dennis said, shaking Mark's hand.

∽∾∽

The guests started leaving after ten, and by midnight the last cars pulled out of the driveway. Joshua and Brooke, who had stayed to help put food away, joined Mark and Pam in the lodge.

"Fine gathering," Joshua said. "I'm amazed how many people

came—there must have been hundreds on the lawn. And they just kept coming."

"I never expected it," Pam said, slouching down on the sofa. "I'm exhausted."

"They were all so kind—so grateful for today as well as for tonight," Brooke said.

"Well, I don't think anyone can question your commitment toward Lumby and its residents," Joshua said.

That reminded Brooke of her chief opponent, and she asked, "So, what did you guys think of him?"

"Of whom?" Mark asked.

"Beezer," she answered.

"Oh, Dennis seems like a great guy," Mark answered. "I can understand why he's such a good friend of yours, Joshua."

"No, not Dennis. What did you think of William, his father?"

Mark looked confused.

"I saw the old man walk past you two and get into his car, so I assumed you finally had a chance to meet him."

Pam asked Mark, "Did you meet Beezer Senior?"

"Not that I know of," he said. "Are you sure it was William Beezer?"

"Positive," Brooke said.

"Why do you think he came tonight?" Pam asked.

"Obviously not to meet us," Mark said with a mystified shrug.

∽

The following morning, like most other Monday mornings, Mark walked out to get *The Lumby Lines* from their mailbox. Hank was still maitre d' of Montis Inn. Skipping all articles and references to the Fork River Festival, Mark turned directly to the Sheriff's Complaints from the prior week for his morning humor.

𝕿𝔥𝔢 𝕷𝔲𝔪𝔟𝔶 𝕷𝔦𝔫𝔢𝔰

Sheriff's Complaints

SHERIFF SIMON DIXON   **AUGUST 20**

6:18a.m. Deer vs. car on Priest Pass. Both reported severe front-end damage. Guardrail relocated to bottom of ravine.

7:02a.m. Man from Hunts Mill Road reported that his mailbox was painted during the night.

7:56a.m. Lumby resident from Hunts Mill Road reported that all the mailboxes on the street had been painted except for hers.

10:44a.m. Couple from out of state reported that their cabin had been torn down since their last visit here three weeks ago. The bulldozer is still on the property. Oops.

11:11a.m. Caller reported a moose was running through his cornfield with tricycle hanging from his antlers.

1:49p.m. LFD responded to tractor fire south of Perimeter Road.

2:32p.m. EMS responded to a call from the lumber mill. A pair of sneakers was found by the auger. They are looking for a body, but no one is missing.

9:09p.m. Lumby man on Pine Street reported sauna heating up out of control.

10:52p.m. Patron at Jimmy D's reported seeing an image of the Virgin Mary in the front window.

11:23p.m. Patron at Jimmy D's reported that Doug Sewell would not hand over the karaoke mike, and that his singing was a crime.

AUGUST 21

6:14a.m. Joy reported that all of her car air bags deployed during the night although the car was locked. She suspects aliens.

8:03a.m. Lumby resident reported pygmy goat stampede down Mineral St. south of landfill.

8:37a.m. Gary Williamson reported striking oil while digging a hole to plant a tree. Requested assistance.

8:41a.m. Gary Williamson reported substance was not oil, but smelly waste bubbling up out of ground. Requested faster assistance.

9:04a.m. Owner of Lumby Hair Salon reported three red wigs were missing, and requested police keep a look out and question anyone matching description (has bright red hair).

9:26a.m. EMS responded to caller who had fallen, gotten up, fallen and couldn't get up again.

11:00a.m. Lumby resident reported that a photograph in new Lumby brochure was picture of Banff.

TWENTY-SEVEN

Hosed

In preparation for the site visit by a representative from the National Historic Landmark Committee, Montis Inn was bustling with activity. The carpenters, having finished the exterior trim a few days before had moved inside and were installing the crown molding and wainscoting on both floors. An additional crew of four was brought in specifically to build the fireplace mantels as well as expansive bookcases throughout the main level and in select rooms on the second floor.

Mark spent most of his waking hours hanging doors, while Pam was in Wheatley making the final selections for rugs, paint and wallpaper. She believed that the more she could show the committee member, the stronger the case would be to have Montis Inn reinstated in the registry. In Pam's mind, it was no longer a question of whether the inn would get historic landmark status but when. Unless, of course, something went radically wrong.

During that week equal attention was paid to the orchard. The second harvest, initially postponed because of the rains, began in earnest, resulting in one-third more yield than planned, with all of the fruit being trucked directly to Saint Cross Abbey.

Chuck Bryson also came that week to complete repairs on the hives and collect the honey. With Joshua, who had offered to become his apprentice, working closely by his side, Chuck was able to systematically progress from hive to hive in half the time it would have taken him working alone. He also liked Joshua's company, as Joshua did his, and the two men spoke for hours. Chuck said the bees were happiest when they felt the low vibration of two friends talking.

"Very good," Chuck said, lifting up a comb. "These really are amazing creatures. Four wings and five eyes, unchanged in twenty million years. These small worker bees make wax from glands on the bottom of their bellies and move it with spines on the hind leg. Then they use their jaws to form six-sided cells." He examined a bee resting on his arm. "Just an engineering marvel."

He continued to work on the hive as he spoke. "A bee will visit a hundred flowers in one flight, and then return to the hive to drop the collected nectar into the honeycomb. They then evaporate it by fanning their wings. They are quite busy in the summer."

"What happens in the winter?" Joshua asked.

"In the cold winter months they only leave the hive to take short cleansing flights; they are fastidiously clean insects. Other than that, they relax and eat the honey that they have stored in their wax honeycomb."

"Are we not taking their winter supply, then?" Joshua asked.

"No, we will only take part of what is here. But honey hasn't been collected from these hives for some time, so there's plenty to go around," Chuck explained.

Joshua, about to ask another question, smelled something so displeasing that it brought tears to his eyes. "Is that smell coming from the hive?"

Chuck stopped short. "Oh, no. That's just awful," he said, smelling the pungent odor in full force.

"What in the world is that stench?" Joshua asked, wiping his eyes. "It seems to be coming from those hives," pointing to the center of the apiary.

Chuck replaced the top of the hive he was working on, while Joshua walked over to the back part of the field where three hives were grouped up against the trees. Circling the hives, Joshua realized that the source of the smell was farther away, being carried by the breeze. He walked through the small clearing to the adjacent field.

Moo.

There stood two Guernsey cows, with marijuana strands dripping from their mouths and dried diarrhea on their legs.

"Oh my," Chuck said, coming up from behind Joshua.

"What a stench," Joshua repeated.

"Well, at least Mark will know who took his crop."

"Which is all gone," Joshua said, seeing a completely foraged pasture. Not one plant remained standing.

"What to do?" Chuck wondered.

"I don't think we should leave them here."

"Good point. They may walk into the apiary. Could cause lots of havoc if they stagger into a hive. And the bees might sting them just for smelling so bad."

Just then one of the cows released some projectile diarrhea, missing Joshua's leg by no more than a few feet, but splattering both shoes.

"Wonderful," he said.

Joshua took off his belt and roped the larger of the two cows, and Chuck used his suspenders for the other. The two men then led the two very doped-up cows out of their land of paradise so that they could be returned to their owner. As the cows sauntered down the orchard, enjoying the last of their cud, they left small piles of chewed marijuana between the rows of apples.

"Looks like green chewing tobacco," Chuck observed.

The larger of the two cows abruptly stopped, released an inordinate amount of gas, moaned, and then continued walking.

From the front porch, Mark had watched the two cows being escorted down the hill, and he called to one of the workers inside.

"Hey Vinny. Is that Bertha?" Mark asked.

"Yeah, that's Bertha."

"I guess she likes it here," Mark said. Just then he caught wind of the cows' smell. Within seconds so did everyone else, and the jokes and catcalls began.

Coming over from the lodge to ask Mark a question, Pam circled around the building and walked directly into the bouquet de bovine.

"God, what is that smell?" Pam asked, stepping onto the front porch.

"Seems Joshua and Chuck are bringing us a present," Mark answered.

"But Mrs. Kincaid is due here any minute," Pam said frantically.

"Well, fine timing, I would say. Is that her in the U.S. Park Service car?" Mark asked as he watched a dark green SUV with an emblem on the door pull into the drive. The driver's eyes were locked on Hank, who stood ready to meet and greet in his casual wardrobe of sneakers, jeans, and a plaid red and blue shirt. Hank knew that it was going to be an upward battle.

Pam went down to greet her just as Joshua and Chuck were crossing the road, bringing the two sources of the intolerable smell with them.

"Welcome to Montis Inn," Pam said, extending her hand to a woman in her fifties wearing a dark navy suit with a straight-line skirt, hose and short-heeled shoes.

"Is that stench from your septic tank?" she asked, trying to step over some wood that she had parked next to.

Oh, this is going to be fun, Mark thought, standing within earshot on the porch.

"No, our tanks are fine," Pam said. "Just some local cows."

Joshua and Chuck crossed Farm to Market Road and walked up, cows in tow, to Mark. The puppies, who had been exploring in the woods, caught wind of the new smells and dashed to join the excitement.

With Cutter and Clipper scrambling at the cows' feet, and the last of the marijuana coming to rest in her second stomach, Bertha had another episode of explosive diarrhea, making the first barrage that Joshua witnessed look like a small trickle in comparison. Unfortunately, Bertha was facing away from the parked SUV, so when the diarrhea took flight, its trajectory hit the side right in the middle of the Parks Department emblem. As semi-digested marijuana slid off the door, everyone watched in disbelief.

Moo.

"What is *that?*" Mrs. Kincaid asked, seeing the long green strands of diarrhea begin to adhere to the car.

"A new strain of alfalfa," Chuck Bryson answered, still holding tight to one of the cows. "Not doing too well for the poor animals, I'm afraid."

"Why don't we go inside?" Pam suggested hastily, and looked at Mark in such a way that there was no misunderstanding that he was to get rid of the cows immediately.

In the lodge, after offering Mrs. Kincaid some coffee, which she refused, Pam reviewed the highlights of her application, focusing specifically on the historical events that would offer compelling proof of the inn's and the abbey's significance to the history of the state as well as the country. She also showed Mrs. Kincaid the photographs and the blueprints, explaining the restoration project in detail.

"Our architect will be here shortly to answer any questions you may have," Pam offered.

"I need to look at the entire compound," Mrs. Kincaid said.

With an inward groan Pam led her outside, where Cutter and Clipper proved that they were not always well-behaved puppies, jumping up on Mrs. Kincaid's legs, snagging her stockings. Pushing them into the lodge and quickly slamming the door, Pam apologized and led Mrs. Kincaid around the compound. As they walked around the grounds, circling the annex and the library, Mrs. Kincaid used several rolls of film photographing Montis from every angle.

"It's hard to see," she said, looking into her camera's viewfinder. "My eyes are still watering from that horrid stench."

"Well, hopefully, the smell will be gone in just a minute," Pam said, looking around to see where the cows had been parked. She noticed a few trees rustle behind the library and wondered if it was caused by the Guernseys.

Pam then escorted her through each of the buildings, beginning with the dining room and then the library. That elicited Mrs. Kincaid's first positive comment; she liked all of the books. She was an avid reader, she confided. They then walked through the sleeping quarters and the annex, with Pam telling the story of the lightning fire that the annex had suffered so long ago.

Pam then led her into the main building, where the men had stopped working to take an early lunch. As Mrs. Kincaid walked about, writing notes on a clipboard and photographing the different rooms, she asked several questions regarding the work that remained. They were in the back room when Pam heard someone enter the vestibule.

"Wheatley Liquor Store is closing, and I just bought us twenty-two cases of rum! Can you believe that?" Brooke said excitedly, coming around the corner, not knowing anyone other than Pam was there.

She stopped dead in her tracks when she saw Mrs. Kincaid, who was regarding her with a disapproving stare.

"It's for the monks," Brooke said, trying to recover, to explain why she would buy enough rum to sink *Lazy Bones II*. Oh, blaming it on monks doesn't sound good either, she thought.

"Mrs. Kincaid," Pam said, stepping forward. "This is our architect, Brooke Shelling. Brooke has done extensive work with historic sites in northern Virginia."

"And where would that be?" Mrs. Kincaid asked, shaking Brooke's hand.

"Well, my office was in Leesburg," Brooke said.

Was? Pam thought.

"Ah, my daughter and son-in-law live in Hamilton," she said.

"That's right down the road," Brooke chimed in.

"Beautiful country. The last time I was there, they took me to a wonderful English pub for dinner," Mrs. Kincaid said, more friendly as the conversation went on.

"Boxer's Tavern. They have the most delicious lamb stew," Brooke said.

"That's the one," Mrs. Kincaid said, pleased. "Are you living here now?"

"Actually, I may be in the process of moving," she answered.

Mrs. Kincaid and Brooke hit it off famously. Walking back to the lodge, where Brooke wanted to use the blueprints to answer some of her questions, she asked, "What is that ungodly smell?"

"Unfortunately, my car," Mrs. Kincaid said dryly.

The rest of the visit was quite enjoyable, and before leaving, Mrs. Kincaid assured Pam that Montis would be reinstated as a national historic landmark at the committee's meeting the following week.

∽

Feeling confident that Mrs. Kincaid was as good as her word, the following day Pam brought the new Montis Inn brochure to Chatham Press for printing.

"Is this also the office for *The Lumby Lines*?" Pam asked after placing her order at the main counter.

"It is," the woman who had been assisting her replied.

"Well, could you tell me who put in an advertisement—actually, it was an invitation—for the Montis Inn last month?"

"Sure, let me just look it up for you," she said, and began to type into her computer. "That's spelled m-o-n-t-i-s?"

"Yes. The Montis Inn."

"Here it is. Only one job in the July 12th edition. It doesn't say who did the layout, but Mr. Beezer gave it final approval. He also waived the billing for the ad."

"So, who submitted it?" Pam asked.

"I'm not sure, but it would appear to be Mr. Beezer himself."

TWENTY-EIGHT
Stones

As Pam walked back to her car, she tried to think why William Beezer would have run the ad, inviting the entire town of Lumby to the Montis Inn. Given Brooke's encounter with him earlier in the summer, she discounted any virtuous reasons. She tried to remember what Brooke had said after the party. Was it Beezer she saw getting in the car, and why didn't he introduce himself?

"You look like you're miles away in thought," Brother Michael said, coming up behind her.

"Oh, it's wonderful to see you," Pam said. "We were just talking about the abbey yesterday, and wondered how everything is going."

"Very well," he said. "Can I buy you a cup of coffee, and we can get caught up?"

They walked down the block to S&T's Soda Shoppe. Walking in, Pam immediately noticed a pyramid of Saint Cross Rum Sauce jars in the window display.

Sitting in one of the old-fashioned booths, Brother Michael ordered a root beer float.

"They have our sauce on their dessert menu now, and it seems to be selling well. S&T's was one of our first restaurants, but we now have our jars in about forty stores and that many restaurants between Rocky Mount and Jefferson. We're just about to expand south of Wheatley and will be delivering to the major cities around the state in about four weeks," he said. "One of my new jobs is to oversee the distribution and deliveries."

"How do you like that?" Pam asked.

He tried not to wince, but his initial reaction was telling. "It's very different being away from the monastery as much as I am now. Before our rum sauce, I used to leave the abbey maybe once every two weeks. But now I'm gone six days a week, leaving after matins and arriving home just before dinner." Michael paused, thinking about how their lives had changed so quickly. "But all of this is still a novelty to me, so it's exciting."

Pam rushed to assure him that the new business would not mean an end to his monastic life as he knew it. "When your volume increases, Saint Cross will be able to hire a company that will take care of the distribution."

The waitress brought the sodas.

"They make the best floats here," he said, smiling.

"Did you get the rum that Brooke sent over yesterday?"

"Yes. Please tell her thank you, and that we'll be mailing her a check this week."

"I don't think it's urgent. She can wait if you need some time to balance the cash flow."

"Actually, we're doing quite well now, so much so that we may be in a position to repay you and Mark some of the money you loaned us within a few weeks."

"Michael, that wasn't a loan," she said firmly. "It was a donation to the abbey to get your business running. We had no expectation of being repaid."

"That's very kind of you. I'll tell the abbot," Brother Michael responded, digging into the root beer float.

"So, sales are good?" Pam asked.

"Better than we could have ever expected. In truth, I didn't fully understand everything in your business plan. I've heard that our costs are what you had estimated, however, and our sales are about twenty percent higher. We're in full production for five different rum sauces, and we'll be in most grocery and specialty stores in the Northwest within three or four months."

"That's wonderful," she said.

"And," he continued, "we have sent out both unsolicited and requested samples to four national food chains and should be hearing their responses in the next month. We are almost sold out of the lot made from the first harvest, and we'll be finished processing the second harvest in about two weeks."

"It sounds like the abbey is doing well," Pam said.

"Almost too well. We need more fruit, so we've met with three other local farms and have signed contracts with them for next year's harvest. I know that Father Andrew would also like to sign a contract with you and Mark."

"Please assure the abbot we have no other plans than to send our fruit to Saint Cross. We promised you our full harvest for as long as the abbey needs it," Pam said.

"That will make him very happy." Brother Michael got the last drops of his float before he continued. "We are also looking at a few different products that we would like your opinion on."

"Oh, really? What are they?"

"Well, Brother John has become quite inventive in the kitchen, and he has developed a different recipe for fruit glazes. Personally, I think they're outstanding. They're thicker than the rum sauce and can be drizzled over just about anything. Also, he's starting to experiment with grilling sauces: apricot for pork and peaches and pears for fish. They're also good, but they need more work—for some reason, lots of the sauce drips off the meat while it's cooking. But the brothers certainly are happy trying out all of his recipes."

"Mmm. They sound wonderful," Pam said.

"Between Brother John's experimenting, and perhaps taking a sip of rum every now and again, I think all of the brothers have put on a few pounds. We joke about having to start an exercise program after Sunday services."

Pam laughed. "And how is Brother Matthew?"

"He is tired but well," he answered simply. "Did you see *The Lumby Lines* this week?"

"No, I haven't read it yet."

"Let me get you one." He went up to the cash register, paid the bill, and on his way back to the table grabbed a paper by the window.

"Free advertising," he winked.

The Lumby Lines

What's News Around Town

BY SCOTT STEVENS   **SEPTEMBER 6**

Yet another extraordinary week in our fine town of Lumby.

Last Wednesday, I had the delightful opportunity to sample a new product that has just become available: Saint Cross Rum Sauce. The monks of Saint Cross Abbey, to include several of the brothers from our own Montis Abbey of a few years back, have gone into the business of making rum sauces. And do they pack a tasty punch. I had a chance to taste all five varieties: apple, peach, pear, nectarine and plum, and each one was better than the last until I got back to the first, which was the best of all. I tried them on both cake and ice cream, and can say that they are, bar none, the best rum sauces I have ever had. The charming blown-glass mason jars are also a delight to keep after every last drop of rum sauce is gone. They are now being sold about town, so I'd recommend everyone go out and buy a case.

Steve Iron Enterprises, Inc. has submitted plans to the town and county commissioners for an eighteen-hole "Arnie Palmer like" golf course to be built on the northwest side of town, somewhere by the landfill. Although so few people in Lumby play golf that Lumby Sporting Goods doesn't carry clubs or balls, Steve believes it's an untapped need in our community. Whatever.

Priest Pass remains the highest-accident stretch of road in the entire county. When I called the Department of Transportation to ask about the state's plan to repair the pavement and reinstall the guardrails, they had no comment. Until they wise up, everyone needs to take care driving those curves.

Lumby Lumber and Construction, Inc. seems to be its own worst enemy these days; the company has bulldozed three cabins at the wrong addresses, due to what appears to be a problem of uncorrected dyslexia suffered by one of its new employees.

Over the last three weeks, there have been an unprecedented number of mailbox paintings. Being one of the recipients of lime green brush strokes, I suppose I'm more curious than angry. If anyone has any thoughts as to why, please call me on my cell phone. All conversations will be kept confidential. I was told that a Kubota riding lawn mower has been parked outside the Wayside Bar for three days now, with the keys still in the ignition. If you can't remember how you got there or how you got home the other night, this could be yours. Check it out.

After arriving back at the inn, Pam walked over to Brooke's cottage to bring her some rum sauce that Brother Michael had sent home with her. The two conversed outside, while Brooke weeded around the front entrance and Pam swung in the hammock.

"It sounds like all is going well for the brothers," Brooke said after Pam told her about seeing Brother Michael.

"Certainly better than I expected. Oh, by the way, Michael said that a check for the rum will be sent to you this week," Pam said.

"That's nice. And what a great idea to diversify into similar products. I wouldn't be surprised if they have a full line of products by this time next year."

"I hope so," Pam said, getting up to leave. "Before I forget, I saw a garden rake over by the cemetery when I walked past. I don't think it's ours."

"No, it's probably one that I left there from a few days go. I'll head back over with you to pick it up," Brooke said, putting the pair of trimming clippers into her back pocket. "I want to tell you about a phone call I got this afternoon."

"Anyone special?" Pam asked, noticing Brooke's mysterious tone.

"Sort of. It was from Spencer Associates."

"The architectural firm in Wheatley?" Pam asked. "They reviewed our final blueprints. Is there something wrong?"

Pam saw a wide smile come across her friend's face. "Oh, not at all. Actually, just the opposite. They were calling to see if I'd be interested in talking with them about joining the firm."

"Brooke, that's wonderful!" Pam exclaimed. "Are you seriously thinking about moving here?"

"It's been on my mind a lot during the last couple of months," she answered.

"Oh, this could be great! I know you've brought it up a few times, but Mark and I always thought it was a long shot at best, so we didn't want to push the idea."

"I'll be the first to admit that I never thought I'd like living in such a small town, but I do."

"Lumby seems to grow on everyone that way." Pam paused. "Do you think you would enjoy working for a larger firm?"

"I'm not sure—it's been a long time since I worked for someone else," Brooke mused aloud, still thinking out the opportunity. "I think in my business, there are some real advantages to working with a group of talented, dedicated people. In truth, I think being alone the last few years has almost been harder professionally than personally."

"Would it be inappropriate if I asked if Joshua is playing a part in your decision?" Pam asked with a shrewd smile.

Brooke answered with a slight nod. "Not at all, and he does, but I just don't know how much. I've asked myself a hundred times if I would still want to be here if Joshua wasn't close by."

"And your answer was?"

"Probably yes, but I'm not sure."

"Well, maybe you're thinking too hard about it."

"How so?" Brooke asked.

"Well, if you love it here, and if you feel strongly for Joshua and he's here, doesn't that answer your question?"

"I suppose it does," Brooke said.

Watching Brooke tilt her head back and forth, having an internal argument about the risks and rewards, Pam added, "You live your life so cautiously, Brooke. Maybe this time you should just follow your heart."

Brooke laughed. "You're right. I don't like to take chances, do I?"

Pam's only response was an appraising smile.

As they passed the side path to the cemetery, Pam continued on to the inn, and Brooke picked up the rake that was leaning against the tree. When she walked into the cemetery, she sensed that something was different, but couldn't place how or why. She began to trim the grasses around the tombstones and smaller headstones. When she stood again, she realized what was wrong: in one area of the cemetery, dried grass cuttings were littered on the ground, and a tombstone was closely manicured when all the others had weeds shin high. Someone had been there within the last week.

She walked over and looked at the tombstone of the grave that was manicured: Benjamin Beezer 1917–1962. But what was startling was a headstone next to Brother Benjamin's grave, a piece of granite no more than two feet square lying flat slightly below ground level that had previously been covered with grass. Someone had not only cleared the grass and soil from on top of the stone and wiped the stone clean, but had diligently trimmed all the grass around the grave, visually connecting it to Brother Benjamin's.

Brooke bent down to read the etching, which had badly weathered because the stone was facing upward and fully exposed to the rain and snow.

WOODROW BEEZER
Beloved husband and father
August 5, 1896 – August 21, 1966

Brooke stared at the headstone. It should have made sense to her; Brother Matthew had told them that after Benjamin had joined the order, his family frequently came to the abbey and participated in the church services. And upon Woodrow's passing, it was probably his request to be buried next to his eldest son, who had died several years earlier. But nonetheless, Brooke felt numb and continued to stare at the wording, even leaning down to touch the engraving.

She didn't understand her uneasiness. Perhaps it was because the headstone had been buried under the grass and would have been so forever had someone not uncovered it. Perhaps it was that someone had come to the cemetery without anyone's knowledge. Mark and Pam would have said something to her had they known about it. Perhaps it was looking at the two graves, side by side, father and son, a long life and a shorter life.

Instead of going back to the cottage, Brooke went to the inn.

Mark was outside tying up some roses. "Pam told me the great news about you and the position in Wheatley. Congratulations."

"Thanks," Brooke said. "You know, I was just over at the cemetery, and I found something unusual."

Pam, hearing Brooke's voice, came outside from the lodge. "What's up?"

"Someone's been in the cemetery," she said.

"Ghosts?" Mark asked, pretending to tremble wildly.

"No, I'm serious," Brooke said. "It's a little creepy." She explained what she saw, after which all of them went to the cemetery to look.

"He died August 21, 1966. August 21st was just a few weeks ago," Brooke said, looking down at the dates on Woodrow Beezer's headstone.

"August 21st was the river festival and the raft race," Mark added.

"August 21st was our party," Pam said.

They all went silent.

"Beezer was here. I'm sure that's who I saw getting into the car," Brooke said.

"Now that you mention it," Mark said, "during the evening when I was talking with Cantor, I saw an older man walk behind the annex. He stopped and then disappeared. I was going to follow him, but was pulled into a conversation. By the time I walked to the back of the building, he was gone."

"How do you know it was an old man?" Pam asked.

"I guess I'm not sure it was. That's just the impression I had. He was smaller with a slight hunchback. He moved more slowly, perhaps with a cane," Mark said, thinking back to that night. "Do you really think that Beezer came that evening just to go to the cemetery?"

"Given his feelings toward Montis, and the editorial he wrote, I'm sure he would have never called to ask your permission," Brooke said.

"And this way he could go to the cemetery unnoticed," Pam added.

"And pay his respects," Mark said.

Pam shook her head in disbelief. "So," she said slowly, "that means that William Beezer ran that invitation in the paper for the sole purpose of visiting the cemetery on the anniversary of his father's death."

Just then Brooke remembered something buried in the hazy past, something she'd read. She looked at the Beezer graves. 1917–1962. 1896–1966. Benjamin entered the monastery in 1937. Oh, my God, she thought.

Pam noticed a haunted expression on Brooke's face. "What's up?"

"I need to look at the Montis journals," was all Brooke said.

Pam and Brooke went back to the lodge, where Pam retrieved the journals from the bedroom. Brooke sat down at the dining table, quickly flipping through the pages.

"What has she found?" Mark asked as he walked in.

"I'm not quite sure," Pam said, watching Brooke.

"Here it is," Brooke said.

"Here what is?" Pam asked.

Brooke took a deep breath. "Do you remember when Brother Matthew was translating some of the ledger entries for us? He said that 'Donativum Talio Incendium' roughly translated as a donation in retribution for the fire."

"Uh-huh," Pam concurred.

"The payments began in 1937, when Benjamin entered Montis Abbey and when, coincidentally in that same week, someone set fire to the orchard."

"How do you know it was the same week?"

"It was in the other journal, the diary," said Brooke. "And the payments ended in August 1966."

Pam looked at Brooke. "When Woodrow Beezer died?"

"Exactly," Brooke said. "I think that Woodrow Beezer was the 'IC,' the anonymous donor who made monthly payments to Montis Abbey for the damage caused by the fire."

"Why?" Pam asked.

"Who do you think set the fire?" Mark continued with another question.

"I think it was William Beezer, Woodrow's other son and Benjamin's brother. Matthew told us that William was profoundly angry when Benjamin joined the monastery, and I think he turned that anger into a fifty-acre blaze. I also think his father and the monks knew he did it, and that's why Woodrow made payments to Montis Abbey every month until the day he died."

Pam and Mark stared at Brooke, who was still holding the journal.

"And William has lived with that secret his entire life," Mark finally said.

"That certainly would explain yet another reason why he feels such anger for Montis," Pam said.

"But it's also anger at himself for doing what he did. For hating what his brother did, for the financial burden he put on his father to repay the monks. For all of it," Brooke said.

"That's unbelievable," Mark said.

"Maybe these are the ghosts in the cemetery," Brooke responded.

"I wonder how much Dennis knows of his son's activities and his father's involvement," Joshua pondered. "I actually feel a little sorry for him. That Brian Beezer certainly is a hell-raiser."

"Yeah, I've seen his name mentioned quite a few times in *The Lumby Lines* sheriff's report," Brooke said.

"Right. The kid Chuck Bryson told me about," Mark said, recounting the discussion during which Chuck had suggested that the youngest Beezer was responsible for the abbey fire last year.

"Strange that both he and his grandson would have committed the same crime against the same abbey," Pam said.

"Like grandfather, like grandson?" Brooke asked.

"Do you think his grandson knew about the first fire?" Joshua asked.

"I seriously doubt Beezer ever told anyone. He probably wanted that secret to go to the grave when his father died," Brooke said.

"I wonder what other secrets those journals hold," Brooke mused.

"Probably more than we want to know," Mark said.

TWENTY-NINE
Direction

"Will we need salad bowls?" Pam said, setting the table in Brooke's small cottage.

"No, I don't think so. I'm just serving tomatoes, which we can put on our plates with the entrée." She continued to slice the heirlooms she had picked from her own garden that morning. "I'm glad you were able to come over before the men arrived."

"I'm glad I had a place to escape to," Pam laughed. "Mark and Joshua are trying to solve a plumbing problem in the annex, so I'm half expecting that corner of Montis to implode under a gush of water."

"Well, the stones in this cottage will protect us from any fallout, I guarantee you," Brooke said, turning up the music.

"Something is starting to smell delicious."

"I'm trying a family recipe Gabrielle gave me." Brooke fell silent for a moment, concentrating on the tomatoes. "I've given it a lot of thought. . . ."

Pam waited and then finally asked, "You've given the tomatoes a lot of thought?"

"No," Brooke laughed. "I'm accepting the job at Spencer Associates. I faxed them my letter an hour ago."

"Brooke! That's great! I was so hoping you would. Does Joshua know?"

"Oh, definitely not."

Pam straightened up and looked at her friend in amazement. "Why not?"

"Because I don't want him to know that he was part of the equation, part of my decision to stay."

Pam scratched her head, trying to understand her logic. "Why not?"

"He may only want what he has now—a casual, no-ties, summer affair."

"Joshua doesn't seem to be an affair type of man," Pam said firmly.

She nodded her head. "I agree. But it may scare him to think I was moving to Lumby because of our relationship."

"That's not your only reason," Pam countered.

"No, but it certainly was a significant factor."

Pam went over to the counter and leaned into her friend. "Brooke, you live so cautiously. I think you should give Joshua the benefit of the doubt. Tell him your plans and let him decide for himself."

∽∾

"We have something to celebrate," Pam said, passing around the wineglasses after the men joined them.

"What's that?" Brooke asked.

Mark explained, "We got a call this afternoon from Mrs. Kincaid, and the committee voted to have the inn reinstated as a historical landmark."

"Oh, that's wonderful," Brooke said, raising her wineglass.

"We can't thank you two enough for everything you did. We know that we could never have done it without either of you," Pam said.

"When do you officially open?" Joshua asked.

"It will take another month to complete and furnish the main building," Mark said. "We also have one final harvest of the orchard."

"Then we were thinking about taking a short vacation," Pam added.

"So I think we're planning on opening the inn the week before Thanksgiving," Mark said. "Cheers." They all toasted to good fortune, good friends and an exciting future ahead of them.

"There are two other things we want to do," Pam began to explain. "One is to convert the marijuana field, which is all but eaten anyway, into a full vegetable garden to grow the produce we will need for the inn's kitchen."

"Ideally, it would be closer to the kitchen, but it's cleared land, and the soil up there is incredibly rich," Mark said.

"I bet," Joshua said, laughing.

"That's a wonderful idea," Brooke added.

"The second," Mark continued, "is to bring livestock onto the property."

"I thought you had your fill after getting to know Bertha so intimately," Joshua teased.

"We think we could tap into the family vacation market if the inn could offer some outdoor activities. We're planning to have a few kayaks, sunfish and bikes but, in addition to that, we're thinking about offering trail rides. We think the place is perfect for it."

"It is, but do you know anything about horses?" Joshua asked.

"As much as he does about cows," Pam teased her husband.

"Interesting idea," Joshua said. "But where would you stable them? I don't think Montis has enough open land for a farmstead."

"You're right, we don't. But a few weeks ago we received a call from our realtor who told us that a twenty-two-acre parcel of land adjacent to our property will be coming on the market as soon as the survey is complete."

"Where is it?" Joshua asked.

"It's across the street, in between the orchard and the lake," Mark said.

"Ah. Mr. Camden's land," Joshua said. "He used to come to the abbey every Sunday. A very nice fellow, very soft-spoken. Did you know that it's surrounded by federal park land on two sides?"

"Yep. And the road is the third, and we're on the fourth side," Pam said, nodding her head.

"It's great acreage if you could get it," Joshua concurred.

"Well, we've put in a fair offer to buy it before it goes on the market," Pam said.

"He always liked the abbey. Maybe he'll fancy the idea of his land becoming part of Montis," Joshua said. "Do you want me to call him?"

"If that would help, and you wouldn't object, we'd appreciate it, Joshua."

"Well, you guys will certainly have your hands full," Brooke commented.

"We know," Pam said.

"But we think this is doable if we get the right person in to manage that part, the outside operations, of Montis for us," Mark said.

Taking her cue, Pam went over and sat on the arm of Mark's chair. "Joshua, we think you'd be the perfect person."

Mark immediately followed. "You know the property better than any of us, you're wonderful with animals, and you know more about agriculture than the three of us combined."

Surprised by the offer, Joshua didn't respond at first.

"I'm flattered," he finally said. "You know how much I care for Montis, but . . ."

"But what?" Pam asked.

"This conversation is too late," Joshua said.

"Too late for what?" Brooke asked, seeing that he was having a difficult time saying what was on his mind.

"Too late to consider their offer. A few weeks ago, I made some commitments that begin in January," Joshua said, looking at Brooke. "I haven't discussed them with you yet but it would happen after you went back to Virginia."

A sick feeling of apprehension settled in the pit of Brooke's stomach. She braced herself. "What's that?"

"I've been accepted into the graduate program at the university."

Brooke was stunned. "Where?" was all she could ask.

He saw the distress in her eyes. "The university—the Wheatley campus. A few minutes south of town. I may have to go elsewhere for thesis work in a few years, but that wouldn't be for longer than a few months."

Mark and Pam looked no less surprised.

"For a master's in what?" Mark asked.

"Biological and agricultural engineering," Joshua answered.

"Ah. Changing the genes of white corn. Interesting for a man who was once a monk," Pam teased.

"So are you moving?" Brooke asked.

Joshua was unsure why there was so much pain in Brooke's voice. "I was thinking of moving to Wheatley. I need to get a job to pay for school."

There was silence.

Then Pam said, excitedly, "But this is perfect! This couldn't be more perfect."

"How so?" Brooke asked, giving Pam an anguished glare, feeling like the rug was just pulled out from under her.

"Joshua," Pam said, "the next few months will be incredibly demanding. We're going to make a strong push to get a stable and a barn built, at a minimum. You could work on that full-time. But come January, everything will move into slow gear, giving you as much time as you need to study. Then we pick up again in the late spring."

Mark saw Pam's logic right away. "Were you planning to take summer classes?"

"No, I need to work, but haven't made any commitments either way," Joshua said, thinking through what was being presented to him.

"Then I agree with Pam," Mark said. "This could be a great arrangement. It would allow you to go to graduate school, and give us the help we need by having you managing the outside operations of Montis, as well as give you the income you need to pay for tuition."

"What do you think?" Brooke hesitantly asked Joshua.

"I think it's an incredible opportunity," Joshua said, and everyone smiled all around.

"So, here's to our future," Mark said.

Mark, Pam and Joshua raised their glasses as Brooke sat silently on the sofa.

∞

Once alone after dinner, Joshua and Brooke sat at the table, neither knowing what to say or how to begin. Joshua felt Brooke's guard go up.

"I'm sorry I didn't tell you earlier, but I wanted to finalize everything before sharing it with you."

"I don't understand," she said, because she didn't. "Perhaps I put too much stock in our relationship."

"No, you didn't. It's just that graduate school is something I've been preparing for for so many years. There were quite a few gaps I had to fill in my undergraduate work, and I was unsure where I wanted to get my master's degree. Also, I just got notification from the schools four weeks ago," he added.

"You applied to other schools?"

Joshua nodded. "Four others."

"And did you get accepted into all of them?"

"No. Only three out of five."

"Where were the others?"

"One in California and the other was the University of North Carolina."

"But you're staying here?"

"Yes, that's my decision," he said, putting her hands in his.

"Why here?"

"Well, this is my home and the little family I have is here." He paused, looking into her eyes. "And you're here. Even though I know you'll be returning to Virginia soon, you'll return to visit, and when you do, I'll be here to see you. I felt those are reasons enough."

She put her head down. "No, I won't," she almost whispered.

"No, you won't be visiting?" It was now Joshua who felt the pit in his stomach.

"No, I won't be going back to Virginia."

Joshua felt as if a bolt of energy had gone through him. "I don't understand."

"I accepted a job this afternoon," Brooke said, wincing slightly.

"Where?"

"Spencer Associates—an architectural firm in Wheatley."

Joshua squeezed her hands. "Why didn't you tell me?"

"I didn't want you to feel responsible for my life, responsible for me moving to Lumby."

"But am I?" Joshua said, confused.

For once in her life, she dropped all of her defenses and opened her heart. "You are the most significant reason I am staying."

"That's wonderful to hear." He took her in his arms and kissed her passionately. It was a kiss that lasted well into the morning.

THIRTY

Bequests

𝕿𝖍𝖊 𝕷𝖚𝖒𝖇𝖞 𝕷𝖎𝖓𝖊𝖘

A Consumer's Report

BY CARRIE KERRY   **SEPTEMBER 20**

The Barkolator: Last Wednesday, at two o'clock in the morning, I was coerced into buying yet another product from a shopping network on satellite television: the Barkolator. The concept behind this high-tech, cross-species translator, for those who have not yet heard, is to allow your dog's bark to be read in English, and convert your words into canine barks. If only communications with my boyfriend could be so simple.

   A team of scientists, animal behaviorists, and clinical psychiatrists in Asia defined nine emotional categories for dogs: fear, happiness, hunger and so on. I would think dogs' fears run high over there since they are often served up for lunch and dinner, but who knows.

Anyway, each bark is transmitted from a receiver in the pooch's collar to a small handheld computer, which then displays the words behind the bark, so to speak.

When I received the package yesterday, I strapped the bright red collar around little Maggie's neck, Maggie being my flat-coated retriever.

"Bark," she sounded. "I'm hungry," the display read.

"Bark," she sounded. "I'm full," it read.

"Bark, bark," she sounded. "I'm jealous jealous," it read. Jealous jealous of what? I thought.

I could neither dispute nor support the translation, but it was fun.

I then decided to take the Barkolator out for a field trial, and went to the Fairgrounds where I strapped it on one of the renegade chickens.

"Cluck," it said. "I'm hungry," it read.

"Cluck," it said. "I'm free," it read.

Fair enough.

My final test was at Mcnear's Farm, where I asked to borrow Bertha, as her emotions are fairly superficial.

"Moo," she voiced. "Dumb," it read.

"Moo," she voiced again. "Dope," it read.

I'll never understand that one, but I acknowledge that I may have pushed the envelope too far by testing it on a bovine.

So, overall, I give it four out of five bananas. Why not? Wouldn't our town be that much better if we all knew what our dogs were telling us?

After reading the paper Monday morning, Pam went to pick up Brooke. Upon leaving Montis she noticed that Hank was preparing for the colder weather to come. He had donned a lightweight green sweater with a striped scarf casually thrown around his neck.

When Pam and Brooke arrived in town, their first stop was at Chatham Press, where the Montis Inn brochures were ready. When they got to the entrance, however, a large "CLOSED" sign hung on the door. As they peered inside, the lights were off, in spite of the business hours printed on the schedule. They agreed to bide some time in the Lumby Bookstore, but found a similar "CLOSED" sign.

"Is today a holiday?" Pam asked Brooke, mystified.

"Not that I'm aware of. Let's grab a bite at S&T's and come back in an hour."

Retuning to Chatham Press after an early lunch, they found the "CLOSED" sign was still hanging on the door, but they saw people working inside.

Pam knocked on the window, catching the attention of a man who was standing away from her, reading galley proofs at the front desk. When he turned around, she saw Dennis Beezer and drew back in surprise.

"It's Dennis!" Pam said under her breath. "In his father's building."

Dennis opened the door but didn't say anything right away.

"Hi, Dennis," Pam said awkwardly. "I came by to pick up the Montis Inn brochures, but it appears you're closed." She ended the sentence more in a question than a statement.

Dennis looked at her and then Brooke.

"Dennis, are you all right?" Brooke asked.

"I'm sorry," he said, shaking his head as if to end a bad trance. "The press will be closed for business for the next few days."

He saw Pam peering inside at the staff at work.

"We're printing a special edition in remembrance," he explained.

"For whom?" Brooke asked.

"My father. He died in a car crash on Priest Pass last night."

"We're so very sorry, Dennis," Pam said. "Is there anything we can do?"

"No. Well, actually, yes. I've been trying to reach Joshua. If you see him, would you please let him know what's happened?"

"Of course," Brooke said.

"Please call us if there is anything we can do," Pam said as Dennis began to close the door.

"I'm speechless," Brooke said, walking back to the car with Pam. "I feel so sorry for Dennis—he looked so distraught."

"It must be painful for him just to be in that building," Pam correctly assumed.

"Gabrielle mentioned that Dennis hadn't stepped foot in his father's business for thirty years. And now, to have to go there under these circumstances," Brooke said. "I was hoping to ask William Beezer about the fires, and about the journals. In fact, I was planning on bringing it up this morning."

"Well, that's definitely not going to happen," Pam said dryly.

After dropping Brooke off at her cottage, Pam went home and told Mark about William Beezer's death.

Within no more than a few minutes, the phone rang. Pam listened to Mark, and his brief responses: "Yes, I just heard. . . . Uh-huh. . . . That's fine. . . . Yes. . . . Yes. . . . See you then."

"Who was that?" Pam asked.

"Russell Harris," Mark answered.

"Is there something wrong?"

"Not that I'm aware of, but he would like to see us in his office this afternoon at three o'clock."

"Why so?" Pam asked.

"He wouldn't say, other than to tell me that he is handling William Beezer's estate and final requests."

Pam had the sinking feeling that something was about to go terribly awry, fearing what she referred to as "the other shoe dropping," although Mark had always wondered when the first shoe dropped.

"Can we be sued posthumously?" she asked.

"Sued for what? We've done nothing wrong. We don't even know him," Mark reminded her.

"I know. But he had such a strong vendetta against Montis. Perhaps it was his final wish that he bring the abbey to its knees."

"Interesting metaphor," Mark laughed. "Don't worry. It will be fine."

"But why do you think Russell needs to see us?" she asked. And Pam repeated that question no less than ten times in the next hour.

∞

"Thanks for coming so quickly," Russell said, shaking both Pam and Mark's hands. "These matters are always so difficult, and usually time is an unfortunate reality. I trust all is going well at Montis."

"Very well, thanks. The weather has been good for the orchard," Mark said, filling in for Pam, who was too nervous for small talk.

"Wonderful party you had. It's nice to see the community come together like that," Russell said.

Pam couldn't hold back. "What can we do for you, Russell?"

"Here, please sit down," he said, offering them chairs around a large mahogany table, the same table on which they had signed their closing papers for Montis Abbey.

"As you know, William Beezer passed away last night, and, as I told Mark, I have been asked to handle his will and last requests."

"But we didn't even know him," Pam said, bracing herself for an expected blow.

"Oh. I thought you might have met him since moving here," Russell said, "but that was just an assumption on my part."

"No. All we knew is that he didn't think too favorably of Montis," Mark said.

"Well, that would be difficult to know," Russell said. "There are actually two different reasons why I needed to see you." He tapped the paper in front of him. "The first is in respect to his will. It was William Beezer's request that he be buried in the cemetery at Montis."

"At Montis?" Pam asked, startled.

"Yes," Russell answered. "On the one occasion when he and I spoke about this, specifically when I was drawing up his last will and testament, he told me that he wanted to be buried next to his brother and father, and that he wanted that request stated as such in both his will and letter of last request."

"I'm shocked," Pam said.

Mark explained, "Given an article he wrote in *The Lumby Lines* last spring, we assumed that he would prefer Montis be torn down, stone by stone."

"Personally, I don't think that was the case. Perhaps he just didn't want the past stirred up by your purchase and restoration of the abbey."

"Why do you say that?" Pam asked. "Are you aware of William Beezer's connection to the abbey?"

"Only slightly." Russell moved on. "I know this must come as an unexpected request—"

"To say the least," Mark interrupted.

Russell continued. "And I would like to give you as much time as you need to consider his request, but unfortunately, matters must be finalized today. Perhaps I can leave you two alone to discuss it."

"Yes, please," Mark said.

"Before I leave, though, I need to give you this envelope. In William's letter of last request, he asked that you do not open it until you advise me of your decision regarding his request to be buried on your property which I have already cleared by the county and state if you agree. Regardless of your answer, though, he wanted you to have this," Russell explained, placing a white business envelope on the table in front of Mark, and then left the room.

"I'm amazed," Pam said, looking at her husband.

"Me, too," he said. "Could we have misread the situation so badly?"

"I don't think so," she said. "I'm sure Brooke was totally accurate in what he said to her. And there was little room for misinterpreting his editorial in the newspaper."

"So, you think no matter how he felt toward Montis, his desire to be buried next to his brother was stronger?" Mark asked.

"I do," Pam answered. "So what do you think?"

"I think we would both feel strange to have William Beezer, alive or dead, at Montis."

"I do, too," Pam said, concurring. "But . . ." she paused.

"But," Mark completed her thought, "all of us will have our own last requests and hope that they will be honored."

"Yeah, I think so," Pam said.

"So we should agree?" Mark asked.

"I think so. Do you?" Pam asked back.

"I do."

They asked for Russell to rejoin them.

"We're fine with William Beezer being buried at the Montis cemetery," Mark told Russell.

"Very good," the lawyer said, and picked up the phone to advise his assistant.

"You said there were two matters?" Mark asked.

"Yes. The other is the envelope on the table, which you can now open," Russell said.

Mark picked up the envelope. Taking out what looked like a slip of paper, he read it and handed it to Pam in silence. They both stared at the paper in shock. In Pam's hand was a cashier's check made payable to the Montis Inn in the amount of fifty thousand dollars.

Pam peered at it more closely. "Persolvo' is written on the memo line. What does that mean?"

"In Latin, it means to pay off one's debt," Russell answered.

"But William didn't owe us anything," Mark said.

"He thought he did."

"For what?" Pam asked.

"For last year's fire," Russell answered more softly, offering no further information.

After gathering whatever composure they could, Mark and Pam thanked Russell and left his office.

When they returned home, they invited Brooke and Joshua over to tell them what had transpired. Joshua had just been in town to console Dennis and was clearly shaken, holding Brooke's hand tightly. Pam poured strong martinis for everyone.

"Do you think we did the right thing?" Pam asked Brooke.

"Yes, I do. Given everything, I would have made the same decision. Interesting how he didn't want you to see the check before giving Russell your answer."

Mark agreed. "I'm sure he didn't want the money to influence our decision."

"And, in truth, it could have," Pam said. "That's a lot of money. I'm glad it wasn't hanging over our heads when we were discussing his burial request."

"Would it have swayed you?" Joshua asked.

"I'm embarrassed to admit it, but yes, I think so," Pam answered honestly. "If I had been strongly opposed to the idea but knew about his check, I would have felt that approving his request was the least I could do for the money he gave us."

"But the money wasn't for that," Joshua said.

"Exactly," Mark concurred. "That's why he wanted to keep the two separate."

Brooke shook her head. "I have to admit that I admire his forethought and sense of objective fairness."

"Me too," Pam said.

"And so it was his grandson who definitely set fire to the main building last year?" Brooke asked.

"Yes, although Russell never said those exact words," Mark said. "He explained that his role was simply to handle any legal issues that came up regarding Brian Beezer's potential involvement in the fire. He never confirmed any of the stories we have heard."

"But a man doesn't give fifty thousand dollars away for no reason," Joshua said.

"One hundred thousand," Pam corrected him. "Today's remittance, if you can call it that, plus the other check that was in the journal sent to Brooke."

"Here," Mark said, handing Brooke the paper. "Before leaving town, we picked up the special edition of *The Lumby Lines.*"

Brooke began scanning the numerous articles about William Beezer, his father, his sons, and their lives. Below the obituary and framed by articles on each side was a series of photographs that showed William Beezer as a carefree young boy, a high school football player, a graduate student at Northwestern, a loving husband and father, and a community leader in Lumby.

Brooke grabbed the paper and held it closely to her face, studying the center photograph. Tears came to her eyes as her hands started to tremble. Joshua looked at her.

"What's wrong, Brooke?" he asked.

"Brooke?" Pam asked, trying to get her attention.

She put down the paper and pointed to a man standing next to William Beezer, one man among six, all laughing, in a photograph that was entitled "Northwestern Medill School of Journalism 1943."

"That's my father."

THIRTY-ONE

Closures

"That's my father," Brooke repeated.

She picked up the paper again and scrutinized the images of both men: her father, tall, lean and so youthful but still wearing the same smile she knew all her life, with his arm resting on the shoulder of the other man, William Beezer.

"I remember this photograph. My father had one in his library next to his Northwestern degrees. I don't know if it's the exact same, but I'm sure it was taken at the same time," Brooke said, tears still in her eyes.

Her friends were unsure what to say.

Then the tears came harder. "He must have known who I was. That's why he looked at me the way he did when I first met him, but he didn't say anything. If only he had told me. If only I had the chance to get to know him the way my father knew him. He could have told me wonderful stories about my dad, about the times they spent together in college."

She was crying now.

"I miss him so much," she said, touching her father's face on the photograph. "It was so unfair to die that young . . . to be taken away from me."

She saw her friends watching her and became embarrassed. "I'm sorry," Brooke said.

Joshua leaned over and kissed her cheek.

"There's nothing to be sorry about. We're as stunned by this as you are," Pam said.

"And now it's too late," Brooke said, shrugging her shoulders, wiping the tears off her cheeks.

❧

The day before William Beezer's funeral, Brother Matthew and Brother Michael brought rum sauces and peach and apple glazes to Montis Inn. Brother Matthew also presented Mark with a small decanter of heavily pulped peach brandy that needed to be aged for many years. Although good friends were once again united, the evening was somber and the quiet conversation ended early.

The following morning, upon leaving for the Presbyterian Church, Mark noticed that Hank was dressed appropriately: a conservative black suit, white shirt, and black tie. As were the many Lumby townspeople who came to pay their respects. When Mark, Pam and the brothers arrived, only a few seats in the back pews of the large church were unoccupied.

William's memorial service was like most others in Lumby; several hundred people remembering a person and the deeds done while alive. A procession of friends and loved ones spoke kindly of William and then sat down to listen to the next.

As the voices from the hymn faded, Dennis walked nervously to the front of the church. Standing at the podium, he looked down at the paper on which he had written his father's eulogy. For several days he had struggled to find benevolent words, and he deeply wished his mother, in her grief and loneliness, had seen the impossibility of her request. Dennis looked out over the pews and down again at his notes. He then folded the paper, creasing it with his thumbnail, and put it in his pocket.

He finally began to speak slowly, and in an effort to hear, a hush came over the church. "Over my father's desk, thumb-tacked to the wall, is a small index card on which he wrote President Reagan's epigraph: 'I know in my heart that man is good. That what is right will always eventually triumph. And there is a purpose and worth to each and every life.'

"My father was haunted by these words and struggled to reach deep within himself to embrace their values, but lived with a constant disappointment that he couldn't find refuge in the optimism they represent. Nonetheless, he had the strength and fortitude to read those words each morning, as his colleagues have told me. And I find that admirable.

"He was quite unsure if man is fundamentally good. If so, he believed we repeatedly show bad judgment as we struggle as best we can to get by. He also doubted if right and honesty do prevail, if our moral fiber is strong enough to defend against the self-gratifying takers of this world. A belief in God and an undying faith in a final judgment certainly address that quandary. But for those who religiously waver, the personal struggle to correct wrongs and ensure an equitable resolve of good over evil is never-ending. Either way, he was, as we all are, constantly angered when good does not triumph.

"As for the last sentence, my father firmly believed that there is worth to each life if it is lived honestly, courageously and meaningfully, but that worth can only be achieved through struggle and sacrifice, protected by a hardness that sees one through difficult times. That same hardness, though, was impenetrable to many of us. But Lumby gave William his worth: in the businesses that he started and grew, and in his involvement in the community. He deeply loved this town and believed in its people. Had he known his own destiny . . .

"I will forever regret assuming that there would be time to bridge the distance between us—that we would be given months and possibly years to heal and grow strong together, but minutes weren't even shared for us to say goodbye. So, we are left with unsaid words of love and forgiveness, knowing how easily those words would now be spoken if only he was here to listen."

૨૦૦

Following the memorial service, a very small procession of four cars drove to Montis cemetery, where William Beezer was finally laid to rest next to his brother and father. Afterward, Dennis and Gabrielle followed the brothers as they walked back to the inn, but instead of going into the main house, they and Brothers Matthew and Michael crossed the road and joined Joshua and Brooke and Pam and Mark, who were standing on a knoll in the orchard. Once together, the eight friends stood in silence and watched the sunset flood golden hues across the valley and onto the stones of Montis Inn.

Brother Matthew raised his head toward the sky, and everyone bowed their heads in anticipation of a prayer.

"Looks like the stars will be out over Lumby tonight," he said, smiling.

The Lumby Lines

What's News Around Town

By Scott Stevens   **September 27**

Another normal week in our sleepy town of Lumby.

Eyebrows are raised as to the origin of numerous twenty-dollar bills that have been found entangled and deeply embedded in a beaver dam on Goose Creek. From all appearances, a bank bag belonging to Chatham Bank was found by an enterprising beaver who, after chewing through the canvas sack, used the money to further strengthen its damish empire.

Chatham Bank has stated that it was missing neither a bank bag nor any currency. Sheriff Simon Dixon has estimated there to be at least fifty to

eighty bills in the dam, and has secured the area.
Dr. Campbell, DVM, has been contacted for advice
on best methods for removing the cash without
endangering the rodent.

Dennis Beezer has assumed the management of
the Chatham Press, *The Lumby Lines*, and other
businesses owned by the late William Beezer:
"I would like to thank the people of Lumby for
allowing my father and his family into your lives,
personally and professionally. Thank you for the
years of friendship you gave him while he was alive.
And finally, thank you all for the support you have
offered our family since my father's death. I look
forward to continuing in my father's footsteps, and
delivering to you, each week, the news of Lumby."

As reported by the Associated Press, last
evening the monks of Saint Cross Abbey received
the highest honors at the International Culinary
Arts Competition in Geneva, Switzerland. The
competition, which is sponsored by the International
Culinary Federation (ICF), is a week-long event that
brings together the finest culinarians and chefs from
around the world, with as many as one thousand
competitors and eight thousand attendees. The
award, accepted by Brother Matthew, is bestowed
upon the person or persons in the competition who
best represent the standards, quality, creativity and
excellence that the ICF embraces.

Finally, the new Chatham County bus that was
commissioned yesterday for servicing Lumby and
Rocky Mount came to an abrupt stop on its maiden
voyage this morning, getting stuck halfway through
Benders Tunnel just north of Gypsum Creek.
Evidently, the original specifications of the one-lane

tunnel that were given to the bus manufacturer were correct, but the pressure of the mountain over the last thirty-four years has compressed the sides of the tunnel inward by no less than fourteen inches. The Army Corps of Engineers and the Department of Transportation are developing a plan for extricating the bus from the tunnel. Until then, drivers need to use SR 621.

Godspeed to all.

Gail Fraser is the author of the acclaimed Lumby series, which thus far includes *The Lumby Lines, Stealing Lumby, Lumby's Bounty, The Promise of Lumby, Lumby on the Air,* and *Lost in Lumby.* She also co-authored *Finding Happiness in Simplicity* with her husband, folk artist Art Poulin. Together they live and work at Lazygoose Farm in rural upstate New York, which has been featured on PBS and in numerous national magazines.

When not writing, Gail tends to her vegetable garden, orchard and beehives. She is also an avid long-distance swimmer and flute player.

Prior to becoming a novelist, Gail Fraser had a successful corporate career holding senior executive positions in several Fortune 500 and start-up corporations, and traveling extensively throughout the world. She has a BA from Skidmore College with undergraduate work completed at the University of London, and an MBA from the University of Connecticut with graduate work done at Harvard University.

www.lumbybooks.com

Contact Gail Fraser and Stay in Touch with Lumby

Visit www.lumbybooks.com

Blog: http://www.lumbybooks.com/newsfromlumby/

and

Sign up for Lumby Emails, Freebies & Newsletters

 https://www.facebook.com/lumbybooks/

 @gailfraser

CPSIA information can be obtained
at www.ICGtesting.com
Printed in the USA
LVOW10s0400220517
535372LV00007B/83/P